nie.

"I'm no_____ael went on. "We made promises to each other five years ago—"

"And you broke your promises."

"I told you why."

"You said you wanted my forgiveness. All right. Fair enough. If I forgive you, will you go away?"

Michael shook his head. "I changed my mind. I want more than your forgiveness. We had something five years ago. Something important."

"Five years ago it was important. Now it's dead."

"I don't think so," he said, reaching across the table and taking her hand. Not to say grace this time, but to force her to acknowledge him physically. If he couldn't persuade her with his words, perhaps he could persuade her with his touch....

Dear Reader,

In my book *Found: One Wife* I created a detective agency called Finders, Keepers, which specializes in helping clients reconnect with their long-lost lovers. *Found: One Wife* told the story of Maggie Tyrell, the skilled detective and incurable romantic who started Finders, Keepers.

By the end of that book, Maggie had found her own true love. Now she's eager to reunite other separated lovers. But as she warns all her clients, finding a lost lover doesn't guarantee a happy ending. Occasionally those lovers don't want to be found. Occasionally the reappearance of a love from their past is enough to destroy their present.

Maggie gives client Michael Molina that warning, but he hires her to find his old sweetheart anyway. In *Found: One Son,* he learns that sometimes it's as difficult to build a future with a woman you love as it is to let go of the past.

Judith Arnold

Books by Judith Arnold

HARLEQUIN SUPERROMANCE
634—CRY UNCLE
684—MARRIED TO THE MAN
715—BAREFOOT IN THE GRASS
763—FATHER FOUND
767—FATHER CHRISTMAS
771—FATHER OF TWO
809—FOUND: ONE WIFE
830—THE WRONG BRIDE

FOUND:
ONE SON
Judith Arnold

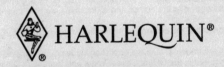

TORONTO • NEW YORK • LONDON
AMSTERDAM • PARIS • SYDNEY • HAMBURG
STOCKHOLM • ATHENS • TOKYO • MILAN • MADRID
PRAGUE • WARSAW • BUDAPEST • AUCKLAND

ISBN 0-373-70856-4

FOUND: ONE SON

Copyright © 1999 by Barbara Keiler.

This edition published by arrangement with Harlequin Books S.A.

Visit us at www.romance.net

Printed in U.S.A.

This book is dedicated to my GEnie sisters.

PROLOGUE

THIS WASN'T GOING to be easy.

Thinking five years back into his past was never easy for Michael. Talking about it was worse. He had formed scars and figured out how to live again—but going back there, getting sucked into the memories as if they were a whirlpool, spinning him around and dragging him down...

It was hard.

He wasn't in the past anymore. He was in the pleasant, sun-filled office of Maggie Tyrell, the founder and president of Finders, Keepers, a detective agency that specialized in locating lost lovers. He had come to see her because once he'd summoned the courage to start thinking about that long-ago time in San Pablo, he'd realized that most of his thoughts centered on Emmie Kenyon.

He missed her.

He worried about her.

He wanted to tell her he was sorry for what had happened, what he'd done, the way he'd disappeared on her. He wanted to hear her say she could forgive him. He wanted to know she was all right.

Discussing the situation with the detective seated across the desk from him, her computer humming and a pencil wedged between her thumb and forefinger, was a trial, though. The only way he could

do it was by reminding himself that seeing Emmie
again would be his reward.

"Her name was Mary-Elizabeth Kenyon," he began. "Everyone called her 'Emmie.' Those were her
initials—M.E." He sounded strange to himself, his
voice gruff, the words struggling to emerge.

Maggie Tyrell smiled and nodded in encourage-
ment. One wall was adorned with a framed poster
of two ballet dancers in an elegant clinch, but Maggie herself seemed anything but elegant. Her hair
was frizzy and wild, her apparel utilitarian, her build
stocky, utterly lacking the ethereal grace of the ballerina.

She seemed all business, which Michael liked. He
didn't think he could bear being pitied or fussed
over, having either his stupidity or his heartache
commented upon.

"We met five years ago," he said when Maggie
remained silent, her gaze expectant. "In San Pablo,
down in Central America."

That tweaked her interest. She stopped fiddling
with her pencil and leaned forward. "An interna-
tional search isn't as simple as a domestic one, Mr.
Molina," she warned.

"I doubt Emmie's still down there. She was
working with a church group, teaching school."

Maggie jotted that detail onto the notepad before
her. "Elementary? High school?"

"Back then, she was working with younger kids.
Elementary, I guess."

Maggie nodded. "What else can you tell me
about her?"

He could tell her that the moment he'd noticed
Emmie standing near a booth at the open-air market,
her windswept blond hair and pale-blue eyes star-

tling in a land where everyone had dark coloring, her lightweight linen skirt pressed against her long legs by the breeze and her cheeks pink from the sun, he'd become enchanted, eager to know who she was. He could tell the detective that he'd been seduced by Emmie's lilting Southern drawl and her gentle hands, and the way laughter bubbled up from deep inside her like an underground spring of crystalline water. He could tell Maggie Tyrell that making love with Emmie was like discovering heaven did exist after all, and you didn't have to die to reach it as long as you were in Emmie's arms.

But none of that would help Maggie to locate Emmie. "She would be about thirty now, maybe thirty-one," he said. "She grew up in Richmond, Virginia. I think her parents were well-off."

Tyrell scribbled notes on her pad.

"I left San Pablo kind of abruptly." Understatement of the century, he thought grimly. "I didn't have time to say goodbye or let her know where I was going. I had to...well, leave."

The detective nodded.

"I need to find Emmie, to explain to her why I had to leave her like that." No, he needed to find Emmie to tell her that when he'd said he loved her, he'd meant it. He didn't love her now—too much time had passed, and they would practically be strangers if they saw each other—but he wanted her to know he hadn't lied to her then, not about love.

Maggie put down her pencil and leaned back in her chair. "Mr. Molina, I've got to tell you, before I take your case, that things might not work out."

He nodded. "I know it's going to be hard to find her."

"Oh, I'm pretty sure I'll find her. Finders, Keep-

ers has been in business for a year and I haven't
struck out yet. But sometimes the person I find isn't
the person my client is looking for. People change.
Ms. Kenyon could be married, for instance.''

"It wouldn't surprise me," he muttered. How
could a woman like Emmie remain single these past
few years? Michael surely hadn't been the first man
to fall for her, and he wouldn't have been the last.

"She might be settled, with a family of her own.
A man from her past might be the last person she'd
want showing up on her doorstep."

"I understand."

"I started Finders, Keepers because I wanted to
bring separated lovers together," she told him. "My
brothers are detectives, too—I share this office suite
with them. But they specialize in digging up dirt for
their clients, working for divorce lawyers, that kind
of thing. I'm the family optimist, and I believe
happy endings are possible."

Michael waited, knowing she had more to say.

"I've done a good job of bringing long-lost lovers
together, but I'm afraid I haven't always made them
happy," she warned.

He nodded. She wasn't telling him anything he
hadn't told himself a million times, ever since he'd
begun his own unprofessional, ultimately fruitless
search.

"So. I'll take your case, but I want you going
into it with your eyes open."

He thought of the months after he'd returned to
the States, when he couldn't close his eyes at all
because closing them would bring on the nightmares. Now whenever he closed his eyes he saw

Emmie. "My eyes are wide open," he assured Maggie Tyrell.

"All right, then," she said. "Let's do it. Let's find Mary-Elizabeth Kenyon."

CHAPTER ONE

IT WAS THE TRICYCLE that brought him up short.

He remembered everything Maggie Tyrell had warned him about how people changed, about how what a client was looking for and what he found weren't always the same thing, about how she couldn't guarantee happiness. And he remembered the more basic warning that the woman she'd located might not be the same Mary-Elizabeth Kenyon he had known five years ago. "Kenyon isn't that unusual a name," she'd reminded him when she'd phoned him a week after he'd signed a contract with her. "Your Mary-Elizabeth might have gotten married and changed her name. Or there could be other Mary-Elizabeth Kenyons."

"Then why did you call?" he'd asked Maggie. "If you don't think this is the same woman as Emmie—"

"You're paying me to find things out. I did a search of the database of the two big teachers' unions, and I found a woman named Mary-Elizabeth Kenyon living in Wilborough, Massachusetts, and currently working as a third-grade teacher at the Oak Hill School in the Wilborough School District. According to her employment records, she's thirty years old and she was born in Richmond, Virginia. Now, I don't know if—"

"It's her," Michael had declared. If the woman

Maggie Tyrell had found *wasn't* his Emmie, his heart wouldn't be pounding like a stampede in his chest. His hands wouldn't be clinging so tightly to the receiver that his knuckles ached.

"As I said, Mr. Molina, there could be other Mary-Elizabeth Kenyons."

"And all of them are thirty-year-old elementary schoolteachers?"

"I'll dig deeper if you'd like. I can try to find out if she was ever in San Pablo."

"No," Michael said. "It's her. I know it."

It wasn't until after he'd gotten off the phone that he'd allowed himself to consider that maybe the woman Maggie had found wasn't the woman he'd lost. The Emmie Kenyon he'd known wouldn't have wound up in Massachusetts. He couldn't imagine her in some white-clapboard town with snow and sleigh bells and winter apples, a town populated by lobstermen and flinty villagers who misplaced their R's when they talked. The Emmie he'd known five years ago had taken great pride in her Virginia ancestry. She wouldn't have chosen to make her home amid all those Yankees.

But that was the point Maggie had repeatedly emphasized: even if she found the right Emmie Kenyon, it might not be the Emmie Michael was looking for. She might be the same person genetically. But five years was a long time. Emmie could have changed.

He stared at her house through the open window of his rental car. It sat on a tidy, tree-lined block of modest, well-kept houses. The lawn was neatly cut and edged, the azaleas were splashed with bright-pink blossoms and the house's white shingles and pine-green shutters looked recently painted. The one-car garage was open, but no car was inside; the interior of the garage appeared uncluttered, although he couldn't see much from his vantage across the street. No lights appeared to be on inside the house, although given the bright late-afternoon sunshine, there was probably no need for indoor lighting. The mailbox on a post at the foot of the driveway bore the number of the house but no last name.

And there, parked on the grass alongside the driveway, was a tricycle.

Michael cursed.

Despite every warning Maggie Tyrell had given him, and every warning he'd given himself, he'd had...*hope.* Hope that so many years after fate had sent him to hell and home again, he could stroll back into Emmie's life, bringing apologies and explanations as if they were generous gifts she couldn't help but accept. Hope that he could somehow convince her the past was truly behind him, and everything he'd felt for her that long-ago spring in San Pablo had been true and real, and now that he'd put his world back together again, maybe he would feel those feelings again. He'd been persuasive then; surely he could be persuasive now.

Maggie Tyrell, detective to the lovelorn, the curious and the foolishly optimistic, could have cautioned Michael from here to Sunday that Emmie would likely have gone on to live her own life, and if he had half a brain he would have recognized the truth in Maggie's words. Of course Emmie had gotten on with it, left San Pablo and forged a new life for herself—in Massachusetts, of all places. He could accept that. But he'd never let himself consider that she might have gotten married and kept her own last name. She hadn't struck him as the sort who'd do that.

The hell with her last name—it was the tricycle that really had him scared.

If she was a wife and mother, Michael would disappear. He'd go back to California and figure out a new strategy for surviving the rest of his life. He wouldn't screw up whatever she'd created for herself.

But still...*hope*. Hope that the tricycle—one of those vibrant-colored plastic low-riders with fat wheels—belonged to a neighbor's child. Hope that Emmie was still single, still gentle, still possessed of the most mesmerizing blue eyes he'd ever seen, the most honest smile he'd ever felt warming his soul. Hope that her eyes would sparkle and her smile would shine when she saw him.

He climbed out of the car. That no one seemed to be home was actually a good thing. Before he actually saw her, he wanted to orient himself to this part of the world where she'd set down roots. Any reunion was bound to be awkward. He wanted to accustom himself to her new environment first. It might make him feel a little more comfortable when he finally saw her.

The air smelled of spring, of afternoon warmth. When he shut the car door, two startled swallows bolted from the foliage of the maple tree near where he'd parked. A minivan cruised down the street, and he waited until it had passed before crossing the road to her driveway.

His gaze swerved inexorably to the tricycle. The front wheel was the color of a ripe banana, and large enough to seem aggressive. Red streamers hung from the molded plastic handlebars. The seat was green.

Birds called to one onother. A flat white petal floated down from a blossoming dogwood in her front yard, swirling and gliding like a scrap of paper caught in a breeze. He wondered if she tended the property all by herself, or if she hired a landscaping service. Or if she had a husband to mow her lawn and prune her shrubs.

More birds sang out, and then he detected the sound of young laughter in the distance, drifting from behind the house. He didn't dare to march up her driveway and around the side to see if the laughter was coming from her backyard—and then he didn't have to. Two young boys scampered into view, veering past the blossoming rhododendron at the front corner of the house, shrieking playfully as they fled from someone. They were moving so quickly Michael could make out little more than logo-emblazoned T-shirts, grass-stained blue jeans and faded Red Sox baseball caps.

Kindergarteners, he'd guess. Five years old, at least. Which meant they couldn't belong to Emmie, because five years ago she'd been in San Pablo with him. Maybe she'd adopted the boys, or they were her nephews. Maybe they were stepsons, her husband's from a former marriage.

Or else maybe Michael had come to the wrong house. Maybe this Mary-Elizabeth Kenyon wasn't his Emmie after all.

That possibility was reinforced when a robust woman chasing the boys appeared. Her dark hair was pulled back into a ponytail, and she wore soccer shorts, a sweatshirt and running shoes. Definitely not his Emmie.

He was disappointed, but also relieved.

"Get back here, you two!" she shouted at the boys. Apparently she was unaware of the stranger lurking near her driveway, observing her. "Right now! You guys are in *so* much trouble…" But she was laughing nearly as hard as they were. Her threats were obviously part of the game.

The boys shrieked louder and tore around the house, out of sight.

The woman could have snagged them if she'd tried, but she clearly wasn't trying. Hands on her hips, she paused in the driveway to catch her breath. She looked too young to be the mother of those boys, and her Williams College sweatshirt made her look even younger. But who knew? Teenagers became mothers all the time these days. Or else she might be older than she looked, wearing a sweatshirt that dated back to her college days.

In any case, she wasn't the right Mary-Elizabeth Kenyon.

Gradually she stopped panting. She tucked a stray lock of hair behind her ear and checked her watch. A breeze carried the giggles of the boys from somewhere behind the house, but she just shrugged and turned, reaching for the tricycle. Noticing Michael, she froze.

Not wanting to alarm her, he remained where he was on the sidewalk near the foot of the driveway. He turned his hands palm out, as if to prove that he was unarmed. He really didn't think he appeared dangerous in his khakis and tailored blue shirt.

Still, he was a stranger, and she was entitled to be wary.

"I'm looking for Mary-Elizabeth Kenyon," he said.

The young woman abandoned the tricycle and straightened up. "She's not here," she said laconically, informing him that she herself wasn't the Mary-Elizabeth Kenyon who lived at this address.

He dared to take a step closer, and let his hands drop to his sides. "Do you know when she'll be home?"

"Who are you?"

"An old friend."

"What's your name?"

He hesitated before answering, then realized his hesitation was making her suspicious. "Michael Molina."

"I'll tell her you stopped by," the woman said, turning back to the tricycle.

No. That wouldn't do. If the Mary-Elizabeth Kenyon who lived here was his Emmie and this woman told her Michael Molina had stopped by, she might pile her furniture behind the door and file a restraining order against him. Not that she had anything to fear from him, but after the way he'd treated her five years ago, he doubted she would want to see him. His plan had been to pop into her life and start apologizing so fast she wouldn't have time to erect any defenses.

Of course, if he was at the wrong Mary-Elizabeth Kenyon's house, the lady in the Williams College sweatshirt would mention that someone named Michael Molina had stopped by, and the woman who lived here would say, "Who?"

"It's really important that I see her," he insisted. He didn't want to scare Williams College off, but he didn't want her to blow him off, either. "I've been trying to find her for a long time."

Williams College abandoned the tricycle once

again and turned to regard him. She scrutinized
him—measuring him for homicidal tendencies, no
doubt. He gave her his most winsome smile and
sensed something thaw inside her.

"Okay," she said. "Are you staying somewhere
in the area?"

"Yes."

"Then I'll tell her you're in town, and she can
get in touch with you. Where are you staying?"

He held his face immobile while his mind revved.
He hadn't even bothered to find a room for the night.
He'd simply gotten off the plane at Logan Airport,
rented a car and headed straight for the Cullen Drive
address in Wilborough Maggie Tyrell had provided.
He'd thoughtlessly assumed that the moment Emmie
saw him and heard his apologies, her heart would
melt and she'd open her arms and her home to him.

Obviously that assumption had been pretty wide
of the mark. He scrambled to recall the names of
the motels he'd passed on his drive. "The Holiday
Inn," he said, praying the motel would have a room
for him, on the chance that Emmie might call that
evening.

"Okay. Michael Molina, Holiday Inn. I'll tell
her."

He understood he was being dismissed. "Say it's
important," he stressed, wondering if he sounded as
desperate as he felt, wondering why he should even
feel desperate. He was arguably crazy, chasing Emmie down so many years after everything had gone
wrong. In all likelihood, she was more necessary to
him as a memory, a fantasy of what might have
been, than as a real woman in the present.

But he'd come this far. He'd paid good money to

a detective to locate her for him. He couldn't give up, not yet.

"I'll tell her," Williams College responded, sounding less than enthusiastic. Clearly she didn't think it was important that Mary-Elizabeth Kenyon get in touch with him. She probably figured him for a pest, if not worse: a stalker, a felon, a dire threat to everything Emmie cared about. At one time, he supposed, that was exactly what he'd been.

If he continued to insist on how vital it was for Emmie to contact him, Williams College would definitely feel threatened. "Thanks," he said, shoving his hands into the pockets of his khakis. "I appreciate it." With a benign nod, he turned to go.

A sudden peal of laughter spilled into the front yard, capturing his attention. The two little boys raced around the house from the back, jostling each other and giggling. The minute they saw Williams College, they burst into simultaneous shouting.

"We saw this thing—" one began.

"It was so big—"

"And it was this big monster—"

They both dissolved in giggles again.

The woman folded her arms across her chest as she turned to them. She looked skeptical, but the corners of her mouth twitched upward, fighting for a smile. "A monster? How big?"

"*This* big!" one of the boys squealed, spreading his tyke-size arms wide.

"No, *this* big!" his buddy said, topping him, stretching his arms outward.

"No, *this* big!" It was obviously a competition to see which one of them could extend his arms wider.

"All right, you guys," Williams College interrupted. "So it was *this* big. What color hair did it have?"

"Green!" hollered one boy, while the other shouted, "Poker dots!" That was silly enough to launch them both into gales of laughter.

The woman eyed Michael conspiratorially. He couldn't resist a smile. In general, children—even cute ones—didn't do much for him. What passed for childhood wisdom generally seemed about as profound as fortune-cookie messages, and adorable kids on TV made him gag. He could stare politely at the stilted school photo of some friend's offspring and make appropriate comments, but he usually had to force himself to pretend he cared.

These kids, though… Their laughter was a tonic at the end of a long day that had begun that morning in Berkeley and had entailed a tiring transcontinental flight followed by a baffling drive from the airport through downtown Boston to this quiet village a half-hour north of the city. He knew he was on Cullen Drive in Wilborough, but he had no idea where he *really* was, at least when it came to Emmie.

What was a man to do at a time like this? He could groan, he could curse or he could grin at two scrappy little boys with huge imaginations who were in the grip of a giggle epidemic.

One of them, slightly taller than his friend, stopped laughing first, petering out with a few snorts and gasps. He gave the other boy a playful shove, then spun around, evidently intending to return to the backyard to deal with the *poker*-dot-haired monster. Michael glimpsed the boy's brown eyes beneath the curved brim of the child's baseball cap and his heart slammed against his ribs.

Beneath that cap, beneath the shock of dark hair, Michael saw his own face gazing back at him.

"I'M SORRY, MS. KENYON, but I simply don't see how we can make it happen," the mortgage officer at County Savings and Trust said. His tone registered a level of sorrow Emmie knew he didn't feel. He was a callow kid in an off-the-rack suit, a recent college graduate, no doubt. He'd likely majored in something utterly impractical and then hastily enrolled in a seminar on bank mortgage policies, and now he had the power to reduce her life to shambles.

She'd already tried the big banks, the megafinanciers with no true ties to Wilborough. They'd been politely chilly as they'd rejected her mortgage application. She'd thought that maybe the one local bank with roots in the community might feel an obligation to keep its neighborhoods stable and its customers satisfied.

But Ronald Petit, the young mortgage officer who now held her fate in his hands, evidently didn't think that satisfying Emmie and keeping her neighborhood stable were compelling reasons for him to stretch his bank's mortgage qualifications. "I've been renting the house for three years," she reminded him. "I've maintained the property. My landlord would love to sell to me. It would make life easier for everyone."

"Everyone except us here at County Savings," Ronald Petit explained. "I've gone over your application, Ms. Kenyon, and I just don't see how you can do it. We have formulas to calculate eligibility, and I'm afraid you don't come close."

"I'll be coming up for tenure next year. I'm sure

I'll get it," she said with as much certainty as she could muster.

"And you're earning a decent income," he agreed, his voice so heavy with condescension she wanted to reach across his imposing desk and smack him. "But even if you do get tenure," he went on, "it's only one income. Most first-time home owners manage the financing by having two incomes." He angled her application before his eyes as if he hadn't already read it a million times—and probably snickered every time at the numbers she'd inserted into the blanks.

"In other words, you think I should moonlight evenings at the local hamburger joint?" Her mother had drilled into her that sarcasm wasn't ladylike, but sometimes, Emmie believed, it was mandatory.

Apparently Ronald Petit was immune to sarcasm—or else oblivious to it. "You have one income and a lot of expenses. Your child-care costs—"

"In one more year, Jeffrey will be starting kindergarten. I'm going to be saving a lot of money on child care."

"But the bottom line," Ronald Petit declared, "is that you have nothing for a down payment. Your savings are negligible." He seemed to have trouble pronouncing "negligible." It was a word he might have been kind enough to avoid, given the pain it inflicted upon her. He attempted a sympathetic smile. "You know, a lot of people in your situation get help from their families. Perhaps your parents could contribute to the down payment—"

"No," she said swiftly. Her parents could not contribute to the down payment. Her parents could not—*would not*—contribute anything at all. And

Emmie would rather fall on a sword than ask them for help.

"That's what a lot of first-time buyers do," Ronald said, persevering.

"I'm not a lot of first-time buyers," she snapped, then took a deep, calming breath. Arguing with the young bank officer wouldn't do her any good. "I don't suppose your bank has done any research on whether its mortgage decisions discriminate against single mothers."

That got his attention. "Discriminate?"

"Well, when you mentioned two incomes, you weren't talking about my taking a second job. You were talking about a husband and wife who both work, am I right?"

"In this economy, that's often the way young families qualify for mortgages," he agreed, watching her as if he expected her to spring a civil rights lawyer on him.

"And you've pointed out my child-care costs as a reason I don't qualify."

"I'm going by the numbers, Ms. Kenyon. There's nothing I can do." His sympathy seemed genuine now. "If I could approve your application, I would. I would love to. But I can't. We've got a formula and we have to stick with it. If you could scrape up a bigger down payment, then you'd be able to handle the monthly payments on your income. But without a sizable down payment, you won't. I'm just going by the formula."

"Fine." She wouldn't beg and she wouldn't weep. She would hang on to her dignity, because at the moment it was all she had.

Being rejected for a mortgage wasn't the worst thing that had ever happened to her, she tried to console herself as, after a few bland words of thanks, she left the bank for the sun-glazed sidewalk outside. Mary-Elizabeth Kenyon, great-great-great-granddaughter of a Confederate officer who'd lost his left leg and his farm in the War Between the States, knew how to survive defeat. That particular talent had been bred in the bone. Kenyons fought, and sometimes they lost, but they never gave up. They simply threw back their shoulders, wrapped their pride around them like a mantle and marched on.

Pride wouldn't put a roof over her head and Jeffrey's, though.

The house on Cullen Drive was the perfect home for her and her son. It was just the right size, with a fine yard for playing in and a beautiful sun-kissed corner of the rear yard for her garden. The rent was manageable, and her landlord never badgered her. She would have been content to remain right where she was until Jeffrey was grown and gone—except that her landlord had fallen and broken his hip, and he'd decided to move to Tempe, Arizona, to be closer to his son and daughter-in-law. For him to buy a place in Tempe, he had to sell the house in Wilborough.

"I'd love to sell it to you," he'd told Emmie. "It would make my life easier, and yours, too. Just to save myself the chore of having to list the place with a real-estate agent, I'd sell it to you at ten thousand below the listing price."

The price was fair. But Emmie's finances simply couldn't accommodate it.

So she had to move. She had to uproot Jeffrey and find new housing, even though she knew she'd never find anything as ideal as her current residence.

Just contemplating the physical labor of moving—changing all the utilities, packing everything into cartons, hiring a mover or renting a truck and corraling a few friends to assist her—brought tears to her eyes. A move could be exciting if you were moving to a better house and if you'd chosen to make the move. But she hadn't chosen it. She had no choice at all.

Sighing, she slung her purse higher on her shoulder and walked across the parking lot to her car, an eight-year-old subcompact she'd bought used right after she'd gotten the job at the Oak Hill School. It wasn't as if she didn't live frugally. She worked hard and loved her job. She drove a clunker and said a little prayer every time she twisted the key in the ignition. She bought Jeffrey's clothing in the discount shops and never entered a supermarket without her envelope of discount coupons. Over the summer she tutored children for extra cash. Vacation trips with Jeffrey were as simple as a day at the Museum of Science or the beach in Rockport. Her only extravagance was the preschool where Jeffrey was enrolled; it was the best preschool in Wilborough, and Jeffrey's well-being was one area where she refused to stint, even if the tuition was astronomical.

When a single woman started with nothing but a degree in education and a baby, saving money for a down payment on a house was all but impossible. She'd done her best, but—as Ronald Petit had pointed out—most women looking for financing for a house were one-half of a two-income marriage, or else they turned to their parents for assistance.

Emmie couldn't turn to her parents. That door was closed and locked.

If she'd survived her parents' rejection, she reminded herself as she settled behind the wheel of her car, surely she could survive rejection by the mortgage officer at County Savings and Trust. Still, as she closed her door and leaned against the steering wheel, a few tears trickled through her lashes and down her cheeks. Damn. She didn't want to lose the house. She didn't want to move. She didn't want to be at the mercy of Ronald Petit or anyone else. All she wanted was a nice, comfortable home for her son. Was that so unreasonable?

Most of the heat had left the day. May was an odd month in eastern Massachusetts, Emmie had learned: some days felt like mid-August; others, the thermometer never inched above sixty degrees. Today had been somewhere in the middle, warm enough at midday for her students to grow restless for recess, warm enough for her to open the windows and fill the classroom with the song of spring birds, but not so hot that the children grew limp from the heat. It was the sort of day Emmie would have liked to spend with Jeffrey, and if Gwyn from the front desk hadn't chased Emmie on her way out of the school building at three-thirty, waving a phone message from Ronald Petit that said he would meet with her that afternoon to discuss her mortgage application, she would have picked Jeffrey up at the Sunny Skies Preschool and driven him to the playground by the community center so he could have played pirate on the colorful, rambling maze of swings and tubes and slides constructed in the center of the park.

Instead she'd raced back into the school building, phoned Claire—blessedly home for the summer break—and begged her to pick Jeffrey up at Sunny

Skies. Claire had baby-sat often for Emmie during her senior year at Wilborough High, and Emmie had been distraught when Claire had left for college. Now she was back for the summer, eager to earn money. Jeffrey knew and loved Claire, which made her worth every penny Emmie paid her.

Her tears spent, Emmie rubbed the knotted muscles at her nape. If she and Jeffrey had to move from Cullen Drive, would they lose Claire as a baby-sitter? What if they had to move so far away that Claire wouldn't want to bother driving across town, or across several towns, just to baby-sit for a couple of hours with Jeffrey?

The entire mess drained Emmie. Her head throbbed, and a lump of emotion, part anger, part frustration, part grief, churned in her chest. As a young woman she had left her comfortable existence and traveled thousands of miles to work with people less fortunate than she…but somehow she'd always thought that eventually, once she'd reached the age of thirty, her life might regain a bit of the ease she'd known as a child. She'd thought she would return to America and continue to teach and do good works here—but she would also be fifty percent of one of those two-income couples, living in a house she owned, raising her children without any financial stress—maybe even eating off nice dishes and taking winter vacations—a week in the Bahamas or skiing at Lake Tahoe.

She'd never thought she would return to America pregnant and abandoned. But she didn't regret what had happened, because what had happened had given her something infinitely more valuable than a nice house and a gainfully employed husband, or winter vacations at the beach or on the slopes. It had given her Jeffrey, and it had given her herself.

Rush-hour traffic oozed through the tranquil streets of town. Much as Emmie wished she were home, she didn't mind driving slowly, especially at this time of year, when daffodils and goldenrod lined the roads with a yellow as bright as sunshine and rhododendrons looked as if someone had splashed shocking-pink paint all over their leathery leaves. Her car lacked air-conditioning, but that was all right. She liked driving with her window down, smelling the season in the air. Springtime seemed more precious here in New England, since it inevitably followed a long, dreary winter.

It took her twenty minutes to cover the three miles from downtown Wilborough to her block. She waved at Glenn Drinan as he steered onto the driveway across the street from her house, then braked when she noticed the unfamiliar car parked in front of the Drinan house, blocking her normal swing and requiring her to make a tighter turn into her own driveway. She was touched that Claire had thought to leave the garage open for her. If she ever had real money, she would install one of those remote-control garage-door openers. After she bought a house, of course.

The garage was dark and cool, filled with the tart scent of fertilizer. How could the bank turn her down when she took such good care of this place? Most home owners wouldn't have bothered to fertilize the lawn. They'd tell the landlord to take care of it, or hire a service. But she'd assured her landlord she would maintain the property, and he in turn kept her rent low.

She loved this house. She'd made it her home. She didn't want to move.

She felt the sting of a few fresh tears and quickly batted her eyes. She didn't want Jeffrey to see her upset. She'd have to put a cheerful spin on the news that he would be moving away from the only home he could remember, away from Claire, away from Adam Kessler, his very best friend in the whole wide world.

Once she was certain she wasn't going to start crying, she got out of the car, pulled her briefcase from the backseat and stepped out of the garage, figuring Jeffrey had to be outside on such a gorgeous afternoon. She didn't hear him, though. Maybe he and Adam were busy plotting some pirate activity in the backyard—when she couldn't take him to the playground, Jeffrey improvised, pretending the redwood picnic table on the patio was his pirate ship.

She started toward the rear of the house, but a movement in the distance teased her attention. Glancing toward the street, she saw a man emerge from the car parked in front of the Drinan house. She turned away, then hesitated and turned back again.

The man was crossing the street toward her. He moved with a loping gait, his shoulders loose, one arm swinging at his side and the other bent, his fingers hooking the collar of a jacket slung over his shoulder. He wore khakis and a crisp blue shirt, open at the collar—a nondescript outfit.

But he wasn't a nondescript man. His hair was blacker than ink, his skin a tawny bronze, his eyes almost as dark as his hair. She knew his face as well as she knew his lanky build, his easy stride, the defiant angle of his chin and the set of his mouth.

Michael Molina.

Momentarily her mind went blank. When it resumed functioning he was several steps closer, his long legs devouring the distance between them.

Michael Molina.

She wanted to scream. She wanted to run. She wanted to grab Jeffrey, lock him in the house and barricade the door.

If there was anything she *didn't* want, it was Michael Molina walking across the street and back into her life.

He was on her driveway now, just six strides away from her, five, four. He stopped at three—and thank God for that, because if he'd kept approaching she definitely would have flinched or fled for her life.

"Emmie," he murmured.

She opened her mouth, but no sound emerged. She had nothing to say to him, nothing she could say without feeling wretched afterward.

He drew closer. "I've been looking for you."

Tell him to leave, she ordered herself. *Tell him you hate his guts and wish him a life of misery followed by a painful death, and then tell him to get off your property. He doesn't have to know you don't own it. Tell him to leave or you'll have him arrested for trespassing.*

"I started searching for you more than a year ago," he continued, evidently viewing her silence as permission to continue talking. "I finally hired a detective."

"Oh." *Oh?* That was the best she could do? A man who had all but ruined her life, except for her uncanny ability to find triumph in the ruins—and he'd hired a detective and tracked her down and all she could say, in a rusty, half-choked voice, was "Oh."

"Can we talk?" His words were soft, lulling. Obviously *he* could talk just fine. She was the one reduced to grunting.

She would have to try harder. In San Pablo she'd never had any difficulty speaking her mind with him. She'd just have to do it now. "No," she said. "We can't talk."

"I've missed you."

"I haven't missed you." More tears beaded in her eyes. She told herself they were caused by the angle of the sun and her defeat in Ronald Petit's office at the bank, but these were different tears. These were tears of long-buried anger and pain, tears of a woman who'd had her heart broken, tears of panic and dread at the sight of the man who had broken it invading her life all over again. "Please go away," she whispered, wishing she sounded strong and forceful instead of teetering on the edge of despair.

Unable to look at him, unable to let him see the dampness in her eyes, she took a step toward the front walk. He reached out and caught her arm in his hand. She felt his fingers on her, warm and strong, and that made her hate him even more.

He urged her around to face him, his hand tightening on her wrist. He was too close to her, his eyes so dark and potent his gaze felt like a caress, like a slap.

"I saw the boy," he said.

CHAPTER TWO

SOMETHING LOCKED TIGHT inside her, a bolt sliding into place in her soul. Michael Molina would not gain entrance to where she and Jeffrey lived. He would not be allowed in.

She stared at him, his posture straight without being rigid, his height imposing even though he wasn't extraordinarily tall, his angular features edged in gold by the slope of the fading sunlight. She remembered the first time she'd glimpsed him in the village square in San Pablo five years ago, the flutter she'd felt along her nerve endings at the sight of such a strikingly handsome man. Nothing about Michael's appearance had been polished, nothing perfect; yet his face had come together beautifully—the dark slashes of his eyebrows, the sharp line of his nose, the slight hollows beneath his cheekbones, the sun-bronzed glow of his complexion. And his lean physique had reminded her of a cougar's, fleet and graceful.

He was just as handsome now as he'd been then. His eyes were just as mysterious, taking in much more than they gave away. She knew his eyes, because she saw them every time she gazed into Jeffrey's face, every time she greeted her little boy in the morning and tucked him into bed at night.

Michael wasn't going to learn why she saw his

eyes in her son's face. Michael had no rights where Jeffrey was concerned. He had abandoned Emmie, and abandoning her meant abandoning any claim to the life she'd created since his departure.

Saying so flat out was impossible. She was too angry to find the right words, too afraid to force them out—and too aware of his fingers wrapped around her wrist to think clearly. His hand wasn't hot, yet it sent a burning sensation into her skin and up her arm. She wished he would let go so she could race into the house and shut the door.

"Is he mine?" he asked.

"No." She could say that without lying. Contributing sperm didn't make a man a father. Jeffrey wasn't Michael's, and he never would be.

"He looks like me."

"He looks like a lot of people." She tried to ease her arm out of Michael's grasp without seeming too obvious. He didn't release her, though, and she couldn't free herself without jerking her hand so violently he would realize how upset she was.

"What's his name?"

"I want you to leave," she said steadily, holding her fear at bay and staring directly into Michael's eyes. "We have nothing to say to each other. Please go."

Michael ignored her request. "How old is he?"

"Go away, Michael. You don't belong here." She lowered her gaze pointedly to her wrist trapped within his hand. Sighing, he loosened his grip.

Oddly enough, she found it impossible to move away from him, even after he was no longer holding her. She smelled the familiar scent of his soap, a spicy, woodsy fragrance that caused a spasm of nostalgia to grip her. He'd used that soap in San Pablo. He'd always smelled so clean, even in the muggy, buggy heat.

She told herself she no longer liked his fresh fragrance. She no longer liked his long legs, his black hair. His soul was blacker, and she despised it. She despised everything about him.

"I'm sorry about what happened in San Pablo," he said.

He sounded earnest. But she knew better than to believe him. "It doesn't matter anymore."

"Of course it matters. I've been looking for you for more than a year."

"Then you wasted a year." She heard as much sorrow as rage in her tone. "We've both gone on to other things. And now I'd like to go on to my house—" the house that, soon enough, would no longer be hers "—and my son—" the son who would always, always, be hers. Neither the decisions of bank mortgage officers nor the sudden appearance of Michael Molina would ever change that.

Somehow she found the will to turn from Michael, to stride up the front walk, enter her house and close the door without slamming it. She didn't dare to peek through the window in the door to see if Michael was loitering in her driveway. Even if he wasn't gone, she wanted to assume that he was.

"Jeffrey?" she called into the quiet living room.

Claire emerged from the kitchen, brisk and bouncy in her athletic apparel and tennis shoes. "Adam came over to play," she reported. "I didn't think you'd mind."

"Of course not." Emmie walked down the hall

that bordered the living room and led to the kitchen at the rear of the house.

"They're in Jeffrey's room," Claire continued, following Emmie back into the kitchen but hovering in the doorway as Emmie tossed her tote bag onto the table and slouched against a counter. "They were playing outdoors, but…there was this man."

Emmie raised her eyes to Claire.

"He asked for you. At first he said you could contact him at the Holiday Inn, but then he decided not to leave. He just stayed out there, staring at the house and waiting for you. It was kind of spooky, so I made the boys come inside."

Emmie nodded, reached for her briefcase and rummaged in it for her wallet. "I spoke to him. I think he'll leave now." He'd better leave, she added silently. He *had* to leave.

"He said he was an old friend of yours. He's way handsome. It was weird—he looked kind of like Jeffrey. His eyes were so intense, the way Jeffrey's get sometimes. I wrote down the guy's name." She handed Emmie the message pad, which said "Michael Molina—Holiday Inn" on it.

"He's an old acquaintance, not a friend." Emmie tore the top sheet from the pad and tossed the sheet into the garbage pail. Then she pulled a ten-dollar bill out of her wallet to cover the two hours Claire had stayed with Jeffrey. "I appreciate your coming on such short notice, Claire—and bringing the boys inside when that man showed up. It was the right thing to do."

Claire accepted the money with a grateful smile. "Well, it's not that I thought there was anything wrong with him. It was just, like, his eyes. And he didn't want to leave, you know?''

"I know." He didn't want to leave because he'd seen Jeffrey's face, noticed the resemblance and decided to make a big deal out of it. The hell with him. If seeing Jeffrey was racking him with guilt over what he might have left behind when he'd fled from San Pablo, that was his problem, not Emmie's.

Emmie's problem was much more immediate: finding housing she could afford for Jeffrey and her. The last thing she needed was Michael Molina and his unforgivably belated explanations.

Claire observed her thoughtfully. "I can walk Adam home if you want," she offered.

Emmie managed a weak smile. "Thanks, I'd appreciate that." A hint of her drawl slipped into her voice. It always did when she was weary, and right now she felt as drained as a punctured balloon. She hated for anyone to see her so deflated, and she forced some spirit into her smile. "I'll go get Adam," she said, turning and heading down the hall to Jeffrey's bedroom.

She heard the boys' giggles through the closed door. After knocking, she eased it open. They were engaged in a battle with Jeffrey's plastic dinosaurs. He had a stegosaurus and an allosaurus in his fists; Adam was armed with a triceratops and an ankylosaurus. The landscape was littered with waffle blocks and the pillows from Jeffrey's bed were on the floor, but the boys were both laughing too hard to wage a war with any effectiveness.

She allowed herself a moment to watch them. Jeffrey's room was raucous with color. His rumpled bedspread was bright red, and above it hung a multicolored felt picture of Noah's ark, the animals fastened to the boat with Velcro so Jeffrey could rearrange them. The bureau had a white frame and drawers of red, blue and green; Emmie had bought it and the bookshelf at the Salvation Army store, sanded off the scratched veneers and refinished them in bright colors. The footlocker where she stored Jeffrey's winter sweaters and linens she'd found in the recycling area of the town dump; she'd whitewashed it and painted vibrant-colored balloons over the white background.

The room was wonderful, as exuberant as the boy who lived in it. The shelves were crammed with all Jeffrey's essential stuff: toy construction trucks; a bucket of Legos; assorted Matchbox cars; his stuffed bears, Teddy and Frumpy; Candy Land; Checkers; half a dozen other plastic dinosaurs; and books. Lots of books. Picture books and alphabet books and a few simple storybooks he could already read by himself, and the books she read to him at night before bed. She and Jeffrey were halfway through *Winnie-the-Pooh,* and it lay on the top shelf, a bookmark protruding from its pages.

She couldn't bear the thought of having to pack up all Jeffrey's things and move them to some other bedroom in another house. Would another bedroom let in so much afternoon sun? Would another bedroom occupy a corner, with windows on two walls, so the room would cool down at night in the cross-ventilation, the breezes lulling her little boy to sleep? Would she ever find a house with a room Jeffrey would fit into so perfectly?

"Adam has to go home now," she told the boys. "Please clean up the floor."

''Can he stay for supper?'' Jeffrey asked, his eyes large and pleading.

Emmie pursed her lips. She'd scolded him about inviting friends over for meals and sleepovers without first checking with her. Tonight was definitely not a good time to have a guest for dinner, even if dinner was going to be nothing more elaborate than macaroni and cheese. She was strung too tight, ready to snap. ''I'm sorry,'' she said, exerting herself to remain calm, ''but he can't.''

''Well, but we had a plan,'' Jeffrey said, his hands still curled around his dinosaurs. ''We thought we could have a picnic—''

''We could eat outside,'' Adam elaborated.

''On account of the monster—''

''What monster?'' she asked.

''The one outside.''

A picture of Michael materialized unbidden in her mind. Was he the monster? Had he frightened the boys? Had he spoken to them? Dear Lord, had he told Jeffrey who he was?

''He's got poker-dot hair,'' Jeffrey continued, ''and he lives in the crab-apple tree.''

''We were gonna feed him some food,'' Adam explained. ''From our supper. We were gonna share it cuz sharing is good.''

Emmie was relieved to learn the monster was only a polka-dot-haired denizen of the crab-apple tree. Better that than the man who had wreaked havoc with her life once, and could do it again simply by pressing her for information about Jeffrey.

''I'm afraid the monster will have to go hungry tonight,'' she told the boys. ''Or he can eat crab apples.''

"There's no crab apples," Jeffrey reminded her. "Only flowers."

"Then he'll eat those. Anyway, monsters mostly eat little boys who refuse to clean up their messes. So what do you say, boys? How about picking up all those blocks?"

The boys conceded, looking only mildly disappointed. She suspected Jeffrey had known all along she would say no to his plan to have Adam stay for dinner, if for no other reason than he hadn't cleared it with her first. The boys bent to the task of gathering up the blocks, and she herself pitched in and scooped up a few. She didn't want to make Claire wait, and besides, she wanted everyone out of the house, everyone but her and Jeffrey.

She needed some peace and quiet. But even after Claire and Adam were gone—and Michael, too, she noticed when she waved off the baby-sitter and Jeffrey's friend—she could not quell her agitation.

Michael was gone, but not really. She felt his presence even in his absence. She felt his nearness like a shadow, just beyond her peripheral vision, hovering. It chilled her to the depths of her heart.

She honestly felt she could have handled losing her home. Not happily, not willingly, but she could have found a silver lining in that cloud, a positive outcome to that calamity. Perhaps she could move to a rental unit in a condominium complex that had a pool. Then Jeffrey could go swimming every day in the summer, and there might be more friends to play with, friends whose homes he could walk to by himself. Perhaps the utilities would be cheaper in a smaller place. Perhaps the shopping would be more convenient.

So what if it wouldn't have a crab-apple tree with a monster dwelling in its branches? She could deal with moving from this house. She'd dealt with worse.

But to deal with moving, she had to be able to think about it, and she couldn't think about anything but Michael Molina.

How had he found her? More important, why had he bothered? What could he possibly want from her?

As she boiled the water for the macaroni and put Jeffrey to work peeling a carrot for the salad, she tried to apply logic to the situation. She knew Michael couldn't have been aware of Jeffrey's existence, so that wasn't why he'd searched for her. She doubted he'd found her through her parents, because they hated him for what he'd done to their precious daughter, even though they were thoroughly disgusted with their daughter.

Was he looking to relive his past? Did he think Emmie would be interested in another fling five years after their last fling?

And why did his eyes still have the power to mesmerize her? Why did his mere touch make her feel shaky and uncertain, no longer in control of herself?

"This carrot is too slippery," Jeffrey complained. "It keeps slipping all over the place."

If she hadn't been so frazzled, she would have stopped stirring the noodles into the boiling water and helped him with the carrot. She would have demonstrated a better way to hold it, a better way to ply the peeler. But she lacked the stamina to turn Jeffrey's struggle with the carrot into a learning experience. "Never mind," she muttered. "I'll do the carrot."

"What do you want me to do?"

Promise me you'll be a better man than your father, she answered silently. *Promise me you'll never disappear without warning. Promise me you'll be honest and noble, and you'll love me at least half as much as I love you.* "You can take some of the peels outside to the monster," she suggested.

Obviously thrilled, he scooped up the stringy orange shreds and raced out the back door. She spied on him through the window, amazed at how easily he moved about the backyard, how utterly at home he was in it. It was his small, safe universe, a world enclosed by dense hedges and filled with grass and trees and the garden. A world of mosquitoes and butterflies, of a redwood picnic table that could double as a pirate's ship in a pinch, and a hose, and a rectangular cement patio suitable for roller skating or scribbling secret runes with chunks of colored chalk.

Where on earth could she and Jeffrey go that would be as ideal as this house?

Someplace where Michael Molina would never find them, she thought with a bitter sigh.

AS IT TURNED OUT, the Holiday Inn did have a vacancy. Not that it would have mattered at that point. He'd already seen Emmie, and if her behavior was anything to go by, she wouldn't be getting in touch with him.

He sprawled out on the bed and closed his eyes. He could see her. She was still beautiful. She still held herself proudly, her chin high and her eyes steady. She was also still transparent. He knew, the instant she'd noticed him, that she would have been much happier if he hadn't reappeared in her life.

He'd hurt her five years ago; of course she wouldn't be thrilled to see him. But he'd come to apologize, and the Emmie he'd known five years ago would have given him the opportunity to do so. Then again, the Emmie he'd known back then didn't have a little boy who looked alarmingly like Michael.

The possibility that he could have fathered a son without knowing about it burned inside him like acid. He wished Emmie had contacted him if she'd been pregnant—as if there had even been a way for her to contact him. If he'd known, he would never have ignored his responsibilities. But she probably hadn't even tried to reach him. She'd probably assumed that if he was irresponsible enough to run away from her, he'd be just as likely to run away from the consequences of his actions.

Still…a boy. His son.

Maybe.

She'd pointed out that the boy looked like a lot of people. Michael had to admit he'd had only a split second to study the kid before Williams College had hustled the children indoors. Maybe the boy did look like a lot of people, and one of those people, not Michael, was his father.

He couldn't count on Emmie to fill him in on the boy's lineage, or anything else. She'd radiated such hostility he wouldn't be surprised to find the police waiting for him if he dared to show up at her place again.

It didn't make sense, though. If he was the kid's father and he proved to Emmie that he was willing to make up for the past five years, to pay child support and get involved in the child's life and whatever it was fathers were supposed to do, wouldn't she be pleased?

No. Nothing he did right now would please her. Nothing other than the very thing that had hurt her five years ago: leaving.

If he was smart, he would do just that. He'd pack his bag, drive back to Logan Airport and hop on the next plane heading west. He would run away again, with Emmie's blessings this time.

But he wasn't that smart.

He glanced at his watch: six o'clock, which would make it three o'clock in San Francisco. Digging into his hip pocket, he pulled out his wallet and located the Finders, Keepers card he'd stashed there. Maggie Tyrell had asked him to telephone her and let her know if the Mary-Elizabeth Kenyon she'd located was the woman he was looking for.

He dialed the number, listened to it ring on the other side of the country and then heard Maggie's voice. "Finders, Keepers. Can I help you?"

"It's Michael Molina," he said. "I'm in Wilborough. It's the right Emmie Kenyon."

"You saw her?"

"Yes." He chose not to expand on his answer. He didn't want Maggie to know that he was feeling bruised and frustrated, that Emmie had treated him as if he were toxic and that all those warnings Maggie had given him about how people changed had proved true in the most painful way.

His succinct reply hung between them for a minute, before she responded, "Well, good. I'm glad we found her."

He pushed away from the mattress and hunched forward, as if that position could improve his ability to think. "I've got a question for you. How does a person prove that a child is his?"

Maggie paused before answering. "Do you mean legally?"

"I mean…" What the hell. Maggie was a good detective. Maybe she could help him with this. "How does a man go about proving he's the father of a child?"

"Ah." She must have figured out what he was getting at. "Your Emmie Kenyon has a child?"

"A little boy." Michael took a deep breath, then added, "He's got my eyes."

"Ah." Her silence this time struck him as respectful, as if she understood how tricky his predicament was. "Is he the right age?"

"I don't know. I thought he looked too old, but…" He swallowed, afraid his voice would crack. "He's got my eyes."

Maggie sighed. "I don't know if you want to go there, Mr. Molina."

"Call me 'Michael,' and I do want to go there."

"All right." She paused again, then said, "You could take a blood test. If your DNA matched the boy's, then you'd be presumed to be his biological father."

"But the boy would have to be tested, too. I know about those tests. The mother usually insists on them when a guy is trying to elude paternity. I'm not trying to elude it—I'm trying to establish it. I'm more than willing to get tested, but I don't know if Emmie would allow the kid to undergo tests."

"She doesn't want you to turn out to be the father?"

She doesn't want me, period, he almost blurted out. "I don't think she was exactly thrilled to see me" was all he could bring himself to say.

Maggie meditated a bit more. "I tell you what. I'm going to hand you over to my brother Jack. Finders, Keepers is affiliated with his detective agency. I think he might be able to help you with this better than I can. I specialize in true love and happy endings, whereas Jack..." She didn't complete the sentence.

She didn't have to. Her insinuation was clear: what Michael was contemplating would surely lead to true hatred and a pathetic ending. "All right," he said, trying not to let pessimism overtake him. "Let me talk to your brother."

He heard a click as he was put on hold, then another click as the phone came to life again. "Michael Molina?" a man said briskly. "Jack Tyrell here. My sister said you wanted to speak to me."

"I've got what looks like a possibly unhappy ending," Michael admitted. "I don't think she wants to deal with it."

Jack chuckled. "She's allergic to unhappy endings. Besides, she's busy planning her wedding these days. All she can think of is rainbows and flowers and romance. So, what happened? Your lost lover didn't want to be found?"

"It's worse than that," Michael warned, then added, "maybe," because he really didn't know how bad it was going to be. "I saw my lost lover and she has a little boy, and the little boy looks like me."

Jack whistled through his teeth. "You know, I'm always telling Maggie these reunions of lovers aren't guaranteed to make everyone happy. Sometimes there's a damned good reason a relationship ended."

"Well, there was a good reason this one did, but it has nothing to do with the boy. It was my fault the relationship ended, and I never knew a baby might be involved. Can you help me figure out if I'm the father? Without a blood test. I'm just guessing, but I don't think Emmie would agree to let the kid be tested."

"You could force her to, through the courts," Jack suggested.

Michael shook his head. What a great way to show Emmie how sorry he was—by issuing a subpoena for her son's blood. "Isn't there any other way? You're a detective."

"Emmie's the mother? Your ex-sweetheart?"

"Yeah. Mary-Elizabeth Kenyon."

"Okay." A pause, as if Jack were jotting something down. "What's the kid's name?"

"I don't know."

"If you could find out his name, I could probably dig up his birth certificate and see who's listed as the father. That might tell you what you want to know."

Michael frowned. How was he going to find out the boy's name? Wasn't it the detective's job to find things out?

"Can't you get the birth certificate through the mother's name?"

"It would be easier with the kid's name."

"Okay." Michael wasn't helpless, after all. He

had a working brain. He'd found Finders, Keepers, hadn't he? He could do what he had to to find out the boy's name. Maybe he could follow the boy to school—although if the boy actually was his son, he wouldn't be old enough for school. He'd be in preschool or day care. Maybe Williams College was his nanny. However, she hadn't exactly been forthcoming with information; he doubted she would tell him anything about the boy.

Maybe, just maybe, Michael could approach Emmie again, and charm her into telling him what he needed to know—if not the boy's parentage, at least his name. "I'll see what I can do," he said.

"Meanwhile, I'll see if I can get anything off the mother's name," Jack promised.

"Thanks."

"And hey, listen, Molina." Jack's voice took on a confidential tone. "I love my sister, but she's got stars in her eyes, you know? She hates to think these things can come out any way other than perfect. She's salvaged our brother Sandy's rocky marriage, and she's engaged to marry Mr. Wonderful, and she's really into the whole true-love-and-destiny thing. But even Cupid can miss his target sometimes. Don't take it too hard."

"I won't," Michael said, although he didn't sound terribly convincing. "It's just...if this is my son, I need to know."

"Of course. I'll do what I can to find out for you."

"Thanks." Michael said goodbye and hung up. Then he fell back against the pillows, swung his legs up onto the bed and stared at the ceiling. It was white, flat, a blank screen for his imagination to play off.

A son? Could he have a son? He'd been careful with Emmie—and buying protection in a backwater town in a staunchly Catholic Central American country hadn't been easy. Only once, that one time... He hadn't known it would be their last time together, but fate had crashed into him, slashing and burning, and he hadn't been able to fight it.

It had just been that one time, that one night.

A low sigh escaped him. He remembered the scent of exotic flowers wafting through the screens into the back room of the *posada*—their room, the place they'd found because he was sharing his living quarters with Max Gallard, a colleague, and she was living with a family in a private home where she couldn't bring a man to her room for the night. Michael remembered the silver edge of the night air, the soft, limp linens on the bed, the swirls of the wrought-iron frame against which the pillows were propped. He remembered the lace cloth covering the round nightstand beside the bed, and on it the bowl of clear water with pink roses floating in it.

Mostly he remembered Emmie asleep within his arms, her skin soft and her respiration deep and slow. He remembered the silken spill of her hair over his arm, and the way her flesh nestled against him, and he remembered believing he had to make love to her one more time before the sun rose, had to do it because if he didn't have her once more he was afraid he would die.

He hadn't realized how close to the truth that fear was. All he'd known then was that this sweet, smart, gentle, beautiful woman was the only good thing in his world, and to keep himself from loving her would be harder than to keep his heart from beating.

He'd already used up the condoms he'd brought with him. His pockets were empty, but his soul was so full he hadn't cared. He'd kissed her until she'd turned in his arms and kissed him back, and then their bodies had begun to move, their hands to touch, to stroke, their arms to cling and their legs to grip and their moans to blend in a passionate song. He'd known making unprotected love to her was risky—but he'd been positive that not making love to her would have been even riskier. It would have destroyed him.

And she hadn't stopped him.

Just that one time.

He had assumed he would see her again after that night, to discuss their future, make plans, even accept the ramifications of their lovemaking, if there were any. The following morning, he and Gallard were finally going to complete their work in San Pablo, and once their mission had been accomplished, Michael had had every intention of returning to Emmie, coming clean with her about what he'd been up to, and figuring out where they could go from there.

He hadn't expected everything to go wrong. He hadn't expected the sky to crack open and hell to come pouring through. He hadn't expected to have to be spirited out of the country before he could grasp what had happened, to wake up in a bed a thousand miles away, his mind filled with pain and confusion and a loneliness so profound that days passed before he realized it was Emmie he was lonely for. He hadn't expected any of it to take place the way it had.

He hadn't expected to kill a man.

After all that, after all the years needed for him to heal...damn it, if he had a son, he wanted to know. He was back, and he wanted to know.

CHAPTER THREE

THE NIGHTMARES RETURNED. He should have expected them—he probably *did* expect them on some subconscious level—but that didn't make them easier to bear.

People always said gunshots sounded like exploding firecrackers. In Michael's dreams they sounded like dry tree branches snapping in a raging forest blaze. The sound wasn't festive. It was hot and mean, the music of fear.

He couldn't recall what the gunshots sounded like then, when he'd been awake, living through it. The reality had been more of a nightmare than the dreams that had haunted him for years afterward. The reality had been a phantasmagorical blur, images piled up on one another, jumpy and incomprehensible. In his dreams, everything was almost painfully crisp and vivid—the foliage too green, the sky too blue. Gallard too confident. The backups too late.

"This is going to be a piece of cake," Gallard had boasted as they'd driven their Jeep up the hilly, twisting road toward Edouardo Cortez's mountain retreat. "Remember, I'm the rich *americano* who supposedly doesn't speak English. You're my assistant and translator."

"I know." Michael had actually been excited at

the time. Maybe he'd been overly confident, too. He and Gallard had rehearsed the scenario dozens of times: Gallard was pretending to be a millionaire looking for weapons, and Michael was with him because he knew San Pablo so well, because he could navigate among the locals and find out where Cortez was operating.

Michael had visited San Pablo frequently in his youth, when his grandparents and other relatives had still lived there, before his father had taken them across the border to California. Michael had grown up knowledgeable about the habits of the region, even though his real home was the sprawling town of Bakersfield, sunken into a valley north of Los Angeles. His father used to be gone for months at a time, traveling to San Pablo to help his parents bring in their crops, then returning to Bakersfield and trying to find work. Sometimes he took Michael with him; sometimes he left him behind with his mother and brother. His father used to call him "Miguel," which his mother hated. "He's 'Michael,'" she'd argue. "He's as American as I am."

They used to argue a lot, his parents.

So Michael knew San Pablo. He spoke the accent. He understood the way things were done there. When he'd learned that a bounty hunter named Max Gallard was heading south to find Cortez, he'd volunteered to help.

Gallard had been warrior tough, his bodybuilder physique as hard as granite, his face a blank mask. Michael had been a recently minted Ph.D. teaching classes in political science at Cal-State Northridge. Unlike Gallard, he couldn't bench-press three hundred pounds; unlike Gallard, he'd never had any de-

sire to. But in San Pablo five years ago, his
strengths—agility and intelligence—had been just as
essential as Gallard's brawn and steel-edged experience. Michael had been in the thick of things. He'd
been eager to act. He'd been determined to get back
at the bastard who had caused his brother's death.

Michael had been exhilarated that morning, his
heart pumping adrenaline. He'd spent the night with
Emmie, loving her until his entire body was taut
with energy, and he wanted to burn that energy serving at Gallard's side.

"It's going to be as easy as one-two-three," Gallard had insisted. "You introduce me to Cortez, I
start talking business, and then, the instant he lets
his guard down, I take him. If anything starts getting
hairy, you just duck. I'll take care of you."

Michael hadn't wanted to think about how hairy
anything could get. That Cortez dealt in illegal arms
should have frightened him, but he'd never been
frightened by anything in his life, at least not for
himself. He'd been frightened by his parents' constant fights and his brother's bad choices. But for
himself, no. He'd always figured out what he wanted
and gone after it. And most of the time he'd gotten
it, whether it was a scholarship for college or a job
or the beautiful blond woman he'd spotted in the
village square.

He'd done his best to put Emmie out of his mind
that morning. He'd needed to stay focused on what
he and Gallard were doing, on Cortez. He'd had to
keep his head clear so that if anything started getting
hairy, he'd remember to duck.

It had gotten hairy, and Michael had ducked. So
had Gallard. They'd raced into the forest surround-

ing Cortez's retreat, but the undergrowth had been dense and the low branches had reached out to snag them like greedy arms. Maybe that was why he associated the sound of gunshots with snapping trees....

And then Gallard was hit.

In the actual living of it, Michael had scarcely been aware of what he was doing. Hoisting Gallard up, dragging him along, babbling to him like a raving lunatic. Dodging bullets. Eluding the man who was chasing them through the jungle-dense woods; tripping over vines; ignoring Gallard, who kept saying, "Put me down, leave me behind. Save yourself."

They'd reached a ravine and descended into it, Michael stumbling but managing to keep Gallard upright. He'd seen blood. He'd felt a searing pain in his shoulder, and Gallard had slid to the ground, groaning and clasping his hands against the wound just above his hip. Someone had charged down the ravine toward them. Cortez, Michael had later learned, though at the time he couldn't see the man's face. All he'd been able to see was Gallard's gun, tucked into the waist of his bloodstained slacks.

Michael had grabbed the gun, swung it toward the man chasing them and squeezed the trigger.

The nightmare he'd lived hadn't lasted more than a few minutes, but when he'd finally awakened from it, days had gone by and he was back in California, in a bed, his arm bandaged and his memory hazy. How had he gotten out of San Pablo? Why couldn't he recall what had happened? Why couldn't he get it clear in his mind?

More important, where was Emmie? Did she

know where he was? Did she know what he'd done? Would she ever forgive him for lying to her and— worse—for killing a man? He *had* killed someone. That was the only lucid thought he owned: he'd killed a man.

He doubted he would ever forgive himself. He couldn't imagine begging Emmie to forgive him.

HE'D BEEN DREAM FREE for a long time now. He thought he was finally healed. But some scars never faded, he supposed. Or else seeing Emmie had torn the scar tissue away.

He opened his eyes to find himself surrounded by black. He didn't recognize the smell of the room, the texture of the sheets or the hum of the ventilation system. As his vision clarified, he noticed a thin white line under the door—hallway light seeping through the crack.

The Wilborough Holiday Inn, he remembered.

He sat up, his heart pounding wildly, his skin damp with sweat. If he could have spent the night with Emmie, maybe she would have warded off his demons. Maybe that was why he'd gone to the effort of searching for her—because he'd always felt safe with her.

No. He'd found her because he had believed himself cured, completely over the past. And if he sat long enough in the darkened room, the sheets tangled around his naked legs and his hair damp and matted against his nape, he would calm down and feel cured again. What had occurred five years ago had ended five years ago. Michael had done what he'd had to do. Some folks considered him a hero. He considered himself lucky to be alive and out of

San Pablo, and he wanted to believe finding Emmie was further evidence of his good luck.

He groped at the lamp on the night table until he located the switch, and clicked it on. His eyes burned in the sudden glare, and he blinked until they stopped hurting. After throwing back the covers, he swung out of bed, padded barefoot across the industrial-strength carpet to the bathroom and cranked on the shower faucet to a stinging, tepid spray. Then he climbed in and let the water sluice down his body, washing away the perspiration, washing away the dream.

"TOMMY CANTRELL! Will Simon! Joshua Kaye! You have to the count of five to get into your seats or come up with a creative reason you're not in them!" Emmie hollered above the din of twenty-three eight-and nine-year-old voices. Most of her students were at their desks, but Tommy, Will and Joshua were a trio of hellions. Although she adored their spunk, they could really disrupt a class, and she had to rein them in when they got to behaving the way they were now—Josh and Tommy tossing a tennis ball back and forth while Will attempted to swat it with a ruler.

It was another warm, sunny day, and her class was restless. She considered whether taking the students outside for a nature walk around the school-yard would settle them down or rev them up. She liked leading her class on impromptu nature walks, finding fascinating insects and unusual weeds for the children to study. Last week she'd dug up a chunk of lawn so they could see the webbed root system of the grass and the earthworms aerating the soil underneath.

Frequently the walks helped the children to unwind, but sometimes it made them want to stay outside and play, and then they were even crankier when she brought them back into the classroom. This morning, she herself was so keyed up she wasn't sure whether stepping outside would inspire her to keep walking, to walk and walk until she was miles from all her problems.

But she couldn't walk away, either from her problems or her class. Her students needed and loved her as much as she needed and loved her job. Her problems—housing and Michael Molina—weren't likely to let her escape, no matter how far she walked.

She hadn't slept well last night. More accurately, she hadn't slept at all. She'd lain awake, gripped by a vague fear that Michael would steal Jeffrey from her. She couldn't imagine a logical reason he would want to. He hadn't raised Jeffrey; he hadn't even known of the boy's existence until yesterday. For five years he'd shown no interest in Emmie or anything that might have happened to her—including her bearing a child. He hadn't come to Wilborough looking for his son.

But she couldn't shake her dread. What she and Jeffrey had was perfect just as it was. She'd constructed that perfection herself, after discovering her pregnancy and returning home to Richmond once the school term in San Pablo ended. She'd been demoralized that the man she'd given herself to, body and soul, had gone and left her pregnant. But she'd believed her parents would accept her choices—the choice to have loved Michael Molina and the choice to keep and raise their child.

Her parents hadn't. "Who was he?" her mother had fumed. "Just some local peasant you picked up?"

"He was an American," she'd retorted, as if that mattered. "A college professor from California."

"A son of a bitch is what he was," her father had railed. "And you! We raised you with morals. We let you go down to that godforsaken country only because you were going with a church group! And now you've come back to us like *this!*"

She'd refrained from arguing that as a twenty-five-year-old woman with a master's degree she was long past the point in her life where her parents could *let* her do anything. But she'd hoped they would respect her new situation and welcome the prospect of a grandchild.

There had been no welcome, no respect. Only condemnation.

So she'd left Virginia and moved to New England. She'd given birth to Jeffrey, spent two years on the substitute-teacher lists of schools in three towns and landed a permanent job at the Oak Hill Elementary School in Wilborough. She'd been a good mother, loving Jeffrey, raising him and nurturing him, disciplining and doting on him. She understood that no matter how much she despised Michael Molina, she was grateful for the weeks she'd known him in San Pablo because those weeks had given her this precious little boy.

No one was going to upset the balance she'd established with her child. Not even Jeffrey's father. Especially not Jeffrey's father.

Josh, Will and Tommy were still playing stickball with the tennis ball. "One," Emmie counted ominously, watching the three rascals scramble to their seats. "Two..." And all three slumped into their chairs and grinned. "I guess none of you are feeling creative today," she teased. "Julie, I bet you're feeling creative. Why don't you start us off by reading the poem you wrote during free writing yesterday."

Julie Markowitz stood, giggled, blushed, held her paper up in front of her face and began to read. Emmie sat atop her desk, listening to Julie's tremulous voice as she recited a charming poem about a dog who longed to climb trees. Emmie loved these children—not the way she loved Jeffrey, of course, but with genuine, loyal affection. She'd watched them grow since last September, and she'd grown along with them. Teaching brought her joy, and teaching at Oak Hill, where the classes were small enough to be manageable and the children came to school well fed and ready to learn, was a pleasure. She'd taught in schools where the mere idea of asking nine-year-olds to write their own poems would be laughable, but here she could take chances with her students, stretch their minds, give them challenges.

She'd loved her students in San Pablo, too. Although they didn't always come to school well fed, they were willing to meet challenges. For some of them, simply getting to school was a challenge greater than anything her Wilborough students had ever had to face.

Julie finished her poem and, in a welter of giggles, sat down. Josh shouted, "I wanna read mine next!"

"You'll have to wait your turn," Emmie chided,

then called on Kyle Dante. His was a gruesome rhyme about explosions and monsters. Emmie remembered the imaginary monster Jeffrey had found in their backyard yesterday. Jeffrey's monster wasn't violent, she thought proudly, recalling how earnestly her son had carried out the carrot shavings to feed the beast.

He couldn't help the fact that his father was a heartless, selfish creep, a man who could tell a woman he loved her one day and vanish the next. It wasn't Jeffrey's fault that the man who'd impregnated his mother was a liar who for five years hadn't bothered to find out what had become of the woman he'd made love to in San Pablo. Jeffrey couldn't be blamed for his father's absence during his birth, during the first weeks of his life, when he and Emmie were up every two hours for feedings, when he learned to focus his eyes, learned to smile, learned that as long as Emmie was with him he would be hugged and adored and cared for. Michael hadn't been there when Jeffrey had caught a rubber ball for the first time, or when he'd caught the chicken pox. Michael had missed Jeffrey's first tooth, his first step, his first day of preschool. How could she even think of Michael as Jeffrey's father? He might have contributed half of Jeffrey's genes, but Emmie had worked hard to make sure the genes *she'd* contributed were the ones that counted.

Midway through Kyle's poem, the classroom intercom buzzed. "Excuse me," Emmie said, crossing to the wall by the door where the wall phone hung. She lifted it and said, "This is Emmie Kenyon."

"Emmie? It's Gwyn at the front desk. Someone

just dropped off a delivery for you. Can I bring it down to your class?''

"Sure." Emmie wasn't expecting anything, but it was possible someone's mother had delivered a tray of cupcakes or a forgotten lunch. She turned from the intercom in time for the climax of Kyle's poem, a depiction of gory mayhem in ragged meter. Kyle bowed, the boys cheered and clapped, and the girls whined, "Gross!" and grimaced in disgust.

"Before we all shriek 'gross,'" she instructed the class, "let's think a little about the imagery Kyle used in his poem. Poetry is supposed to touch your emotions. So if Kyle managed to gross you out— and I'll admit he grossed me out—can we see this as a successful poem?"

"It's too gross to be successful," Amber Laughton complained.

"Yeah, but he did what he set out to do," Tommy argued. "So that means it *was* successful."

Debate on poetry and the nature of success erupted throughout the room, almost loud enough to drown out the knock on the door. Emmie opened it and fell back a step at the sight of a bouquet of flowers so large it hid Gwyn's face. "Here's your delivery," the school secretary announced cheerfully, peering out from behind the flowers as she handed the heavy glass vase to Emmie. She was grinning curiously. "I wonder who they're from."

Emmie could guess—and her guess made her queasy. Her discomfort increased as the class lost interest in their discussion of successful poetry and turned their attention to the enormous bouquet. "Wow!" Amber bellowed. "They're beautiful!"

"They're gross!" Kyle disputed her. His comment prompted a chorus of smooching sounds and snickers from the boys.

"Okay, quiet down," Emmie said, gritting her teeth and carrying the flowers to the windowsill. She plucked the card from its plastic holder and tucked it into the pocket of her denim skirt. "Let's get back to our discussion—"

"Aren't you gonna open the card?" Shawna Sikorski asked. Shawna was a tiny girl with huge eyeglasses, and she had such a plaintive voice Emmie couldn't ignore her. She glanced toward the door, to see that Gwyn was still perched there, waiting to learn whom the flowers were from.

"Is it your birthday?" Nicole Evigan asked. "My grandma sends me flowers on my birthday."

"Yuck," one of the boys muttered.

Undeterred, Nicole added, "Maybe those are from your grandma."

Highly unlikely, Emmie thought, pulling the card back out of her pocket and opening it. "Please talk to me," it said. "Michael." A local telephone number was printed below his name.

It took her a moment to realize that the classroom was as close to silent as a gathering of twenty-three third-graders could be. She swallowed the knot of distress in her throat and squared her shoulders against the chill that ran down her spine. Her students mustn't know she was upset. They mustn't know that her personal life was currently under assault from several directions at once.

"They're from an old...*friend*," she said, forcing out the word. "And they're pretty, aren't they? Now, let's get back to our poetry."

She made it through the rest of the school day

without letting on how distracted she was. Even if she hadn't already been preoccupied with thoughts of Michael Molina, she smelled those accursed flowers and thought of him every time she inhaled. The card that had come with them felt stiff in her skirt pocket. When she walked and the denim swirled around her legs, she could feel his message against her left thigh.

At least he hadn't sent red roses. If he'd intended the flowers as an unambiguous love offering, she would have been twice as distracted—and twice as angry. She knew what a profession of love meant coming from Michael—absolutely nothing. Surely five years after telling her he loved her and then disappearing he couldn't have tracked her down and expected her to believe him if he told her he loved her again.

Five years was a long time. Things must have happened to him during the interval. *Women* must have happened to him. Maybe he'd gotten burned a few times and didn't like his odds with the female population as a whole. Maybe he figured old Emmie Kenyon was a pushover, someone he could con as easily a second time as he'd conned the first.

By three o'clock, she was fatigued from the effort of teaching while thoughts of Michael were weighing her down like a leaded belt. Her head ached and her neck was stiff. She sent the children out of the room to their buses and let out a long, weary breath.

Ordinarily she loitered in her classroom for a while after the children were dismissed. Jeffrey could stay at the preschool until a quarter to four, and she liked a few minutes of quiet to assemble her materials and her agenda for the following day.

Today, though, she wanted to get to Jeffrey as quickly as she could. She wanted him with her, just in case…she didn't know what. She just knew she needed to have her son close by.

She stuffed the day's spelling tests and her lesson plans into her tote bag and reached into her pocket for her key ring. Her fingers grazed the card Michael had sent with the flowers. She stared at the bouquet standing on the windowsill, a festive array of daisies and carnations, pink baby roses, ferns and Queen Anne's Lace, and shuddered. Of all the times in the world for Michael to show up, now—when she was facing something akin to an eviction—had to be one of the worst.

Then again, any time he'd shown up would have been bad. She didn't want to see him. It was too late for them to repair the damage, too late for her to care anymore.

She tossed the card into the trash and left the flowers behind in the classroom when she headed outside to her car. At the preschool she found Jeffrey navigating a traffic jam of toy cars in the center of his group's play area. He sent her a smile and then went back to his game, making race-car *vroom-vrooms* and screeching brake noises with his mouth.

"I guess I'm a little early," Emmie said apologetically to the teacher.

"No problem. Do you want him now?"

"Let him finish his game." Emmie retreated to a chair and watched as Jeffrey and two of his buddies maniacally steered their toy vehicles across the floor. Eventually the three cars collided, and the boys whooped and vocalized booming explosions. Finally, the carnage complete, Jeffrey was ready to leave.

Emmie wanted to crush him in a hug, but she didn't dare, not in front of his play group and his teacher. She didn't want anyone to recognize the turmoil she was operating under, and she didn't want to embarrass Jeffrey, who had recently decided that public displays of affection were inappropriate, unless *he* was the one who needed the hug.

Emmie needed a hug now, but she exercised self-control and waited until she was strapping him into his car seat before she peppered his face with kisses. In truth, she needed more than a hug from her son; she needed reassurance that her entire life wasn't about to crumble into a million pieces. Jeffrey couldn't give her that reassurance, but at least he could convince her they were still a solid team.

"Since I came early, I thought maybe you'd like to go to the community center and play on the pirate ship," she suggested. What she really wanted was to delay going home, back to the place where she'd seen Michael last night.

"Okay!"

They spent a half hour at the community center playground, and then Emmie delayed the inevitable further by taking Jeffrey out for burgers for dinner. She bought a small sandwich for herself, knowing she'd wind up eating most of his French fries while he played with the toy that came with his meal.

By six-thirty, she'd run out of ways to put off going home. Jeffrey still needed a bath and some reading time, and she had that stack of spelling tests and tomorrow's lesson plans to review. Reluctantly she drove toward Cullen Drive in the fading day-

light, pointing out sights to Jeffrey along the way:
"Did you see that robin? Robins are sometimes
called robin redbreasts because they have reddish
feathers on their bellies. Look at the tulips! Aren't
they pretty?"

Jeffrey was more interested in his new toy.

Reaching her block, she slowed her car—and bit
back a curse. Parked in front of her house was the
car she'd seen Michael emerge from yesterday. He
was back, and for a moment she saw nothing but
her own black rage.

If ever she'd wished for an automatic garage-door
opener, it was now. She'd love to be able to push a
button, watch the door slide open, drive in and have
the door shut behind her without her leaving the
safety of her car. Sighing, she turned into the driveway, shifted into neutral and climbed out of her car
to open the garage door. Just as she'd feared, Michael got out of his car the instant he saw her, and
bounded up the driveway toward her.

She cut him off before he could speak. "Don't
say a word."

He pressed his lips together and glanced into her
car, as if he thought she was silencing him so she
wouldn't disturb Jeffrey. Jeffrey was wide-awake,
though, peering out through the window in the
driver's side door, his dark eyes so eerily similar to
Michael's that Emmie wanted to slap her hands over
Michael's face so he wouldn't notice the resemblance.

He'd already noticed. Maybe she just wanted to
slap him, period.

"I didn't invite you here," she said emphatically,
her voice low and tight with anger. "I don't want

you here. If you persist in barging into my life, I'll have you charged with harassment. Or stalking.''

"I'm not stalking you,'' he said with such self-assurance she definitely wanted to slap him. It wasn't fair that he should be so much more poised than she was. "All I want to do is talk.''

He sounded so insufferably reasonable she knew she would come across as neurotic if she kept fending him off. She needed to consider herself strong and self-assured—and strong, self-assured women weren't threatened by talk. "I've got some things to do,'' she said, determined to maintain control over the situation. "If you want to talk, you'll have to wait.''

"Fine. I'll wait.''

"Outside. I'm not inviting you in.''

His mouth twitched, as if he couldn't decide whether to smile or scowl. "So—what do you want me to do? Stand out here until midnight and then give up?''

"I'd be thrilled if you gave up, but I'm not counting on it,'' she muttered. "You can stand or you can sit. By midnight I'll be fast asleep. But I've got to get Jeffrey down for the night, and I don't want you in my way. You can wait on the patio if you'd like. There are chairs there.''

"Jeffrey,'' he said, gazing through the window at her son in his car seat.

She didn't like the way he was looking at her son. "I should be done by around eight-thirty,'' she said, just to stop him from staring at Jeffrey. "Maybe you ought to get yourself some dinner and come back.'' *Because I'm not going to offer you anything to eat,* she added silently.

"No, that's all right. I'll wait on your patio." He seemed downright pleased with her brusque instructions. Before she could halt him, he waved at Jeffrey, then headed around the house.

If luck was with her, he would grow bored in the time it took her to give Jeffrey his bath. He would realize how much she loathed him, how wrong it was for him to have hunted her down, and he would disappear while she was stretched out atop Jeffrey's blanket, reading him the chapter about the Heffalump in *Winnie-the-Pooh*.

Of course, if luck had been flowing her way, Michael would never have shown up in the first place.

She couldn't count on luck. She could count only on whatever bravado she could muster within herself. She would take her time attending to Jeffrey, and then she would steel herself and go outside and do Michael Molina the undeserved favor of listening while he said what he'd gone through so much effort to say. Then she would tell him to get the hell out of her life.

JEFFREY, HE REFLECTED. *Jeffrey Kenyon.*

Maybe.

Maybe she'd given the boy his father's last name. Maybe his legal name was Jeffrey Molina. Or maybe—he mustn't deny the possibility—Jeffrey was the result of some other union with some other man.

Still, Michael had something to work with. Something to tell Maggie's brother Jack at Tyrell Investigative Services. Something that might lead him to the truth about that little boy's origins.

The patio was a neat, recently swept slab of cement abutting a rear door. The door had a window in it, and there was another window next to the door. Peering in, Michael saw a relatively tidy kitchen. A yellow cloth covered the table, and the windows were framed with patterned yellow curtains. A pile of mail stood on one counter. A plate and matching cup with cartoon characters on them were propped in a drying rack next to the sink. The appliances didn't look particularly new or top-of-the-line. Several refrigerator magnets shaped like brightly colored fruits clung to the fridge door.

Turning from the window, he settled into one of the upholstered chairs near a picnic table and surveyed her backyard: trees, grass, a small garden tucked into one corner. The modest size appealed to him.

She'd made a nice home for herself and her son. It wasn't fancy or pretentious, but it seemed cozy. The yard was the perfect size for a young boy—big enough to explore but small enough to feel safe in.

He would bet Emmie was a good mother, wise and attentive and patient. He'd bet she was well-read in the current theories of childrearing. He'd bet she was goddamn perfect.

Yeah, sure. If she was perfect, she would have welcomed the arrival of her son's father—assuming Michael was his father. Assuming Michael *wasn't* his father, perfection would have compelled her to introduce the boy to Michael and inform him that he had no ties to the kid. Emmie might not be as imperfect as Michael was, but she was a long way from perfect.

He awaited her with an edgy anticipation. He'd managed to win her ear for a few minutes, and he couldn't afford to misplay the moment. He needed to keep her attention long enough to apologize, to win her forgiveness, to explain what had happened five years ago...and to find out about the kid, if he could.

Jeffrey.

Surely she would tell him whether Jeffrey was his son if he did a good enough job of explaining himself. That was his only hope: that he would explain what had happened in San Pablo so well she wouldn't be able to refuse him the truth.

CHAPTER FOUR

San Pablo, five years earlier

HE COULDN'T HELP but notice her. She was like a circle of sunlight in a dense forest, bright and beckoning.

He was seated at an outdoor table at a cantina with Max Gallard, sipping a cola and lemon while Gallard guzzled a bottle of *cerveza*. The main street was Saturday-morning busy—cars, wagons and bicycles competing for road space, mothers browsing in the shops and open-air stalls while their children bobbed and darted among the throngs, looking for goodies to filch. Michael knew what they were up to: he'd spent enough time in San Pablo to have learned the trouble idle children could instigate while their *madres* dickered over the price of a liter of milk or a sack of rice.

She wasn't anyone's mother, though. She looked too young and not nearly tired enough. Her hair hung soft and pale around her face and down past her shoulders. Her complexion reminded him of cream kissed with the golden sweetness of honey.

Gallard was blustering about how the clutch kept slipping on the Jeep he'd rustled up for them to use in San Pablo. Michael tried to remember to nod at the appropriate times, but his gaze was riveted to the slim blond woman down the street as she studied a display of peaches.

"We've got to find a mechanic," Gallard insisted. "Do they even have them in this godforsaken place?"

Michael wanted to retort that San Pablo wasn't godforsaken. It was too hot for May, and too dusty, and the gnats had a way of dive-bombing people like kamikaze pilots in a World War II movie—but San Pablo also had spicy food in the cantinas and lively music spilling from the open windows. It had clever, if not completely honest, children and strong women and lazy, lolling men filling the tables around him and Gallard, smoking cigarettes and arguing politics. A man could buy a Coke on ice on a steamy spring morning, and he could admire a beautiful woman as she admired peaches half a block away. San Pablo was hardly godforsaken.

"Where there are cars there are mechanics," he pointed out.

"Because we can't risk grabbing Cortez and then having our wheels die on us before we can bring him in."

"I'll find a mechanic," Michael promised.

Max Gallard was all business. His brush-cut hair and burly shoulders gave him the appearance of a marine drill sergeant nursing a deep nostalgia for the darkest days of the Vietnam War. In fact, he looked like the role he was playing—a shady gun merchant—much more than Michael looked like a shady gun merchant's assistant.

Michael looked like what he was: a half Latino, half Anglo guy who taught college courses in political science. He was on the thin side, his hair on the long side, his skin darkly tanned and his apparel campus-cool—faded blue jeans, a white T-shirt and leather sandals with thick, treaded soles. His nose was narrow but too long, his chin blade-sharp, but he'd never wasted time worrying how his features came together. He wondered what a woman like the pretty blonde shopping for peaches would think of him.

He decided to find out. "Look, Max—I'll find us a mechanic this afternoon. I've got other things to do this morning."

"What other things?" Gallard asked, then twisted in his wrought-iron chair and peered over his shoulder to see what had captured Michael's attention. He turned back. "Don't mess with her," he warned. "We're here to do a job."

Michael drained his glass of Coke and stood. "Saying hello to a woman isn't going to keep me from doing my job."

"You want to stay focused—"

"I will," he assured Gallard. "I'll take care of the clutch, all right?" Before Gallard could delay him with further argument, Michael shoved away from the table and headed down the street toward the woman at the produce stall.

He sidled up to her just as she was handing the clerk a bag of peaches to be weighed. Michael pulled out his wallet and handed the clerk enough money to pay for them. Startled, the woman spun around, and he discovered that she was even more beautiful up close than she'd been from a distance. Her skin was exactly as lovely as he'd thought, smooth and satiny. Her eyes were blue, wide with surprise above the elegant contours of her cheeks.

Her loose-fitting cotton dress revealed as much as it concealed, the sleeveless bodice exposing the delicate hollows of her collarbones and the feminine curves of her shoulders, the loose skirt pressing against her long legs whenever a breeze skipped down the street.

"*¿Habla inglés?*" he asked.

She stared at him for a moment, apparently sizing him up. "*Sí,*" she said, then smiled shyly. "I mean yes."

"You're American," he guessed. Three words of English were enough to tell him that. Three words inflected with a slight Dixie drawl.

"Yes, I am." Her smile still reserved, she fidgeted with the paper bag, rolling the top down to protect the peaches. "You shouldn't have paid for these."

"Why not?" he asked.

Stumped, she smiled again. "Now you'll expect something in return."

Not expect, he wanted to explain—but he had hopes. "I'd settle for a peach," he said, grinning to put her at ease.

Her gaze never moving from his face, she unrolled the top, passed him a plump yellow peach and rolled the top shut again.

He took the fruit in his left hand and extended his right. "Michael Molina," he introduced himself.

She glanced at his hand, once again seeming to take his measure, and then shook it. Her skin was softer than the peach's. "Emmie Kenyon," she said.

He wasn't sure he'd heard her correctly. "Emily?"

"No, Emmie. Like the letters M-E. For Mary-Elizabeth."

He liked that—not just that her name was Mary-Elizabeth shortened to Emmie, but that she'd told him. If she'd wanted to blow him off, she wouldn't have bothered explaining all that.

"What brings you to San Pablo?" he asked, pleased just to be standing next to her, watching the breeze flutter through her hair, inhaling her simple talcum-powder fragrance, wondering whether her eyes could truly be that blue. Maybe she was wearing tinted contact lenses. Or maybe the glaring sun was affecting his vision.

"I'm a teacher," she said.

"No kidding? So am I."

"Really?" Her eyes glowed, and he realized that, yes, they truly were that blue. "Are you here with a church group?"

A church group? Hardly. He was here to help Max Gallard capture a gunrunner who had jumped bail and fled from Los Angeles. San Pablo's convoluted bureaucracy might take years to process an extradition, and the bail bondsman who'd hired Gallard to bring Cortez back didn't want to wait years, especially given that it would take a lot less time for someone like Cortez to come up with a new identity and get back into the business of supplying deadly weapons to the street gangs of Los Angeles.

But if Emmie Kenyon was with a church group, she could be…pious. Maybe a novitiate or something, too pure and saintly to entertain the erotic kinds of thoughts Michael entertained every time he glimpsed her unearthly blue eyes.

"I'm a college professor back in California," he

said, overstating his position just a bit. He was an assistant professor in his first year on the faculty at Cal-State Northridge, and the odds of his moving into a tenure-track slot were too iffy to bet on. "I'm down here doing research."

That interested her. "What kind of research?"

"I teach political science. I specialize in Central American political history."

She chuckled. "There's plenty of that, I suppose. Politics in this part of the world seems to provoke as much passion as soccer."

"I think there's just a bit more bloodshed in soccer," he joked. Then he braced himself for the worst and asked, "So, are you with a church group?"

"More or less. My parish back home sponsors Americans who come down here and contribute to the society in some way. They've got a team building houses, and several nurse practitioners are helping to staff a clinic across town. I came to teach for a year. I've got my own class, plus I'm working with the teachers to set up computer classes for their students. Our church donated a computer to the school, too."

That sounded noble without being too virtuous. Michael regained his optimism. "You don't teach on Saturdays, do you?" he asked.

"Not usually." Her smile lost its reticence. She appeared to find him amusing and harmless. If she was aware of the sharp tug of lust her smile awakened in him, she probably wouldn't be so amused, nor would she consider him exactly harmless.

"Are you free this evening?"

Her smile changed again, this time taking on a

skeptical edge. "I don't rightly know," she drawled. "It would depend."

"On what?"

"On what you're really asking me."

It was his turn to smile. For all her delicate beauty, she was no fool—and he was glad, even if her discernment made his life a bit more challenging. "I'm really asking," he said, "whether you'd like to have dinner with me tonight."

She contemplated his invitation, her fingers smoothing the paper bag, her gaze drifting past him. A couple of dogs snarled and barked at each other near the cantina where he and Gallard had been talking. Gallard was gone, he noticed when he turned to watch the sparring mutts. Someone shooed them away from the tables and they scampered down the street, dodging bicycles and a wheezing bus.

Emmie turned back to him. "I'm staying as a guest in a private house," she told him. "I don't think my hosts would be pleased if I had a man calling for me there. So perhaps we'd better meet somewhere."

There were no elegant restaurants in San Pablo. This was a third-rate town in a third-rate country; if anyone was rich here, it was due to illegal activity, and he'd know better than to flaunt his ill-gotten wealth. But there were cozy *hosterías* scattered about, places were the meat was perfectly spiced, the beans perfectly cooked and the rum and beer strong enough to balance the food.

"Do you know Casa Rosita's?" he asked. "Will you meet me there?"

One last, lingering assessment and she said, "All right."

"Eight o'clock?"

"All right." She gave him a final smile, this one warm enough to melt a polar ice cap, then turned and walked down the street, as regal and graceful as a ballerina.

"I'll see you tonight," he called after her, but she didn't stop, didn't acknowledge hearing him. He grinned. She'd said "All right"; she'd be there.

He took a hearty bite of his peach and felt his mouth fill with its sweet flavor. Emmie Kenyon's lips would taste even sweeter, he suspected. Maybe tonight he would find out for sure.

In the meantime, he'd have to scrounge up a mechanic.

WHATEVER HAD MADE HER AGREE to meet a stranger for supper?

Emmie was smart and self-protective. She didn't court trouble or take unnecessary risks. But for some reason, she had decided Michael Molina was safe.

Well, not really safe. He had a wicked gleam in his eyes, a charisma that could test the willpower of even a smart, self-protective woman. He had the kind of lean, athletic build that could inspire a prude to fantasize, and Emmie was no prude.

But she believed she could trust him, at least out in public on a Saturday night. She'd been in San Pablo long enough to know a fair number of locals, and she had Rosita's daughter in her class, so if Michael started any trouble at the restaurant, she would holler for Rosita and her husband.

Michael Molina was an American. A college professor. His smile seemed honest. Even the mischief in his eyes seemed honest. She truly didn't think she would have to holler for help tonight.

She was going to be in San Pablo only one more month. In June she would be returning to Richmond, her grand adventure over. She'd loved every minute she'd spent in the country, loved working with her students and her fellow faculty members at the rustic village schoolhouse, wiring the building for an Internet connection and then linking the tiny educational outpost to the rest of the planet. She'd loved living with the Cesares, becoming an honorary member of their family, honing her fluency in Spanish and absorbing a culture that was in some ways utterly alien to her but in others—the claim of tradition, the deep family roots and loyalties—nearly identical to her own. She'd loved learning how to haggle with merchants, how to use the local currency and navigate around town on the local buses, how to view life from a different perspective.

But she'd been here nearly a year, and not once had she sensed even a glimmer of romance in the air.

Until now. Until Michael Molina, his seductive grin and his seductive eyes, had entered her world.

She wandered down the street, passing the rest of the food vendors but pausing at a table arrayed with painted pottery. She wanted to bring her mother a gift from San Pablo, but she hadn't yet found a souvenir she thought her mother would appreciate. Not that there was anything wrong with the pottery—the terra-cotta bowls, fat and round and decorated with geometric slashes of black and white paint, were actually quite beautiful—but the ceramics wouldn't be to her mother's taste. Her mother liked things that were classy and pricy and...well, American. The local crafts enthralled Emmie. She'd already bought a woven blanket for herself, and a pair of festive beaded earrings. But her parents were conservative and terribly limited in their tastes.

Sighing, she abandoned the potter's table and strolled down the street to the block where the Cesares lived. Their house was a modest stucco structure, but the plumbing worked and she had her own room. More than that she didn't need.

She entered the house and carried the peaches into the kitchen, where she found Señora Cesare scrubbing dishes. She placed the peaches in a bowl and carried them to the sink to wash. "They look ripe," Señora Cesare said in the San Pablo-accented Spanish Emmie had come close to mastering this year.

She pictured Michael Molina taking a peach from her. She imagined him biting into it. She imagined juice dribbling down his chin, and his eyes brightening in delight at the wonderful flavor. "I'm not going to be here for supper tonight," she said to alert Señora Cesare. The afternoon meal was the major one of the day, and the evening meal usually entailed a light snack. But Emmie owed it to her hostess to let her know she'd be out. "I'm meeting friends in town," she explained, reassuring herself that it was only a small lie. If she'd said she would be meeting *a* friend, Señora Cesare would want to know who the friend was. And if considering Michael Molina a friend was stretching reality, Emmie hoped it wasn't an outright falsehood.

"When will you be home?" Señora Cesare wanted to know.

Feeling like a teenage girl negotiating a curfew

with her mother, Emmie smiled tolerantly. "Not too late," she promised. "Before midnight."

"I'll start worrying at a minute past midnight," Señora Cesare declared, flashing an answering smile Emmie's way. Emmie stood a good six inches taller than the short, plump woman, but despite her superior height, she looked up to Señora Cesare. The woman's ash-gray hair and weary eyes hinted at how many years she had overseen the courting rituals of her own three daughters, keeping each one on a short rein until she settled on an eligible man and got married. When Emmie had moved in with the Cesares, they had all discussed the fact that she would be a rent-paying boarder, not another daughter in need of mothering. But Señora Cesare couldn't fight her ingrained habits, and Emmie couldn't resent her for it.

She spent the hottest part of the afternoon in her room, sipping glasses of lemon-laced iced tea and reviewing her students' math work sheets. She let one of the other teachers at the school work with her children on language skills, but Emmie taught math, science and computer science. Although her Spanish was strong enough for her to communicate with her pupils, her spelling wasn't much better than theirs.

The schoolwork helped to distract her from thoughts of her impending date. But Michael Molina managed to sneak into her mind every now and then. Checking the row of multiplication problems on a work sheet, she found herself distracted by a vision of him standing on the walk beside her, the sun lending his skin a coppery glow. Correcting a borrowing error on a long-division problem, she recalled his

voice, low and husky, as if a laugh were threatening
to break through. Circling an illegible answer on a
work sheet, she recalled the warmth of his smile,
and her memory ignited a matching warmth inside
her.

She mustn't allow herself to think of him in terms
of warmth. He was a near stranger, a handsome
question mark. She shouldn't let down her guard.

But as the afternoon heat seeped out of the air
with the fading sunlight, she filled the tub with cool
water and splashed a few drops of cologne into it,
because even if Michael turned out to fall far short
of her expectations, she wanted to smell nice. She
wanted to look and feel fresh. She wanted to remember that she was an attractive woman, entitled
to risk a little hope on the possibility that an evening
spent with Michael Molina would turn out to be a
lovely thing.

MICHAEL STUDIED HIS reflection in the mirror above
the dresser. The warped glass presented him with a
shivery image of himself. In the thirty-six hours he
and Gallard had been here, he'd grown used to the
mirror's distortions, the scratched and chipped chest
of drawers, the narrow beds and the smothering,
stagnant air of the small room tucked behind a *farmacia* in an alley a block from the town's main
plaza. As accommodations went, he'd had better, but
the room had been available, and he and Gallard had
been happy to get it. San Pablo wasn't the sort of
place where the Four Seasons would choose to erect
one of its luxury hotels.

His reflection might be wavering, but he wasn't.
In ten minutes, he was going to be in the company

of a gorgeous woman who had more class in her left eyebrow than he had in his entire family tree. A blond Southern belle teaching school under the auspices of a church group? Talk about being out of his element!

But Michael had always enjoyed mixing elements and watching them react. If he'd let nonsense like class distinctions get in his way, he would never have wound up on a full scholarship at U.C.-Berkeley, earning a Ph.D. The greatest thing about America, his immigrant father always used to tell him, was that class didn't matter.

What mattered now was that Michael would be spending the evening with Mary-Elizabeth Kenyon.

It had been a good day all around. He'd found a mechanic that afternoon, down in the neighborhood of shanties south of town. The man's front yard had been cluttered with cars and trucks in various states of disrepair, with chunks of engine and detached doors and piles of tires scattered around the tiny yard and scrawny chickens pecking in the dirt between the heaps of junk. He'd looked at the Jeep, said he could fix the clutch next week and cited a price that seemed remarkably cheap to Michael, although it would probably buy a month's worth of groceries in San Pablo.

If he and Gallard had been in Mexico City, they could have rented a car from Hertz or Avis and not worried about getting it repaired. But things were done differently in San Pablo. So he'd agreed to bring the Jeep back the following Wednesday.

Gallard hadn't been pleased. "Wednesday? That's four days from now! Why can't he do it sooner?"

Michael had pictured the fellow's chaotic yard, the rusting trucks with their hoods raised, the stripped-down Camaro on blocks, the Volkswagen van without an engine. "He's got other jobs ahead of us," Michael had explained, not the least bit annoyed at having to kill four days waiting for the Jeep to be made reliable before they attempted to do anything that might require a quick getaway. Four days in San Pablo meant four days he could be getting closer to Emmie. "Besides," he'd added to mollify Gallard, "the mechanic had information."

Gallard's expression had remained impassive. "What information?" he asked.

"We got to talking," Michael had told him. It was exactly what Gallard had brought him along to do: get to talking. Michael moved easily within San Pablo. He glided from English to San Pablo-Spanish slang and back again without missing a beat. He knew these people, knew how to befriend them, how to get them to fix a clutch or reveal some important fact.

With the mechanic, he'd mentioned, in the oblique way San Pabloans preferred to discuss subjects of great importance, that he and a friend had come to town on business, that they were looking for a specific businessman by the name of Edouardo Cortez and were having a bit of difficulty locating him, although they'd heard he was in the vicinity. The mechanic had stiffened and sworn. "That *bastardo,*" he'd muttered. "Nobody knows him, but everybody hates him around here." A few more minutes of circular dialogue, and Michael had learned that Cortez was holed up in the hills somewhere outside town, that everyone despised him because he'd hurt a young *señorita,* a good sweet girl who would have made a man a fine bride but for what Cortez had done to her. Everyone in town wanted him dead, but he had too many guns and a few henchmen who knew how to use them, and the *policía* were scared to confront him.

"Nobody's going to stop us if we take him in," Michael had told Gallard.

"Forget the 'we,'" Gallard had scolded. "I'll take him in. You don't have the training. You just keep finding out stuff like this, and when the time comes, I'll take him in. And these folks'll probably have a fiesta when I do. They'll probably stand in line for a chance to kick him in the *cojones.*" It figured that that was one of the few Spanish words Gallard knew.

Michael didn't want to think about Cortez tonight, or about Gallard, who'd gone off for an evening at a local establishment staffed with sweet young *señoritas* whose work did not qualify them to become any man's fine bride but who were paid handsomely for their services. Gallard had invited Michael to join him, but Michael had better plans for his Saturday night.

Emmie Kenyon. Mary-Elizabeth, with eyes like flawless turquoise and skin like ivory, and a smile that could light up the sky.

He pocketed his wallet and left the room. Gallard had the Jeep with its tricky clutch. Michael didn't need it. He could walk to Casa Rosita's, which sat on a corner near the village center just a few blocks down from the *farmacia.*

He arrived five minutes early. She was already there, waiting for him.

He tried not to smile too broadly at the realization that she was eager enough to come early. For all he knew, she'd come early to tell him she'd decided not to spend the evening with him after all. Pessimism wasn't his style, though. Ignoring Rosita's stocky husband, who lurked in the doorway of the cozy cantina, he strode over to the table near one of the arched, unscreened windows overlooking the town's plaza. The table was round, lit by the flame of a waxy red candle that cast her face in a golden glow.

Emmie Kenyon was the most beautiful woman he'd ever seen.

"Hi," he said, suffering an uncharacteristic twinge of shyness as he pulled out the chair across the table from her.

She smiled slightly. "Hello."

"Did you wait long? I'm sorry."

"Not a problem," she said.

He relaxed. This was going to go well. Emmie might be gorgeous, she might be a cultivated and elegant Southern belle, but if his arriving after her for their rendezvous was not a problem, he doubted anything else would be.

Rosita's husband materialized at their table with bottles of beer. Had Emmie already ordered it? Apparently it didn't matter. Emmie simply gave him a smile of thanks when he filled her glass for her.

Michael and Emmie didn't talk much until they'd ordered some food. Once they were alone, Michael lifted his glass to her. "Here's to strangers in a strange land," he toasted.

Her smile warmed him. "Here's to someone who speaks English."

They drank. Michael relaxed some more. He would have been satisfied just to while away a night gazing at her and imagining sharing more than gazes with her, but the possibility that she had wit and intelligence and was good company delighted him.

"I'm picturing you as the mistress of a plantation, in a huge, pillared mansion," he told her. "Is that what you're like at home?"

She threw back her head and laughed. Her neck was pale and slender, and a tiny gold locket on a chain dipped toward the shadow between her breasts. He liked the loosely draped neckline of her dress, the slim strong muscles of her arms, the elegant angle of her chin. He especially liked the locket, a filigreed heart of gold resting against skin he wanted to kiss.

"I'm not Scarlett O'Hara," she said. "I grew up in a nice house, but I assure you there are no slave quarters on the premises." She sipped her beer and he decided he was in love with her fingers. He remembered how her hand had felt within his when they'd introduced themselves that afternoon. Her fingers were long and tapered, the nails filed smooth and layered with a clear polish that glinted in the candlelight. Fingernails like hers could scrape down a man's naked back, leaving heat in their wake.

"Why did you come to San Pablo? You mentioned that you're with a church group, but I'm sure your church could have found a position for you stateside if you'd wanted to do good deeds there."

She held her answer while their food was delivered: a plate of steaming corn tortillas; a plate of spiced, shredded beef; a plate of grilled vegetables chopped into small pieces to be rolled with the beef

inside the tortillas. Once they were alone again, she
sent Michael a playful smile. "My parents wanted
me to find a position back home. That seemed like
a good enough reason to come here."

"Ah, so you're a rebel." For some reason, he
hadn't expected her to be one. He knew plenty of
rebels, even beautiful blond ones. College campuses
were full of them, and he'd lived the past twelve
years of his life on college campuses, as an under-
graduate, a grad student and now as a junior faculty
member. He knew that lovely young women could
rebel against their parents, against their teachers,
against any damned thing that rubbed them wrong
on a given day. But their rebellions were usually the
result of boredom or bitterness and didn't carry them
all the way to an underdeveloped town in Central
America.

"My parents want me to be safe. They want to
protect me, and I appreciate that. But I don't want
to be protected. I don't want to be complacent.
There's more to life than belonging to the right
country club and wearing the right shoes with the
right dress."

As far as Michael was concerned, everything was
right about her. "I wasn't aware some country clubs
were more right than others," he joked.

She chuckled. "My parents are very aware that
some are. They're a bit bigoted, I'm afraid. They
say they're open-minded, but they really like to sur-
round themselves with people just like themselves.
I think it's a stifling way to live." She lifted a tortilla
off the serving plate and onto her own dish. "I take
it you don't belong to a country club?"

"The only club I ever belonged to was a Boy's

Club, when I was a kid," he told her. "They'd corral us barrio kids on a basketball court and tell us to have fun so we wouldn't be tempted to join gangs."

"Did it work?"

"Sometimes." His smile faded as he thought about his brother. "Not often enough."

"Where did you grow up?"

"Bakersfield. Not really a barrio town," he added. "My father thought he'd found the American dream. He married a woman whose great-grandparents were born in this country, and they moved out of East L.A. But it was a pretty rough neighborhood we lived in. We used to call ourselves 'barrio kids.' We knew where we'd come from."

"And now you're a professor," she observed. "That's remarkable."

He shrugged. He hated being viewed as a model minority. "I liked to read," he explained. "I liked to think. And I didn't want to wind up dead from a drive-by."

They ate, they drank, they talked. He told her about his thesis, a comparative analysis of the political structures of three Central American countries, and about the occasional papers he was asked to write for foreign policy experts in Washington. He told her about the many visits he had made to San Pablo over the years, his most recent while he was still in graduate school, and about his love of the place. "It can drive you crazy," he said. "There's so much we take for granted in the U.S.— like public water fountains or easy modem hookups. You have to function at a different speed here. Life moves slower, and it takes patience to get things done.'' More patience than Max Gallard had, he thought to himself. "But you can't get spiced beef like this anywhere else in the world. And the people are great, most of them.''

"Do you still have family here?'' Emmie asked.

"No. My father gradually brought the whole clan to the States. One of his brothers died here as a child, and his parents were really resistant about moving to the U.S. when they had a baby buried here, but eventually my father convinced them to come. Their other children were all in California. There was no one down here to take care of them.''

"One of the things I love about San Pablo,'' Emmie said, "is how the generations take care of one another. We've really lost that in America. Everyone moves on and families spread out, and we can't look after our elders.''

"And the elders can't look after the *bebés*,'' Michael agreed. "Are you going to return to Virginia when you leave here?''

"It's my home,'' she said with a shrug, then took a sip of her beer. "It's where my parents are. I can't imagine living anywhere else.'' And just as he'd told her about his family, she told him about hers. She was an only child, her parents pillars of the community, her mother active in the Daughters of the Confederacy—a fact about which Emmie seemed somewhat embarrassed, and even more embarrassed after Michael asked her what the "Daughters of the Confederacy'' was. "It's a social organization for women who can trace their ancestry to Confederate soldiers. Both my parents can do that. Sometimes I swear they still believe the South didn't really lose the War Between the States. It's just been a very long truce, and we're rebuilding our armies until we can march back into battle and defeat those damned Yankees.'' Her laugh was surprisingly throaty.

"Do you feel that way?'' he asked. Perhaps because he was a first-generation American, he had always found American history fascinating, like an epic novel he would read for entertainment, safe in the knowledge that it didn't have much to do with him personally.

"I never felt that way,'' she clarified. "My parents do, and their friends. I love Virginia, but I don't want to turn back the clock. I prefer to look forward.''

"So you're a rebel,'' he teased.

"I suppose I am. A loyal Virginia rebel, though.'' She didn't laugh this time, but her smile was as sultry as her laughter.

Their food was gone. As he left money on the table to cover the bill, he scrambled to think of a way to prolong their evening. San Pablo had a movie theater, but he didn't feel like sitting in a darkened auditorium with Emmie, all conversation shut down because talking would disturb the other viewers. He could take her to a cantina for a drink, but he didn't feel like getting her—or himself— drunk. What he wanted was to talk more with her, to listen as she told him more about Virginia and her Civil War ancestors, to hear her describe her students. He wanted to look at her, bask in her smile, touch her. He wanted to feel if her skin was as smooth as it appeared, her hair as soft. He wanted to taste her smile with his lips.

"Why don't we take a walk around the plaza," he suggested.

"All right."

The plaza was small, nothing that couldn't be circumnavigated in under five minutes. But a band was performing in an open-air cantina abutting the square, a combo comprising a horn, two guitars and percussion. Along the walkways people lingered to listen. Evening strollers on the plaza gravitated toward the cantina, and a few of them danced, moved by the music.

Michael realized that he wanted to dance with Emmie. He'd never been much of a dancer, but he wanted to gather her into his arms and let the music infuse them. He wanted to have her face close to his, her eyes gazing into his, her hand enveloped in his. He wanted Emmie Kenyon.

He still hardly knew her—although they'd covered an awful lot of ground in just one evening. Their conversation had come so easily, and everything she'd told him about herself had fascinated him. Nothing was ever going to come of it—he would be back in California long before she'd be back in Virginia—but he wanted her. Life was for living, experiences ripe for picking. A lot could happen in a few days.

She stood on the edge of the plaza, listening to the lively music, moving to the rhythm of it. Above them the sky was a sheet of black sprayed with stars. The air was as warm and soft as velvet, scented with roses. One of her sandaled feet began to tap.

It occurred to Michael that he hadn't asked a woman to dance for years. Maybe not since high school...he couldn't remember. He hadn't gone to many dances in his adolescence; they'd seemed hokey and uncool. His best friend's sister had taught him a few basic steps, and fortunately he'd been popular enough that the girls he danced with apparently hadn't minded that he wasn't the most graceful guy in the room.

But he wanted to dance with Emmie. He wanted to hold her in his arms.

The band finished their number and all the onlookers, both inside and outside the cantina, applauded. They began another song, this one slower, more romantic.

Michael opened his mouth and then shut it. He wasn't used to insecurity or self-doubt. When he wanted something, he went after it.

So he didn't ask Emmie. He simply took her hand, turned her toward him, slid his arm around her waist and began to dance.

CHAPTER FIVE

HIS TOUCH SURPRISED HER—but not much. The intimacy that had blossomed between them over dinner felt so natural it seemed just as natural that he would close his hand around hers and tuck it between their chests, and he would bring his other hand to rest at the small of her back, and he would sway to the melancholy folk song the band was playing.

She couldn't back away, and she didn't want to. In truth, she wanted to move deeper into his embrace, to rest her head against his shoulder and clasp his hand beneath her chin, close to her lips. It was unusual for her to respond like this to a man—but Michael Molina was an unusual man.

Her parents would hate him. They would say he wasn't white, a distinction that seemed meaningless to her. He'd told her his father was Hispanic, his mother as American as her own. His skin was a bronze shade, warm and tawny, and his hair was blacker than the night sky. She couldn't really think of him in terms of a specific race or color, and she didn't want to.

She wondered briefly whether her attraction to him was nothing more than a rebellious urge. She couldn't dismiss the possibility that she was drawn to him because she knew her parents would disapprove of any man whose name ended with a vowel, and because she'd found him here in San Pablo, a place they hadn't even wanted her to go.

But there was more to it than rebellion, more to it than his being a singularly handsome man. More than the power in his dark gaze, more than the warm strength of his hands, more than his lean, graceful physique.

Actually, *graceful* wasn't the first word that sprang to her mind as he began to dance with her. Not that he was clumsy, but there was something endearingly awkward in the way he moved his feet, as if they had found the rhythm of the music but weren't quite sure what to do with it. Michael didn't dance like the well-tutored young men she was used to dancing with at cotillions and country club affairs, gentlemen in expensive suits who moved with the practiced precision of an army drill team. Michael wasn't practiced, but his soul was in his dancing.

She liked the feel of his fingers curled around hers. She liked the heat of his chest close to hers, so different from the heat of the spring air. She liked the dense texture of his hair, the way the lanterns from the cantina glazed it with a layer of gold light and the way that same light edged the angles of his face.

She liked the way his nearness affected her. He made her feel interesting, as if what she had to say was important to him. He made her feel pretty, as if gazing at her brought him genuine pleasure. He made her feel sexy, as if dancing with her was the most erotic experience of his life.

Around them other people were dancing, too. One of the things she appreciated about San Pablo was the lack of inhibition in its people. Folks didn't seem to care whether they looked silly dancing in the plaza while a band played in an open-air tavern. No one bothered to notice the two *gringos* in the crowd. One young man in obscenely tight black jeans danced all by himself, as if to advertise his virility to the immediate world. Not far away, two innocent-looking teenage girls danced together, pretending to ignore him.

San Pablo was a magical place, Emmie acknowledged, a place where people danced freely in the public square, where Saturday night meant being outdoors in the starlight with music and beer and absolutely no worries. It was a place where a stranger could approach a woman shopping for peaches and make her feel more appealing than she'd felt in years.

"You're beautiful," Michael said, as if he had read her mind.

Her cheeks grew warm, and she bit her lip to keep from blurting out that she disagreed. His compliment hadn't come across as manipulative sweet talk. Maybe it was the beer and the starlight and the magic of the night, but she believed he was expressing his honest opinion. "Thank you," she murmured bashfully.

He moved his hand over the lightweight linen of her dress, tracing her spine upward until his fingers reached the blunt-cut ends of her hair. "I didn't come to San Pablo looking for romance, you know," he said.

She peered up into his face, a good six inches above hers as they faced each other. She had stopped looking for romance long ago, after the man her parents had deemed the perfect match for her—a strapping young fellow from what her parents called a "good" family—had broken off their engagement because she'd decided to spend a year teaching children in San Pablo instead of planning the most lavish wedding Richmond had ever seen. She hadn't meant to cause a ruckus or dash anyone's hopes, but she'd been secretly relieved when Martin had demanded that she choose between him and her silly fantasy of exposing children in the developing world to the glories of prealgebra and the Internet. The choice had been an easy one for her to make.

She would have been miserable married to Martin. Her parents had made sure she was miserable when he ended the engagement. They'd called her self-destructive, self-centered, unrealistic, narcissistic, impractical—and a rebel. That they were inordinately proud of their rebel ancestors during the Civil War was an irony that escaped them. Emmie simply considered herself the newest breed of Kenyon rebel.

So here she was in San Pablo, having been labeled a troublemaker and made to feel like a loser who would never attract the attentions of an appropriate man again. Yet the way Michael held her in his arms, the way he looked directly at her when he talked to her, the way he absorbed her words when he listened to her... He made her feel like the world's biggest winner.

Maybe he wasn't appropriate. She didn't care.

The song ended. She felt bereft, afraid that without the music he wouldn't want to keep her hand entwined with his, his arm arched around her. But another song began, this one fast, and he started

dancing with her again, bouncing with enough verve
to compensate for his lack of smooth moves.

Emmie decided right then that she didn't like men
with smooth moves.

"I'm not too good at this," he said apologetically,
taking both her hands in his and swinging their arms.

"You're fine," she assured him. "I gather you
didn't attend dancing school in your youth."

"Dancing school?" He snorted. "A *hermano*
wouldn't have been able to show his face in the
neighborhood if he'd gone to dancing school."

"Boys went to dancing school in my neighborhood," she told him, then smiled and added, "their
parents made them."

"I think," Michael said, pulling her slightly
closer, "that you and I grew up in very different
neighborhoods."

"But we're in the same neighborhood now," she
pointed out. She didn't just mean they were standing
on the same patch of pavement near the same street
corner. She meant that where they came from didn't
really matter. All that mattered was where they
were, *who* they were, what they wanted.

What she wanted was vague to her, a swirling coil
of undefined thoughts and yearnings. She didn't
want a fling with a stranger passing through town.
Maybe all she wanted was to be held for a while,
her body rocking to the music. She wanted to feel
wanted by a man as special as Michael Molina.

They danced until the band took a break, and then
Michael took Emmie's hand and strolled with her
across the patterned, tilelike slabs of cement that
paved the plaza. The dry air had lost much of its

heat, but as long as he held her hand she wouldn't be cold.

"One thing I remember about San Pablo is the smell," he commented. "Not just the plant smells and the cooking smells, but there's this dusty smell. I used to think it came from the adobe."

"Adobe doesn't have a smell," she argued.

"Sure it does. It's sun-baked mud. Why wouldn't it have a smell?"

She laughed and shook her head. San Pablo smelled very different from Richmond; the air had an alien lushness to it, even though it was arid. But the fragrance had nothing to do with the construction material of the buildings.

He sped up, tugging her hand as he strode briskly across the street to the building that housed the municipal offices. It was a squat structure of beige stucco, with a red-tile roof and wrought-iron grilles covering the lower-floor windows. He pulled her into the arched alcove that led to the main door, then guided her against the wall. "Smell it," he dared her.

She inhaled. "I don't smell anything."

"Are you kidding? It's as strong as smoke." He leaned toward the wall and filled his lungs. "Different from smoke, but just as strong."

She sniffed again but smelled nothing. "You're pulling my leg," she muttered, although she was having trouble containing her laughter. "There's no smell."

"Come closer." He drew her deeper into the alcove, into the cool shadow of the doorway. All she could smell was him, the spicy tang of his shampoo, the clean scent of his skin. For a moment she couldn't see him. She could only smell him and feel the heat of him. Then her eyes accustomed themselves to the darkness, just in time for her to watch him dip his face forward and brush her mouth with his.

If she'd wanted to inhale the building's smell, she wouldn't have been able to. Just that one light kiss seemed to paralyze her lungs. And her arms, her legs, her back—everything but her heart, which suddenly beat fast and wild, as if desperate to keep her alive, to keep her senses drinking him in.

It was barely a kiss, yet it swamped her with sensation. She tasted beer on his lips, and salt and masculinity. The flavor of Michael filled her.

"Are you okay?" he murmured.

Bewildered, she bit her lip again. Okay? He'd scarcely kissed her; why wouldn't she be okay?

Gradually she realized what he was really asking: was his kissing her okay? She nodded, then leaned toward him as he bowed to take another kiss. This one wasn't as restrained. It wrapped around her the way his arms wrapped around her and the music and the tropical air, as dark as the shadows, as mysterious as the night.

She lifted her hands to his shoulders and he placed his at her waist, urging her closer. He angled his head and moved his lips on hers, slowly, seductively, until she was moving hers, as well, until they were moving together. This dance was much more elegant than their public dance by the cantina. This dance in the shadows found them perfectly synchronized.

When his tongue ventured out to caress her lower lip, she opened to him. When his hand glided up her back to her nape she nestled against his palm, welcoming his touch. When he slid his tongue into her mouth she met his thrust willingly, bravely, fiercely. When he groaned, she groaned, too.

What she felt for Michael was more than a mere rebellion, more than a giddy adventure in an exotic land. It was hot and pulsing and hungry. It was deep inside her, in her heart and her womb, a desire so keen it made her shiver with pleasure. His fingers swirled through her hair and his other hand stroked the width of her waist, and she wanted nothing more than to melt into him, to give him everything and take everything from him, to be generous and greedy all at once.

"Where can we go?" he whispered, easing his mouth from hers. He kissed the tip of her nose, the bridge of it, her brow, the crown of her head. "I can't take you back to my room. I'm sharing it with a colleague. Where can we go?"

If she'd been a little less mesmerized by his kiss, she would have announced they couldn't go anywhere. She had only just met him that morning, after all. It didn't matter how much she felt she knew him; she hadn't known him long enough to consider *going* anywhere with him.

But she wanted him, insanely.

"I don't know," she admitted. "I'm boarding with a family. We can't go there."

A reluctant laugh escaped him. "I love San Pablo, but it's really lacking in accommodations."

"Maybe..." Her voice emerged broken, and she paused to collect herself. "Maybe it's too soon, anyway." She hated being reasonable at such a time, but she couldn't help herself. It *was* too soon.

He leaned back, scooping handfuls of her hair and sifting it through his fingers as he studied her face. He looked concerned, and she thought about explaining to him that even if it was too soon, she hadn't minded his kisses. She'd cherished them, in fact. She'd adored them. She'd wanted more. She'd wanted to find somewhere private, somewhere even more magical than this alcove near the plaza, and make love with him. She could tell him that even though they'd only just met and she wasn't foolish enough to sleep with someone she hardly knew, making love with Michael would have been okay with her.

More than okay. It would have been sublime.

But to say so would take too many words. So instead she rose on tiptoe, holding herself steady by gripping his shoulders, and lightly kissed his mouth.

His lips parted, luring her in. Then he laughed and sighed, all in one sound, and drew back. ''Don't get me started, or I swear I won't stop.''

She nodded sheepishly. He cupped the back of her head with his hand and guided her down to his shoulder. Wrapping both arms tightly around her, he stood with her, their bodies pressed together, cooling off.

''What are you doing tomorrow?'' His voice floated down to her. She could see only the edge of his shoulder, a horizontal line of bone and muscle extending to his arm. He felt so solid. She wished she had the nerve to slide her fingers inside the open collar of his shirt and touch his skin—but then he definitely wouldn't stop.

She digested his words. He wanted to see her tomorrow. Obviously his interest in her extended beyond a few stolen kisses in a dark alcove. "It's Sunday," she said, her lips moving against the soft cotton of his shirt. "The Cesares usually have a family dinner after church. Their daughters and sons-in-law and the grandchildren come. They like me to be there."

"Okay."

"Maybe you could come, too," she suggested. "It's always a big crowd. Señora Cesare might not mind." She pulled away to gaze at him. He looked hesitant. "Unless you'd rather not."

"No, I'd like to."

"You could meet us at church. We go to the nine-o'clock mass, every week without fail."

"Is that part of your church sponsorship?" he asked.

She grinned and shook her head. "My family's church is Methodist. I'm just staying with the Cesares. I don't think they even know what Methodists are." A laugh escaped her. "I don't mind, though. While I'm in San Pablo, I like doing things the local way—which, when it comes to church, is the Catholic way."

"Then I'll meet you at church tomorrow," he agreed.

She rested her head against his shoulder again, because it felt so right there, because she felt so right in his embrace. A smile curved her mouth as she realized that she and Michael had traveled from the mindless yearning for a place to make love, mere hours after they'd met, to a plan to meet at church. Yet that also seemed right.

Magic, she thought. Magic or amazing good luck. Or else maybe just serendipity, two people crossing paths at this one instant in time. Perhaps tomorrow Michael wouldn't show up in church. Perhaps after tonight she would never see him again.

She ordered herself to be prepared for that possibility. Magic could falter, luck could turn. What felt right tonight might feel very wrong tomorrow.

"I should probably be getting back to the Cesares' house," she said, forcing herself to step back. When he released her she felt a chill ripple through her, but she resisted the temptation to fling herself back into his arms. It wasn't like her to take such risks with a man, or to want so much so soon. Maybe the magic was all in her head. Maybe she desired Michael for no better reason than that she was homesick and he was an American.

"I'll walk you," he offered, weaving his fingers through hers and leading her out of the alcove.

They strolled in silence for a while, Emmie indicating the route with simple gestures of her hand. As they passed the cantina, the band began an elegiac piece, San Pablo's version of the blues. The mournful melody made her want to take shelter in Michael's arms once more, to dance just one final dance. But they kept walking, and she shook off the urge.

"Maybe tomorrow afternoon you could show me where you teach," he suggested.

He really seemed serious about spending tomorrow with her. "I'd like that," she said.

"When I used to come down here as a kid, there was a one-room schoolhouse. Lots of the children didn't even go to school then. That was my idea of heaven—not having to go to school."

"And now you're a college professor." She chuckled.

"I grew up and rethought a few things," he said with a shrug.

"I'm still trying to get some of my students and their parents to rethink things. The ones who live outside town say there's no good reason for their children to stay in school. They believe the children will only wind up being like their parents, working the land. They don't need algebra for that."

"So how do you change their minds?"

"I tell them they *do* need algebra to manage their farms. I don't want to tell them that if the children get a good enough education, they won't have to be poor like their parents. The parents don't want to hear that. They don't like thinking their children could outgrow them."

Michael nodded. "That's not just a thing down here. My parents were really proud of me for getting an education, but it scared them, too. They still yell at me every chance they get, warning me not to think I'm smarter than they are just because I have a Ph.D." He sighed in a way that hinted he had outgrown his parents much as she had outgrown hers. She heard love in his voice, but also a bristling frustration that his parents wanted to force him to fit a model of their choosing, just as hers did.

She cautioned herself not to read too much into his words and his wistful tone. She mustn't assume that she and he were alike. Such assumptions might be nothing more than her way of justifying the swift, uncharacteristic desire she'd felt in his arms.

"This is the Cesares' home," she said, drawing to a halt in front of the small, tidy house wedged between two other equally small houses. Vining roses climbed the walls, and the rear yard was fenced in to keep the chickens from straying. Even in town, many residents kept their own chickens for fresh eggs.

This late at night the chickens were quiet. The noise and bustle of people at the plaza seemed far away. The house's windows were dark, everyone asleep.

"I'll see you tomorrow, then," Michael said, turning her to him for a good-night kiss. She sensed him holding back as his mouth touched hers, and she was glad. Like him, she didn't trust herself to stop if they got caught up in another passionate embrace.

"All right," she murmured, gazing up at him and wondering if she looked as awed as she felt.

He smiled, causing tiny lines to fan out from the corners of his eyes. His hair flopped boyishly onto his brow as he backed up a step and plunged his hands into his pockets. "Tomorrow," he said again, then spun on his heel and strode down the street and out of sight.

HE HADN'T BEEN TO CHURCH in a long time. During his childhood, church had been a bone of contention between his parents: his father had wanted him and his brother to attend *la iglesia católica* in their neighborhood, while his mother had preferred what she called "the American church," where the mass was given in English. "This is the U.S. of A.," she used to complain. "My boys are American. You're an American, too, Al. We should all pray like Americans."

His mother had nothing against Hispanics. She'd married one, although Michael had learned he was the main reason for that marriage, an unintended consequence of his parents' raging hormones. But despite their being forced to wed, his mother had always appreciated his father's heritage. She'd learned how to cook rice and black beans, and she'd developed a rudimentary grasp of Spanish so she could talk to his family as, one by one, they immigrated to California. Still, she was adamant about her sons being raised American. His father resented that.

His father had probably resented having to marry her in the first place. He'd had the hots for the cute redhead who worked in the office of the warehouse where he'd been employed driving a forklift, but he had always assumed he would marry a proper bride, someone from San Pablo, perhaps, someone chosen for him by his parents.

He hadn't counted on his *cariña* becoming pregnant.

Church was just one thing they fought about. His insistence on bringing his family to the U.S. was another. Money, or the lack of it, was a major source of conflict. They argued about what time dinner ought to be on the table and what the meal ought to include; they argued about how clean the house should be and how late the boys could stay outdoors shooting hoops with their friends at the park on summer evenings. They argued about whether Michael ought to be allowed to quit his job bagging groceries in the evenings once he was selected for an honors program at his school. But mostly they argued about Michael's younger brother Johnny—"Juan," his father insisted on calling him. Johnny didn't get invited into any honors programs. He was smart but bored, and he wanted to fit in with his friends, who weren't smart at all. He loathed authority figures and resisted them. He fully expected to wind up working at a warehouse like his father, and that didn't seem like a particularly worthwhile future to him, so he poured his energy into other pursuits—cruising around town in low-riders, hanging out, drinking tequila with beer chasers and strutting his machismo.

Then one day he was dead, shot in the chest by a gun someone had gotten from someone in Los Angeles who'd bought it illegally from Edouardo Cortez. And Michael, who had spent a lot of time praying his brother would not be felled by gang violence, developed a serious problem with the church.

But he was looking forward to attending mass that morning—because Emmie Kenyon would be there.

Last night had been special. Today would be special, too. Emmie was special, and he didn't mind praying with her and her hosts in San Pablo.

Gallard was still asleep when he left the room at nine-thirty, dressed in the only shirt he hadn't yet worn, crisp white cotton with a banded collar and sleeves that rolled up loosely. The morning was already hot, and despite nearly two decades of maternal brainwashing, he skipped socks and shoes for a pair of leather sandals. He knew how people dressed for church in San Pablo, and it didn't conform to his mother's concepts of what was suitable.

He would get through the church service okay. Returning to the home of Emmie's hosts for a family dinner afterward had him a little edgy, but he would get through that, too, as long as he remembered he was a college professor in town to do research—and as long as he didn't kiss Emmie in front of her chaperons.

The Catedral de Santa María did not live up to its grandiose name. Hardly a cathedral, it was a cube-shaped structure that looked a bit like a bunker with a spire glued on top. The bells were chiming in the tower as he neared the building; he accelerated his pace, jogging toward the carved-oak front doors that stood open to the congregants funneling into the church. He didn't see Emmie, but he wasn't going to bulldoze his way through the crowd in search of her. He waited until the people in front of him had entered the building, then followed them inside.

The church's interior was stuffy, despite the ceiling fans churning the air. People crowded into the plain wooden pews, most dressed in attire his mother would have approved of. He scoured the room with his gaze, searching for Emmie or at least for a space on one of the benches where he could perch himself.

He didn't see any available seats. However, he did see Emmie. Her blond hair was as out of place in this congregation as a forest fire at the North Pole. She sat facing forward, her posture erect, her shoulders draped in the plain white linen of a short-sleeved blouse.

He couldn't tell if she'd managed to save him a seat, but he worked his way down the side aisle toward her, hoping to catch her eye and let her know he'd come as promised. When he was even with her pew, he wiggled his fingers unobtrusively. She didn't notice.

He nudged the person at the end of the row, a chubby man in a rumpled suit and tie who was sweating profusely and fanning himself with his straw hat. When he'd won the man's attention, Michael pointed down the row to Emmie.

"¡A, sí!" the man bellowed, as subtle as an air-raid siren. His voice soared above the din of people greeting one another and nestling into their seats. *"Muy bella chica. ¿Es su novia?"*

Michael doubted that every single person in the chapel, including the altar boys lighting the candles and the men at the rear of the room unstacking the baskets for the collection, had turned to gawk at him. Yet it felt like a good ninety percent of them had their eyes either on him or on Emmie. She glanced his way and smiled shyly.

He sent her a contrite grin and angled with his head to indicate he would find a seat in the back. But people were already sliding along the pew, squeezing together to make room for him next to his *novia,* his fiancée. He couldn't very well ignore their generosity.

Mumbling numerous *perdóns* as he jostled into the people seated on the pew, he inched his way down to the narrow space beside Emmie. An older couple sat next to her, the woman in a prim cotton dress and a jaunty hat with netting on the front, and the man in a suit that was shiny with age and snug over his shoulders. They each gave Michael a dubious look, then turned forward as the priest strode to the pulpit.

Michael wedged himself onto the pew next to Emmie and smiled again. There was no time to talk. The mass was beginning.

They sat in silence, their hips jammed together, her shoulder pressed into his, her hands folded neatly in her lap, luring his eyes not only to the slender beauty of her fingers and wrists but also to her thighs, their sleek shape outlined by the drape of her skirt. "God have mercy on me, Christ have mercy on me," the priest intoned in Spanish, and Michael watched Emmie's hands, the subtle movement of her right thumb against her left palm, and the nearly imperceptible shift of her knees.

He swallowed. What he was feeling right now didn't belong in a house of God. Except that just as God oversaw a world where street gangs could get hold of illegal weapons without much difficulty and use those weapons to kill people who had brothers who loved them, God also oversaw a world where a man and a woman could meet and connect so suddenly, on so many levels, that the yearning to possess each other was as forceful and heartfelt as prayer itself.

He listened to the priest not for his words but for the familiar cadences of the language. It made him remember his childhood, his parents and their constant tug-of-war, his brother slipping away while they fought. It made him remember why he'd come to San Pablo...but then Emmie stirred beside him, trying to rearrange herself in the confined space, and he forgot his rage about Johnny's death and Cortez's indirect role in it.

He dropped to his knees at the right times, stood, crossed himself. He couldn't recall the last time he'd gone to confession, so when it was time to take communion, he remained at his pew while the people around him rose and swarmed toward the altar. Being Methodist, Emmie probably couldn't take communion, either. The entire congregation flowed into the aisles and forward, leaving them behind.

He stole a look at her and found her smiling at him. She was lovely, her eyes an uncanny blue that reminded him of mountain lakes beneath a clear sky. He'd never seen a mountain lake beneath a clear sky except in photographs, and her eyes had that same startling perfection to them, the almost unreal clarity of a snapshot. With everyone facing the altar, no one could witness him covering her hand with his in her lap. Her fingers fluttered against his palm, but she didn't try to break free.

Lust sheared through him just from that slight motion of her hand. He wasn't sure what it was about her—that she was beautiful wasn't enough. Finding good-looking women had never been a problem for him, and he was too mature to be driven by hormones.

But he wanted Emmie. Last night, he'd wanted to hold her so badly that he'd made a fool of himself dancing with her, and here he was again, making a fool of himself in church. People were beginning to file back to their seats, so he reluctantly let go of her hand.

He got through the rest of the mass, praying for God to forgive him for thinking about sex during mass. Once the church bells started to ring and everyone stood, the older couple with Emmie scrutinized him and then conferred quietly with Emmie. He couldn't hear their words or hers, but she seemed pretty fluent in Spanish, her accent a bit European but understandable.

After their powwow, she turned to him with a

smile. ''Señor and Señora Cesare would like you to be their guest for Sunday dinner,'' she said in Spanish.

He bowed his head politely and said, ''I would be honored.'' Señora Cesare looked mollified.

Leaving the church, Emmie tucked her hand into the bend of his elbow, allowing him to escort her. They walked a few paces behind the Cesares, exhibiting the proper deference to their elders. Michael's grandmother used to describe to him the rigid courting rituals of her youth in San Pablo, the chaperons who always accompanied young ladies, the semiarranged marriages in all classes of society. Emmie must have seemed terribly brazen to her hosts, finding a man all by herself and inviting him back to their house. Michael would do his best not to embarrass her.

The sun beat down on his head and shoulders, making his scalp steam. He missed air-conditioning. He missed drinking fountains spurting icy water. He missed his apartment, with its broad, comfortable bed and the freedom to bring a woman to it.

The Cesares' house had a window fan, at least. Propped into a kitchen window, it whined and hissed, spewing outdoor air into the crowded kitchen. Michael wished he could stand there to catch the breeze, but he knew men weren't allowed in the kitchen when the women were preparing dinner.

He watched from the doorway as Emmie pitched in, carrying thick porcelain plates to the table in the dining room, chatting easily with several other young women. She towered above the others, who all had toddlers clinging to their knees and skirts.

Señor Cesare sidled up next to him and pointed to the women. "My daughters," he said. "Elena, Lourdes, María. If you marry Emmie, be sure to have sons."

Smiling, Michael allowed Señor Cesare to usher him into a parlor that was smaller and hotter than the kitchen. The husbands of Elena, Lourdes and María sat there, drinking hard cider and smoking cigarettes. Michael accepted a glass and let the familiar scent of smoke fill his lungs. His father smoked. All men in San Pablo smoked, and if Michael hadn't spent two torturous years quitting in graduate school, he would have helped himself to a cigarette from the wooden box on the table near the door. He still missed the burning rush of smoke in his lungs, the drugging relaxation of it. But having quit once, he never wanted to have to quit again.

The men didn't talk much. A few comments about the weather, a brief discussion on the decline in profits at the grocery store managed by one of the sons, but mostly the men occupied themselves by giving Michael long, assessing stares. He kept his mouth shut, figuring the less he said, the less likely he'd be to offend them.

After a while the men were called to the table. Pork stew filled a tureen at its center, chunks of meat mixed with peppers and tomatoes and redolent with spices. Orange rice was heaped in another bowl, and a pitcher of lemonade sweated in the heat. Señor Cesare took his place at the head of the table and said grace. Then they sat.

Emmie wound up across the table and several seats down from Michael. He couldn't even glance at her discreetly. Surrounded by one Cesare daughter and another son-in-law, he decided that much more than air-conditioning and water fountains, he missed America's more casual approach to dating. What was he going to say to all these Cesares and in-laws? He could compliment the cooking only so many times before they'd start wondering what was wrong with him.

Emmie must have sensed his discomfort, because she stepped into the breach. "Michael is a university professor," she told the Cesares. "He's here to do research."

The daughter next to him gave him a shiny-eyed look. "What research?" Señor Cesare wanted to know.

Michael took a deep breath, using the pause to review the cover story he and Gallard had worked out. "My father grew up in San Pablo," he told them. "My research involves monitoring the social and economic changes in the region."

"What changes?" one of the sons-in-law muttered. "Nothing changes here."

"There have been changes," Michael argued gently. "Your school now has Internet access." He shot a smile at Emmie, glad for the chance to look directly at her. "The economy is much stronger than it was twenty years ago."

This provoked a chorus of derisive laughter. "The corrupt politicians have gotten richer," Señor Cesare grumbled. "The rest of us are where we were a hundred years ago."

Michael knew he shouldn't say anything risky— but he couldn't help himself. Not after sitting in church for ninety minutes, thinking about why he hadn't been in a church in seven years. "I'll bet the criminals have gotten richer," he remarked.

"What criminals?" one of the Cesare daughters asked. But Señor Cesare outshouted her. "The vermin! They're worse than the politicians!"

"What criminals?" Emmie chimed in, sending Michael a quizzical look.

"I was talking to a mechanic yesterday," Michael said with feigned casualness. "He mentioned that a gunrunner lives in the hills outside town."

His observation was met with gasps and tongue clicking. "Don't mention that beast in my house!" Señora Cesare hissed, crossing herself. "I don't care if he's rich, and I don't care if murder is a sin. Someone should kill him."

Emmie's eyebrows arched higher. "Why?"

"What he did to a girl in town. It's terrible. I can't even talk about it." Señora Cesare shook her head and crossed herself again.

"I hear he's afraid to come into town," one of the sons-in-law remarked. "He knows he'd get torn limb from limb if anyone found him. He does all his business down in Aranal, where they don't know him."

Michael stored that bit of information in his memory bank. Aranal was a good twenty miles to the west. If Cortez was hiding in the mountains, he was likely hiding in the mountains west of town.

"We will not talk about that anymore," Señora Cesare announced. "We will talk about what a fine mass Father Esteban gave today."

The conversation bent to Señora Cesare's will, and they all discussed the mass. Michael ate his stew, sipped his cider and let his gaze veer to Emmie as often as he dared. Whenever he looked at her he found her looking back, her eyes bright with curiosity and amusement and something else, something he wanted to believe was an accurate reflection of what he was feeling: passion.

Passion and a whole lot more.

CHAPTER SIX

"THAT WASN'T SO BAD, was it?" Emmie asked.

They were walking to his temporary residence to get his Jeep. He'd warned her that the clutch was temperamental, but she'd agreed to chance a drive with him anyway, figuring that if he was plotting to have the vehicle conveniently break down so he could have his way with her far from town, he wouldn't have mentioned the clutch problem.

She also figured that, after last night, after that morning in church, after every minute she and Michael had spent in each other's company, he must know he wouldn't have to come up with a complicated scheme if he wanted to have his way with her. The attraction between them was raw and real and obviously mutual.

What pleased her was that that attraction wasn't the only thing between them. His behavior at the Cesares' house had doubled her respect for him. He'd been polite and sociable, and she'd loved listening as he chatted with the Cesares' extended family. She loved the way Spanish words glided off his tongue in the same tangy accent she'd been hearing since she'd arrived in San Pablo last summer. He seemed so patently American, yet surrounded by native San Ploans, he was utterly at home. He knew just how much to praise Señora Cesare's cooking—

too little and she would have been insulted, too much and she would have been skeptical—and he knew how to jog the conversation when it lulled. His smiles for the Cesare daughters were discreet, containing just enough mischief to flatter the young women. He was even reasonably patient with the Cesares' grandchildren. He didn't get down on the floor and play with them, but he tolerated them with good humor.

By one-thirty, he and Emmie had won their freedom. Señora Cesare approved of him; when Emmie said they were going out for a while, the older woman nodded and smiled. "He seems like *un buen hombre,*" she murmured. A good man.

"We could take the Jeep for a spin," he'd suggested once they had left the house. "Assuming my colleague isn't using it. I sort of doubt he would be, though. He has a lot more trouble with the clutch than I do."

"Who is he?" Emmie asked.

"A research assistant," Michael said vaguely, his tone saying he didn't want her to question him further.

They passed the church where they'd attended mass that morning, and she might have only imagined the shadow that drifted across his face as he glanced up at the stark white spire. As soon as they were beyond the church he seemed to brighten again. "I haven't had any real home cooking since I got here," he remarked. "That dinner was great."

"Does your mother cook San Pablo cuisine?" Emmie asked, then rolled her eyes. "I forgot—she's American."

"My grandmother taught her a few things," Michael said.

The plaza was crowded, and Michael took Emmie's hand as they ventured into the throng. A sunny Sunday afternoon tended to lure everyone out of doors. Children careered about on their bicycles, young couples pushed toddlers in strollers and old people sat placidly on the benches, observing the activity around them.

Michael moved purposefully through the swarming humanity, his hand folded snugly around Emmie's. At the far side of the plaza they came to the cantina where the band had played last night. He paused to stare at one of the open-air tables, where a man in a T-shirt that displayed an abundance of muscle sat nursing a beer. The man's aggressive physique and short hair made her think he might be a marine. His coloring—the buzz-cut hair was sandy brown, and his fair complexion was dotted with freckles—made her think he might be an American.

"That's my research assistant," Michael announced.

Emmie frowned. The man looked too old to be Michael's assistant—he was clearly older than Michael—and he looked too rugged to be an academic. His blunt, thick fingers didn't seem to have spent a great deal of time flipping through books and scribbling notes.

She did her best to conceal her surprise, however, reproaching herself not to judge the man by his appearance. Just because he resembled a body builder didn't mean he couldn't be a brain builder, too.

Michael wove through the tables until he reached

the man. Somewhere along the meandering route he let go of Emmie's hand. "Hey," he said quietly.

The man glanced up from his beer, grinned at Michael and then lost a bit of his grin as his gaze expanded to take in Emmie. "What's up?" he asked.

"Emmie, I'd like you to meet my research assistant, Max Gallard. Max, this is a friend of mine, Mary-Elizabeth Kenyon."

Max gave her a sweeping inspection with his eyes. They were hard and gray, like chips of flint. "How do you do," he said blandly, extending his hand.

She shook it, once again hiding her surprise. His palm, tough and callused, felt like an overcooked slab of steak, and his fingers were strong enough to squeeze the life out of a snake. "How do you do," she echoed, forcing a smile.

"We need the wheels today," Michael told Max. "Any problem with that?"

Max shook his head. "I don't know if you should trust it. That damn clutch—"

"I can handle it," Michael assured him, then grinned. "It requires a level of sensitivity that's way beyond you."

Max laughed. Emmie wished someone would explain the joke to her, but neither man did. "Look," Max said, "we've got stuff to take care of. There's research we've got to do."

"It'll get done later," Michael said. "Don't sweat it. We'll be back in a couple of hours, barring a breakdown."

Before Max could say anything more, Michael touched his hand to Emmie's elbow and steered her from the cantina. She waited until they were half a block away before daring to ask, "If he's your research assistant, how come he's the one telling you you have to work?"

"That's just his way," Michael answered with a shrug. "He likes to think he's in charge."

She glanced over her shoulder and saw Max's head bowed over his beer bottle, his shoulders as hulking as rounded mountains. "He doesn't look like a scholar," she remarked.

"He entered graduate school after a stint in the military," Michael explained, ushering her around the corner to a block of small shops separated by narrow alleys. He led her down an alley next to an apothecary and opened the door at the rear of the building.

The room was shrouded—the roller shade was lowered in front of the one window, which overlooked the alley. Despite the gloom, Emmie could see that the room was relatively tidy, neater than she would have expected of bachelor lodgings. One of the two narrow steel beds was made, and she couldn't keep from hoping that that bed was Michael's. The dresser top held assorted guy stuff— thick wood-handled hairbrushes, two different brands of aftershave, a casually tossed handkerchief, a set of keys. Michael scooped up the keys and turned toward the door.

Still in the doorway, Emmie blocked his way. She could have stepped aside, but she was still studying the room. Her gaze lingered on the unmade bed, and the dark-red canvas duffel stowed underneath it. Next to the duffel stood a pair of mud-spattered hiking boots.

"Do you hike a lot?" she asked Michael.

He traced the angle of her vision, then shook his head. "Those are Max's."

She opened her mouth, then shut it and moved back out into the alley. She wanted to believe Max was a research assistant, but she was having difficulty. If she couldn't believe that, then she couldn't believe Michael. The possibility that she might be wrong to trust him was disturbing.

She'd trusted him so much yesterday, trusted him enough to consider making love with him. She'd trusted him enough to bring him into the Cesare household today, to include him in a family dinner. She wanted to trust him…but Max Gallard tweaked her suspicions.

She slowed to a halt in the alley. The stone walls on either side reflected the heat of the day, a dry warmth that seeped into her without causing her to sweat. Michael stood before her, peering down at her, obviously perplexed.

"I don't believe Max is a research assistant," she said bluntly. She could think of no other way to deal with her doubts.

Michael's expression remained perplexed. She sensed no hesitation in him, no defiance or denial. "Why?" he asked.

"He just…" The truth sounded so petty and close-minded. But she'd opted for honesty and saw no point in backing off now. "He doesn't look like one. He doesn't sound like one."

A faint smile curved Michael's mouth. "What does a research assistant sound like?" he asked.

She was being foolish—but still, doubt niggled at her. "Erudite?" she suggested. "Scholarly?"

"Pompous? Pretentious? Just like me, right?" Michael's smile grew. "Just let me know if you want me to lapse into academic jargon. I've got a whole lot of thirty-dollar words at my fingertips. I had to learn them before the university would hire me."

"I'm sorry." She managed to laugh at herself. "It's silly, I know. But when I think of graduate students, I think of skinny, sun-deprived bookworms anxious to get their research completed. And I say this as a former graduate student myself," she added apologetically. She'd spent two years at the University of Virginia earning her master's degree in education. "Skinny, sun-deprived and anxious" accurately described her at graduate school.

"He's anxious, for sure," Michael confirmed. "That's why he'd rather be working with me right now, instead of sitting by himself while I escort a lovely teacher around town."

His comment made sense. Emmie decided to shrug off her misgivings. Assuming Max wasn't what Michael claimed didn't reflect his lack of credibility but her narrow-mindedness.

The Jeep was parked at the rear of the alley. Rather than one of those swanky suburban models that filled the parking lot of her parents' country club, it was an old, canvas-topped model of army green scarred by shapeless blemishes of rust. Michael helped her up into the passenger seat, which was cracked and patched with duct tape, then settled himself behind the wheel. He twisted the ignition key and the engine rumbled to life.

"I want to see where you teach," he told her,

bouncing along the rutted alley to the street. "Where's the school?"

She gave him the address and he nodded, steering down the crowded side road. Wagons and cars parked at bad angles formed an obstacle course, but he navigated deftly around them, cruised past bicyclers and pedestrians and avoided the stray dogs and cats that roamed the street, sniffing and scavenging for food. Emmie thought to give him more detailed directions as they proceeded, but he clearly knew the route.

As they neared the drab building where she taught, Michael let out a low breath. She was afraid he was going to insult the building, which resembled a small prison, its walls intimidating gray slabs of cinder block and its windows tucked high beneath the flat tin roof. The building was indisputably ugly, but it had reliable plumbing and heat in the winter, plus sufficient electricity to run a computer and enough phone lines to link that computer to the Internet.

She was gearing up to defend the building when Michael spoke. "I can't believe it! It almost looks like a real school!"

"As opposed to what?"

He chuckled and shook his head. "When I used to come down here as a kid, the school was this rickety wooden shack. One room, well vented thanks to all the cracks in the walls. There was an outhouse…and that tree. See that tree?" He pointed to the lone palm at one corner of the dusty school yard. "They'd hold classes under the palm tree when the weather permitted. It was too crowded in the one room inside, so the kids would come outside and sit in the dirt and try to concentrate while the teacher taught. No blackboard, no maps—certainly no computers.''

''So…you're saying you think this school is good?''

''Compared with what used to be, it's fantastic.'' He shook his head again. ''I bet even the rural kids come to class.''

''Most do,'' she agreed. ''Sometimes their parents hold them out of class when there's fieldwork to do.''

''The parents hold them out of class because they don't want their kids rising above them,'' Michael said, his voice tinged with bitterness. She remembered his comment as he'd walked her home last night—that his parents resented his rise into the ranks of the professionals—and she wanted to question him about it.

But she had already risked offending him by questioning him about Max. She couldn't risk offending him by questioning him about his parents.

He gave her a measuring gaze. Perhaps he read her questions in her eyes, because he said, ''I'll show you where I came from.'' He pulled back onto the road.

''I thought you were born in the U.S.''

He grinned, but his eyes were pensive. ''Yeah, I was born in the States. But this is where I *came* from.'' He headed north, leaving behind the bustle and traffic for the outskirts of town. The road slithered up into the hills, where the houses were more widely spaced, more rudimentary, surrounded by vegetable gardens, chattering ducks and chickens, pens of grunting pigs and fields of corn. Some yards had the carcasses of stripped automobiles on display; some were nothing more elaborate than packed dirt. Scrawny children chased scrawny dogs and lugged buckets of water from outdoor pumps.

The Jeep groaned when Michael downshifted on the inclining roads, which gradually deteriorated into crumbling strips of rutted asphalt. She watched him play the gear stick gently, his touch light and graceful. "The car isn't going to die on us, is it?" she asked, not sure how safe they would be, stranded so far from town in such impoverished surroundings. She had little on her worth stealing—a wristwatch, her locket and simple gold-hoop earrings—and Michael had said he came from here. He would know how to extricate them from a bad situation.

"It wouldn't dare," he said, tapping his foot on the clutch and steering around another S-shaped wiggle in the road. He slowed the Jeep as they crested a hill, slowed it some more as they came upon what might have been an archeological ruin had it had any grandeur at all.

It had none. The house was barely a skeletal hut, its corrugated roof torn away in spots, its walls—adobe slapped onto wooden beams—disintegrating, its front door gone and the door frame rotting. Scruffy grass grew in dust-caked tufts across the front yard, short and blanched near the remains of a stone fire pit, taller and greener near the water pump. The sun baked the ground mercilessly, fading the scene to a bleak pallor.

Across the road was another shack in only marginally better shape. A woman hunched over a cauldron on her fire pit, stirring its contents with a stick while steam rose from the pot. "Is she cooking?"

Emmie asked, puzzled about why anyone would cook such a huge pot of stew, unless she was planning to feed an army battalion.

"Laundry," Michael guessed, yanking the parking brake and turning off the engine.

A bone-thin girl came out of the house, her eyes wide and her mouth pinched. She darted toward the woman and hid behind her skirt. Chickens cackled raucously at the intrusion of two strangers into their afternoon. A swaybacked dog whimpered and limped over to a patch of shade beneath a wood wagon.

"Wait here," Michael whispered as he got out of the Jeep.

Emmie watched anxiously as he crossed the road to talk to the woman. A few words drifted back to her, but she learned less from them than from Michael's body language. He leaned toward the woman, bowed so he wouldn't loom so tall above her. He tilted his head to listen, nodded, looked compassionate. After a minute, he returned to the Jeep, chased by a brown rooster that seemed to view him as a threat, given the way it squawked and scampered and flapped its wings indignantly.

Michael continued around the Jeep to Emmie's side and helped her out. "This—" he gestured toward the abandoned shack "—is where my grandparents lived, where my father grew up."

Emmie swallowed. She had seen poverty in Virginia, but nothing like this. Even if she added a solid roof and walls and a door in her imagination, the shack was pitiful. She approached it slowly, unable to picture a family growing and thriving in such a wretched dwelling.

He angled his head toward the woman boiling her laundry across the road. "She told me the place has been empty for five years. The people who moved in after my grandparents left brought nothing but trouble with them. The woman finally ran off with a flashy man passing through, and her husband had drunken rages for a while, but then he took off, also. The place has sat abandoned ever since." He glanced over his shoulder at the woman and smiled. "I think the missing pieces from this roof are sitting on her roof. If I looked harder, I bet I'd find the front door doing service in her house, too."

"Doesn't that bother you?" Emmie asked. "I mean—it's like a desecration of your father's home."

He tossed back his head and laughed, then tested one of the splintered beams holding what remained of the house upright. "Let her help herself to what she needs. There's nothing worth saving here. I told her she should use what's left of the walls for fire-wood."

Emmie circled the house. The side wall was a mess of ragged boards and paper-thin pasteboard. The inside appeared to be one room.

"Two," he said, answering her unvoiced question. He climbed through a gaping hole in the wall and extended his hand to her, helping her through. "This front area was the kitchen. The back was the bedroom. My father and his brothers and sisters slept there. My grandparents slept in the kitchen."

Her eyes filled with tears of shame for having grown up in wealth when so many in the world had so little. Tears for Michael's father, whom she'd never even met, because this hovel had been his home. Tears for Michael because he'd been one of San Pablo's children, even if he had been born in America. Michael, though, was one of those children who had outgrown his ancestors. He'd gotten an education. He was a professor.

But this was where he'd come from.

She picked her way around the fallen bits of wood, moving in and out of the thin shafts of sunlight that leaked in through the holes in the roof. She was ashamed of herself for having doubted that Michael's colleague, Max, was really a research assistant. Michael didn't look like someone this horrid place would have produced. He was strong and tall and healthy, his eyes bright and his mind even brighter. She shouldn't judge any man by his appearance or his environment. She should only be grateful that Michael's father had given his son a chance for a better life by leaving San Pablo for California.

She felt Michael move close behind her. He looped his arms around her waist, pulled her back against him and rested his chin on the crown of her head. "I didn't bring you here to depress you," he murmured.

"Why *did* you bring me here?"

He considered his reply. "I have wonderful memories of my grandparents' home," he said, not a trace of irony in his voice. "My father and I used to come down here every year for the summer. He'd spend the visit trying to convince his family to move to America, and I'd learn about the land in my blood. That was what he called this place—'the land in my blood.'" He sighed, his breath ruffling her hair. "I have good memories."

And he'd brought her here so she could share this place with him. She didn't quite understand how such a dismal setting could evoke good memories, but having seen this place, this land in his blood, made her feel close to him, closer than his arms holding her against him, closer than she'd felt last night when they'd danced and kissed and ached for each other.

They stood in the shack for an endless minute. Dust motes danced in the light spilling in. Michael savored his memories in silence, and Emmie savored the feel of his arms around her. Without having to speak, they both knew how long to stand there and when to leave.

Their silence lasted as they climbed into the Jeep. The engine growled, the dog under the wagon whined and the rooster stormed across the road after them, forcing Michael to yank the steering wheel sharply to avoid hitting him. Emmie twisted in her seat for one last look at Michael's grandparents' house. Through the plumes of dust kicked up by the Jeep's tires, it appeared even more desolate.

She turned back and glimpsed Michael. He looked peaceful, even pleased by his pilgrimage. His smile was enigmatic, but his chin was high, his eyes luminous as he maneuvered around pits and stones in the curving road.

She felt a pressure in her chest, something swollen inside her. Respect for this brave, proud man. Respect mixed with love.

The road began its slow, winding descent from the foothills. The houses they passed stood closer together and appeared a bit more substantial. Fences penned the livestock; no rambunctious rooster was going to charge across the street at them in this residential district. He drove slowly, very slowly. The Jeep alternately coasted and groaned.

Gradually it dawned on Emmie that something was wrong with the car. The engine wasn't groaning—it was revving, overworking. She watched Michael's right hand long enough to notice that he hadn't moved the gear stick.

"Is the car all right?" she asked.

He made a sound that was half a laugh, half a snort. "I can't shift out of first," he told her. "No big deal."

"The engine sounds weird."

"Fortunately we're heading downhill. We can roll most of the way. If we pick up a little speed, I might be able to pop the gear."

The streets in this part of town were too congested to pick up much speed, though. Children were celebrating their day of rest by doing anything but resting—playing tag and soccer in the streets, riding bicycles and skateboarding on homemade boards constructed of plywood and skate wheels. If Michael let the car accelerate, he might hit one of the children.

She moved her gaze to his knees, noting the smooth play of his feet on the pedals. Whether or not the clutch was throwing a tantrum, she had utter faith that Michael would get them back to town safely.

Her faith flagged just a bit when she saw the first curl of white smoke rise from the hood of the Jeep. "Michael—I think we're on fire," she murmured, struggling to keep her voice calm when her impulse was to scream.

He, too, must have noticed the streams of white coming from under the hood. He muttered a curse, then steered cautiously around a corner to a tree-shaded side street and braked. "No, it's not on fire," he said. "It's overheated. That's steam, not smoke."

"Oh." She was mildly reassured. She knew an overheated engine wasn't a disaster, although she'd never experienced the problem herself. Her parents bought all their cars new and traded them in after three years, never owning them long enough for their parts to start breaking down.

"What should we do?" she asked as he turned off the ignition.

He leaned back in his seat, sighed, then shot her a sheepish grin. "We'll let it cool down, then add some water to the radiator and say a prayer. I should have prayed for the Jeep while I was in church this morning."

"I'm sure you had more important things to pray about then," she said, remembering the shadow that had briefly darkened his face when they'd walked past the church. "You didn't enjoy church this morning, did you?"

He glanced at her, then smiled reluctantly. "I haven't been to church in a long time. Sitting there reminded me why."

It seemed odd that she felt no qualms about asking him such personal questions. It felt utterly natural that they should talk this way. "Is it church or God you don't like?"

"My brother died a few years ago," he told her. "Neither God nor the church had anything to give me when I needed them."

"I'm sorry, Michael." She reached across the seat to touch his wrist.

He rotated his hand and laced his fingers through hers. His expression grew more pensive as he regarded her. The leaves of an ancient elm threw mottled shadows across his face, but his eyes cut through the shadows with their force. They were dark and radiant at the same time, studying her as if they could see right through her.

Did they see how moved she'd been by their excursion to his grandparents' old house, and by his revelation now, by his willingness to share so very much of himself with her? Did they see that she was smitten with him, falling more and more deeply under his spell? Did they see that she considered him the most fascinating, courageous, complex man she'd ever met?

Apparently what he was gazing at wasn't her but something behind her: a house converted into an inn, judging by the sign above the front door: *Posada.* "How about a drink?" he asked, motioning toward the inn. "We've got to wait for this baby to cool off. We may as well cool ourselves off, too."

"All right." It was probably just as well that he hadn't been reading her mind and her heart. She ought to be more cautious. Just because she was falling in love with him didn't mean she wanted him to know it.

They got out of the Jeep. He strode to the hood, gingerly released the latch and lifted it. Hot vapor ballooned out into the air. He jumped back a step, then propped the hood on its metal support rod and backed away. "That'll teach me to drive five kilometers downhill in first gear," he muttered.

"How about if *I* treat you to a drink?" Emmie offered. "You've got a disaster on your hands. The least I can do is pay for the drinks."

"No, that's okay." He took her arm and steered her up the short front walk to the open door. A wizened old woman appeared and asked him, in brisk Spanish, what was wrong with his car.

"Why don't you stay here," he said to Emmie, pointing to a couple of chairs on a small patio overlooking the street, "and keep an eye on the car. I'll go inside and buy us some drinks. What would you like?"

"A lemonade," she said.

He nodded and followed the woman indoors. Emmie watched the white clouds of vapor rise from the engine. At least she and Michael weren't too far from the center of town. If the Jeep couldn't be resuscitated, they could walk back to the Cesares' house from here.

Michael emerged from the inn carrying a tall, frosty lemonade for her and a *cerveza* for himself. He handed her the lemonade and took a seat next to her. A glance at the Jeep told him it hadn't begun to cool down yet. He shrugged, turned to her and smiled, a magical smile that made her breath catch in her throat.

She took a sip of her drink. Icy and tart, it refreshed her, but she felt warm inside, hot, as if her soul was steaming like the engine. She wasn't sure why, except that Michael's gaze seemed to do to her what his first-gear driving did to the Jeep. She was overheated and under pressure. She sighed without meaning to.

"She has a room," he said.

Emmie frowned. "What?"

He angled his head toward the front door, where the wizened woman had stood. "The innkeeper. She has a room." He paused, then added, "I took it."

The frown left Emmie's forehead but settled deeper inside her. "You took a room here?"

"For us." He watched her, gauging her response. "It's ours."

"Now?"

"For the week." Evidently he read her bewilderment as discouragement. He turned away, observing the Jeep as the flow of steam diminished. "We don't need to use it. I probably shouldn't have taken it, but it wasn't expensive, and I figured it would be here if we wanted it...."

The full impact of what he'd done sank into her, rattling her. They had a room. They had it now, and they'd have it tomorrow, and the next day, as well. No Señora Cesare chaperoning her. No muscle-bound research assistant honing in on Michael's privacy.

They had a room. It was theirs, waiting for them, if they wanted it. All they had to do was walk inside, follow the innkeeper to the room, thank her and shut the door behind her and then face each other. All Emmie had to do was admit what she wanted, what she needed, what she felt for Michael.

"Yes," she whispered.

CHAPTER SEVEN

THEY LAY ACROSS the broad bed, naked, holding each other.

He hadn't even bothered to inspect the room before he'd paid for it, but luckily it was clean and pretty, with a dark oak floor, pale-peach walls and oak beams striping the ceiling. Wrought-iron grilles covered the windows, and a clothing tree occupied one corner. Another corner held a small chest of drawers with an oval mirror above it; a ceramic pitcher and basin stood on the embroidered runner that lay across it. A bowl of pink roses decorated the night table. Fresh linens covered the bed.

Those linens were a bit rumpled now. Not that he cared. All he cared about was the soft, beautiful woman in his arms.

He hadn't had anything with him. He hadn't planned for this, and when he'd impulsively rented the room, he hadn't expected Emmie to agree that they should put it to use right away. But she had. She was with him, and although he hadn't thought to slip a condom into his wallet—hell, he wasn't even sure where a man could buy a condom in this part of the world—they'd still managed to make some kind of love.

Shutting his eyes, he relived it in his mind: Emmie's initial shyness as he'd unbuttoned her blouse.

The flush in her cheeks as he'd bowed to kiss her breasts. Her gasp as he'd moved his hands over her skin, following the elegant slope of her back, the sweet roundness of her bottom, the silken length of her legs. He remembered thinking about her legs in church that morning. Now he could touch them, stroke them, slide his knee between her thighs, and he felt closer to God than he had hours ago in that hot, crowded chapel.

He continued to caress her in the aftermath. She was still descending from a peak, still breathing erratically, her eyes shut and her lips parted. He played his fingers gently between her legs and she tensed and moaned and covered his hand with hers. She arched against him, and he slid his finger inside her. She cried out and shuddered, lost again.

He could do this forever. Watching her come was almost as exciting as coming himself.

"Michael," she whispered faintly, her eyes fluttering open.

He rose on one elbow and bowed to kiss her lips. That brief taste made him hungry for more, and he angled himself so he could kiss her breasts. They were fuller than he'd realized, plump and pale, her nipples the same delicate pink as the roses in the bowl beside the bed. He flicked his tongue over one and she moaned. "Don't," she protested, sounding far from convincing. "I can't…"

He lifted his head and peered down at her. "You can't what?"

She gave him a dazed, helpless smile. "I can't keep feeling like this. I'll die."

"I don't think it's fatal," he assured her, sliding his finger deep once more.

"No…" She convulsed again, her breath escaping her in a ragged groan.

He waited until she'd caught her breath, then kissed her forehead. "See? You're still alive."

"Barely." She smiled, but her voice grew somber when she asked, "Why does this feel so right?"

"It *is* right," he told her.

She shook her head. "It shouldn't be right, Michael. We only just met yesterday. We're practically strangers."

He pulled his hand away. She would resent him if he made her come again when she was so unsettled, so unsure. "We're not strangers," he argued. "You know everything about me." Everything except the truth, he added silently. But she *did* know the most important things—who he was, where he was from, how far he had traveled from the land of his father and how tied he still was to that land. She knew about his brother; she knew about his ambivalence toward religion; she knew where he was living in town and whom he was living with.

The only thing she didn't know was that he'd come to San Pablo to help Max Gallard bring in a bail-jumping gunrunner—and right now, that simply didn't seem relevant.

"If we were strangers," he pointed out, "we wouldn't be feeling this way about each other."

"What way?"

"This way." He rolled on top of her, wanting to feel the hollows and swells of her body against his. His mouth covered hers, coaxed hers open, and his tongue curled against hers. He felt himself grow steel hard, pressing into the surface of her belly.

She ran her hands down his back to his hips and

dug her fingers into the taut muscles there, causing him to grow even harder. He wanted to bury himself inside her, to make her come one more time, around him. He was going to have to find condoms. If he had to fly down to Panama to get them, he'd do it.

She rocked her hips against him and he caught his breath. He understood what she meant when she'd said she was afraid feeling so good would kill her. She kneaded his buttocks, then drew her hands around and between them until she could wrap her fingers around him. She squeezed and stroked the length of him, and dying from the excruciating pleasure of her touch began to seem like a real possibility.

She stroked him again, again. He propped himself up on his arms, intending to roll off her, but she took advantage of the space between them to tighten her hold on him. He closed his eyes, wondering if this was her revenge for what he'd done to her, and if it was, thinking that revenge could be awfully sweet…and then he stopped thinking altogether and gave himself over to the sensations building inside him, the pressure, the heat, the need. He held back as long as he could, then succumbed in a wrenching release that convinced him for at least as long as it lasted that he was madly in love with Emmie.

After his body unclenched, after he sank back onto her, not caring that both of them were damp and sticky and spent, after he remembered how to breathe and his heart settled back into its normal rhythm, he decided that he was still madly in love with her.

"We aren't strangers," he whispered, brushing

her lips with a light kiss. "This feels right because it is right."

She reached up and pushed a lock of hair back from his brow. It was such a thoughtful, caring gesture he had to kiss her again. Then he eased off her, pushed himself to his feet and crossed the room to the pitcher and basin. Two clean towels lay folded beneath the bowl. He soaked one with water and carried it back to the bed.

She watched him as he swabbed her belly clean, her eyes wide and shining. He realized part of the shine was from tears rimming along her lashes. "Are you okay?" he asked, wondering what could have her so upset.

"I'm fine."

"You look sad."

"No. This is just—I never met anyone like you before, Michael. I never expected someone like you to come into my life. It's...a little scary, that's all."

"I shouldn't have rushed you," he apologized. Sure, she felt overwhelmed, making love with him barely twenty-four hours after they'd met. She could have said no, he reminded himself—but still, maybe she felt he'd railroaded her.

"I think..." She sighed, her eyes still glistening but clear and steady as she gazed up at him. "I think I'm in love with you."

He smiled. "That's no reason to be scared."

"Actually—" she allowed herself a smile, too "—I think it's a very good reason to be scared."

He returned to the dresser for the dry towel and brought it back. He dabbed her skin dry, then ran the towel over himself. "I won't hurt you, Emmie." He could feel his smile melt away as the gravity of his words struck him. "You have my word. I won't hurt you."

"Then I won't be scared," she said.

They didn't talk much as they dressed. He wondered if it was true that he wouldn't hurt her, if he could finish his business with Gallard and Cortez and come back to her without hurting her. He wondered what she would think if she knew his real reason for being in San Pablo, whether she would think he was a hero or a fool, or maybe both.

But he'd promised not to hurt her, and he would do whatever he had to to keep that promise.

They emerged from their room to discover that the Jeep had stopped steaming. The engine was cool to the touch, and the radiator barely hissed when he unscrewed the cap. He prevailed on the innkeeper for a jug of water, then filled the radiator, helped Emmie into her seat and gave the jug back to the old woman. He returned to the Jeep and climbed in behind the wheel. "Cross your fingers," he muttered before twisting the key.

The engine purred. The gear stick moved fluidly from gear to gear. Michael shot her a cocky grin as he cruised down the road.

"Can you remember how to get to the inn?" he asked as they approached the street where the Cesares lived.

"I think so."

"We can meet there whenever you want."

Her cheeks flushed an adorable pink and she laughed quietly. "I have to teach tomorrow."

"I've got things to do tomorrow, too." He slowed to a stop in front of the Cesares' house. "How about after you're done teaching?"

"Before supper, you mean? Or after?"

"Before, during and after. Whenever you say. Just tell me, and I'll be there."

A shaky sigh escaped her. "God, don't tempt me."

"Before, during and after, then," he said with a chuckle.

"No." She eyed him evenly. "After teaching. I can get there by four. But I really should be back at the Cesare house for supper."

"Whatever you say. I'll be at the inn by four, waiting." It didn't matter what Gallard had on the agenda for tomorrow. If Emmie could meet him at four, he would stop whatever he was doing and be there for her.

If that meant he loved her, he didn't find the thought scary at all. In fact, he found it exhilarating.

"I DON'T GIVE A DAMN what you've got in mind," Gallard growled, stabbing his eggs and sausage with the tines of his fork. They were seated at one of the outdoor tables at the cantina, working their way through breakfast. Michael's coffee tasted strong enough to strip the enamel off his teeth—which was fine with him. "You're wasting time diddling around with that chick," Gallard lectured. "We're here on a mission, Mike, and don't you forget it."

"She's not a chick," Michael retorted, then grinned, realizing that defending Emmie to Gallard would be a waste of breath. In truth, he didn't care what Gallard thought about Emmie. As far as he was concerned, there was no need for Gallard's and Emmie's paths to intersect. "We can't go out hunting for Cortez until the clutch in the Jeep is fixed."

"There are still things we could be doing."

"Yeah, well, I've done plenty of them already," Michael said, pausing to swallow a forkful of fried plantain. "I found out Cortez is living in the hills west of town. He's been going down to Aranal for supplies. If he were east or north of town, he'd be going to Puerto Bianca, so I figure he's gone into hiding west of town. He can't show his face around here. He assaulted a girl."

Gallard stopped chewing. His jaw slack, he gaped at Michael in amazement. "Where did you learn all this?"

"I've been working," Michael said mildly, shoveling another chunk of plantain onto his fork. "What have you been up to?"

Gallard continued to stare at him. "He assaulted a girl?"

"As best I can tell. No one actually came out and said it—they were all too busy cursing his evil soul. But that was the gist of it."

Gallard added his own curse on Cortez, then resumed eating. "This is not good, Michael."

"Why not?"

"If the guy committed an assault, we might not be able to get him out of the country. The local constabulary might not allow him out if they've got charges pending against him."

"If they wanted to arrest him, they would have done it by now."

"They may not want to go head-to-head with him. It could be he's paid them off. As long as he's floating around in the hills somewhere, out of sight, they don't have to deal with him. If we try to move him across the border, they might feel obligated to do their jobs—or to protect him, if he paid them enough. This could get messy, Mike.''

Michael acknowledged Gallard's point with a nod. "What do you think we should do?''

"Maybe we could have a chat with a local officer of the law, find out Cortez's status and see what they're willing to let us do. The cops are bribable in San Pablo, aren't they?''

Michael laughed. "They're in uniform. Of course they're bribable.''

"Then we'll bring money with us.''

They finished their breakfast in silence. Michael tried not to let thoughts of Emmie creep in to fill his mind. She blurred his concentration, sucked the energy out of his brain and sent it to another, equally vital, organ. She made him want to concentrate only on his watch, marking the minutes until four o'clock arrived and he could be with her again.

Gallard was going to need him to navigate a discussion with the local police, and he couldn't afford to be distracted by X-rated notions of a sensitive blond schoolteacher with trusting blue eyes. Shrugging resolutely, he gulped down the rest of his coffee, winced at its potency and followed Gallard from the cantina.

The *cuartel de policía* overlooked the main plaza where he'd danced with Emmie Saturday night. He ordered himself not to think about her as he and Gallard strolled across the square to the station house, which looked only a little less like a fortress than the *banco* next door. The front room resembled Michael's idea of an American police station from fifty years ago—jangling telephones, piles of paperwork stacked on clunky wooden desks and tabletops, an abundance of people and a pathetic lack of computers.

Gallard nudged him forward. A doe-eyed young clerk peered up at him, her smile coquettish. In brisk Spanish, he told her he and his friend needed to speak to *el capitán*. She was still wearing a flirty half smile as she turned from her desk and sauntered through the bustling room. Her skirt clung snugly to her rear end, which shimmied with each step.

Michael remained unmoved. He glanced at Gallard, who scowled but tracked her with his gaze. "I asked to speak to the precinct captain," Michael told him in a near whisper. "I don't want to speak to some low-level guy. The street cops are likely to take a bribe and then do nothing."

"If we've got to skip-step around immigration, the captain might have more juice," Gallard agreed in an equally muted voice.

The voluptuous clerk returned with a stocky, balding man in tow. He had on the tan uniform of the local police; a large brass badge glimmered above his breast pocket, and a thick, mean-looking revolver was strapped into a holster that circled his shoulder. He appeared a bit past his prime but still powerful.

Michael shook the captain's hand, introduced himself and Gallard and asked if they could go somewhere private to talk. "*¿Ustedes americanos?*" the captain asked.

"*Sí.*"

The captain beckoned them to follow him through the teeming room and down a hall to an office. Once they were inside, he closed the door, shutting out the front room's cacophony. He gestured to two chairs, then took his seat on the leather armchair behind the desk and nodded.

"Tell him we're looking for Edouardo Cortez," Gallard coached Michael. "See if that pushes a button."

Michael asked the question. The captain sat straighter in his chair. "Why are you looking for him? Are you friends of his?"

Michael translated for Gallard. "Tell him the truth," Gallard urged.

"He jumped bail in California," Michael told the captain. "We heard he was in San Pablo. We've come here to bring him back to California."

The captain eyed them speculatively. He leaned back in his chair and tapped his fingers together, clearly trying to decide whether he believed Michael.

"He was arrested for dealing in illegal arms," Michael continued. "A bail bondsman is out a million dollars because he fled the country. We want him back in America so he can stand trial."

"You don't want to kill him?" the captain asked.

Michael shook his head. "We just want to take him back to stand trial."

"That's a pity," the captain muttered. "Around here, we'd rather see him dead."

Michael quickly translated for Gallard, who laughed. Michael didn't think there was anything funny about wanting Cortez dead. "Why do you say that?" Michael asked the captain.

"He's a monster," the captain said. "He's done damage here. We tried to arrest him, but he got away. My men are not as brave as you two. They're afraid of him. They know he has guns and he'll use them."

That should have made Michael afraid, too. He hadn't come to San Pablo to get into a gunfight with a monster. But he wanted Cortez brought to justice, and that desire, that need to avenge his brother's death, was stronger than fear. "We need to know," he told the captain, "that if we go after him, you and your people won't stop us from taking him out of the country."

The captain laughed. "We'll throw you a parade if you take him out of the country! You'll be heroes." He leaned forward, once again sizing up Michael and Gallard, this time with respect gleaming in his eyes. "Do you need assistance? Perhaps I could find one or two officers brave enough to back you up if you go after him."

Michael relayed that information to Gallard. "Tell him we accept his backup. We'll let him know when we're going to make our move, and we'll take whatever manpower he can spare."

The thought that a couple of courageous cops would escort them when they went after Cortez eliminated the last of Michael's fear. He was also encouraged that they wouldn't have to bribe the officers. This was going to go well. He and Gallard would get the son of a bitch and take him back to California.

And then Michael could go back to thinking only of Emmie Kenyon.

EMMIE'S LIFE HAD CHANGED the day she told her parents she was going to San Pablo. It had changed again when Martin told her he didn't think they ought to get married after all.

Those had been monumental changes—changes that marked her growing up, becoming her own person, determining her own destiny. Those changes had pulled the props out from under her—but she'd discovered that without those old, familiar props she could still stand quite nicely on her own. The changes had been traumatic, but she'd emerged a better person.

Now Michael had changed her life yet again. In a mere flicker of time, it seemed, she had suddenly figured out what love meant, what it felt like, how it energized her and elevated her and illuminated the entire world with its shimmering glow. Emmie was in love, and she would never be the woman she'd been just days ago.

They met every day at four, at the inn. Michael was always there, and he always had something with him—a bottle of wine, a bag of plums, a rose wrapped in paper so she wouldn't prick herself on the thorns. And condoms. They were difficult to come by, he'd told her, his eyes glinting wickedly, so he felt they ought to value each one, and make each time as splendid as possible. It would be a crime of nature if they wasted a single condom.

He could be so funny, joking about birth control—and a moment later he could be serious, talking to her about California, describing the ragged shoreline and the vast silver storms of the Pacific Ocean, the placid valley where he'd grown up, the deserts and forests and the exotic beauty of San Francisco. He couldn't believe she'd never been to

California. "That will have to change," he'd insisted.

They made love. Sweet, surging love. Fierce, fiery love. She learned the textures of his skin, smooth and warm and golden, and the thickness of his hair. She learned that brushing her fingertips over his mouth made him groan, and that kissing his sternum had a particularly arousing effect on him. She learned his scars—the faint line under his chin, from when he'd tumbled off his bicycle as a child, and the pale seam along his thumb, from when he'd gotten his first pocketknife and tried to whittle a tree limb into a toothpick, but he'd whittled a bit of his thumb, instead. She learned the scars on his soul, too: his brother's death, his parents' turbulent marriage, his father's unspoken bitterness over losing one son to the streets and the other to the uppermost levels of academia.

She still enjoyed teaching. Her students were still immensely important to her. But now she had something else to live for.

Michael.

"I want to spend the night with you," he said Friday afternoon. "I want to hear if you snore."

"I don't snore," she told him, giving him a playful poke in the arm.

"Prove it. Spend the night with me."

"Tonight?"

He nodded.

She wanted to spend the night with him, too. She wanted to feel his arms around her all night, and his legs woven through hers. She wanted to feel his breath on her nape, slow and even, like a lullaby. She wanted to see what he looked like with a layer of moonlight spread across his skin. She wanted their dreams to merge.

But what would the Cesares think? Would they be shocked? Would they kick her out of their home?

For Michael she would face their disapproval. "I have to tell the Cesares," she said, because she knew Señora Cesare would worry herself sick if Emmie simply stayed out all night. "And I have to get a change of clothes."

"No problem."

Not for him, perhaps. For her—no, it wouldn't be a problem, either. She had learned to stand on her own two feet. She was twenty-five years old, an adult living her own life, and while she had great respect for the Cesares, she would not deny the yearnings of her heart for them.

He walked her to the Cesares' house, then left her there to return to the room he shared with his research associate in the alley behind the pharmacy, having promised that he would meet her back at the inn within an hour. She ventured into the house cautiously, hoping Señora Cesare wouldn't chastise her. She could stand up to the steely matriarch, but she would prefer to avoid a fight.

"We're taking an excursion," she told the *señora* in explanation for her planned absence that night. "Michael and I thought we would take a little trip, so I won't be home until tomorrow." *A little trip,* she thought wryly, wishing she didn't have to dress up the truth. Well, that *was* the truth. They were taking a little trip into the darkest, most passionate part of the night.

"You love Miguel, eh?" Señora Cesare said with

a nod. "He seems like a good man, but there's always a risk when a woman loves a man."

"A life without risk isn't worth living," Emmie pointed out.

Señora Cesare gazed up at her, her lips pursed and her brow furrowed. "You know how much risk you can take, Emmilita. You know how much pain you can bear. Go, but be careful."

"I will," Emmie swore, then impulsively bent down and kissed Señora Cesare's cheek.

She spent the night with Michael. She made love with him, and laughed with him, and rested her head on his chest and listened to his heart pulse against her cheek. "I have an early appointment with Max tomorrow," he told her, "but I have the whole night with you. That's all that matters."

It was all that mattered, the whole night. In the thin pink light of dawn, he made love to her one last time. They'd used up his condoms, but she didn't care. She had Michael. She loved him. He loved her.

And then he was gone.

CHAPTER EIGHT

CRICKETS TRILLED in the waning evening as Emmie rose from her chair, five years after Michael had disappeared. She had listened to him, taken in all his words, filled herself up with them—but her brain was having difficulty processing what he'd told her. Maybe if she walked around, maybe if she burned off some of her agitation…maybe if she put some distance between herself and the man she had once loved so deeply, who now sat on the bench of the picnic table on her patio in safe, sleepy Wilborough, Massachusetts, his shoulders stiff and still, his dark gaze on her, his fingertips drumming against each other…

Maybe if she walked to the edge of her yard and then kept on going until she reached the very end of the earth, she might be able to regain her perspective.

"You killed a man." She wasn't sure if she was asking a question or stating a fact. He'd just told her it was a fact.

"That wasn't our plan," he explained. His voice was so quiet she wouldn't have heard it if she hadn't been hardwired into everything he said, his every gesture and nuance. "Our plan was to drive up to his mountain hideaway, get him and escort him back to California. We were supposed to lure him to the

Jeep and then take off. If we got into any trouble, there were supposed to be two local cops backing us up. But the backup never came.''

"And you got into trouble." She almost laughed at that absurd understatement. Getting into trouble was what happened to Jeffrey when he didn't come home from Adam's house on time. Getting into trouble was what happened to her students when they forgot to do their homework or neglected to bring an absentee note from their parents. Getting into trouble had nothing to do with telling lies and getting shot at and killing people. "Gallard knew what he was doing. He'd done it many times before. It was his profession. He'd gone after guys just as dangerous as Edouardo Cortez and brought them back. So I figured this would be okay, too. It was just…bad luck, I guess.'' Michael held his hands palm up and shrugged. "Things went wrong. Stuff happens.''

Emmie stopped at the edge of the patio and turned to face him. "No," she snapped. "Stuff happens, but this wasn't just stuff. Your buddy—your *research associate*," she emphasized, hating the sarcasm she heard in her voice, "got shot. You got shot. And then you shot that man. You killed him, Michael. You killed him.''

Michael's hands fell to his knees, but his gaze remained on Emmie. The sky had faded to night blue, but she could see him clearly in the light from the amber bulb above the back door. She could see each angle in his face, each line. More lines than she'd remembered from five years ago. Harsher angles.

"I didn't want to kill him. If I'd had a chance to

stop and think…'' He shook his head. ''I probably would have done exactly what I did.'' His hands clenched and relaxed in his lap, as if all his tension was stored in his fingers. ''I'm not a murderer, Emmie. I was never into violence. My brother was the one who hung out with a street gang, not me. I was the intellectual.'' He laughed derisively. ''None of us knows what we might do under the right conditions. Even after I killed him, I couldn't believe I was capable of such a thing.''

''Obviously you were capable,'' she said, steeling herself against the sympathy she felt for him. She, too, believed she was incapable of violence. Yet if someone threatened Jeffrey, she knew she'd do anything—even fire a gun—to protect her son.

''When I realized what I'd done—afterward, a long time afterward—'' he shook his head again ''—it frightened me. It made me crazy. I really wasn't fit for society for a long time. I just sort of withdrew.''

She didn't want to hear this. She didn't want to lose her anger. If she stopped resenting Michael for having vanished without a word, she might allow him back into her life—and then he might leave her again. He might hurt both her and Jeffrey. She had to maintain her resistance to him.

''Things started out okay that morning,'' he said, returning to his story. ''We'd gotten Cortez as far as the Jeep. We had him convinced we wanted to talk to him about buying guns, and we told him we wanted to sit in the Jeep to negotiate because we didn't want his associates overhearing.'' His fingers furled and unfurled, fisted and flexed. ''Gallard had left the keys in the ignition so the instant we got

Cortez into the Jeep we could take off. But he saw
the keys and grabbed them. And then he and Gallard
started tussling. I tried to help, but one of his goons
started shooting at us.''

She tried to come up with a way to stop him, to
spare them both. He'd told her enough. She didn't
need to hear the details. They weren't going to make
her feel more kindly toward him.

But he seemed determined to get it all out. ''Gallard let go of Cortez. Cortez headed straight for his
cabin up there in the hills—we figured he was going
to get a gun. He had the key to the Jeep, so we
couldn't escape that way. Gallard said we'd better
hide in the woods until the cops showed up. They
didn't show up until it was all over.''

''After you'd shot this man dead,'' Emmie said,
mostly to remind herself of what Michael had done
and why she mustn't soften toward him.

He pushed himself to his feet and risked a step
toward her. She instinctively fell back, and he halted
where he was. ''There's a part of me that says Cortez deserved it,'' he admitted. ''I'm not proud of that
sentiment, but it's true. Gallard was shot—either by
Cortez or by one of his buddies. More important,
Cortez was responsible for Johnny's death. For that
alone, maybe he deserved what happened to him.''

''That man didn't kill your brother,'' Emmie
pointed out, her tone gentler than she would have
liked.

''My brother died because people like Cortez supply street gangs with guns.'' The words came out
hard and cold. ''You can tell me it's wrong, or heartless or immoral or whatever you want to call it, but
a part of me doesn't care that Cortez is dead.''

She closed her eyes. She should have been glad to hear this, to glimpse Michael's ugly side. It should have kept her from responding with anything but revulsion to what he was telling her. Yet...she wasn't proud of it, either, but she could understand his lust for revenge.

If only he hadn't acted on that lust. Other people might get into brutal, bloody situations, and maybe they might rationalize their deeds—and maybe she wouldn't mind, at least not on a personal level. But Michael wasn't other people. He was a man she had given herself to, body and soul. He was the father of her son.

"That's the nasty part of me, Emmie, the part that killed Edouardo Cortez. That's the part of me I couldn't bear to have you see. And that's why I stayed away from you."

She swallowed. Emotions seemed to clog her throat, a confused knot of them. Rage and grief and regret were in there. Horror and disgust and bewilderment. "I'm not sure leaving me in the dark like that was the best way to handle things."

"There was no good way to handle things," he argued quietly. "It was a disaster. Gallard was seriously wounded, and I'd gotten shot in the shoulder somewhere along the way, and there was this dead man. It's not the sort of circumstance a young college professor usually finds himself in. So I let the local police spirit us out of the country. They got us back to California. They were glad to be rid of Cortez, and incredibly grateful to us for doing what they'd been too afraid to do."

He studied her, apparently trying to gauge her reaction. His scrutiny made her uncomfortable, so she turned and stared at the crab-apple tree, the one with Jeffrey's imaginary monster in it. She wanted her son to live in a world where the only monsters were make-believe, not a world where his own father became embroiled in acts of terrifying violence.

"There's another, less nasty part of me," Michael continued, addressing her back when she refused to face him. "The part that was devastated by what happened. The part that couldn't forgive myself."

"Maybe I can relate to that part a little better than the part that's so pleased you killed this man," she muttered.

"Maybe you can. Maybe I can, too." He sighed, and it sounded almost like a groan. "Look at me, Emmie. Please. Don't make me talk to your back."

Reluctantly she turned to him. He hadn't moved from where he'd been standing, but he seemed closer. The way he watched her was curiously intimate, as if he were seeing her not as she was now but as she'd been five years ago, completely open to him, trusting and loving and believing in him.

"Tell me what you're thinking," he demanded.

"I'm thinking…" She let out a long breath, buying time to figure out for herself what she was thinking. "It's a strange story you've just told me. Either you're lying now, or you lied to me in San Pablo."

"I didn't lie, then or now," he insisted. "I *was* doing research down there—research on Cortez."

"Oh, sure. You were doing *research*." Arguing with him would only prolong this discussion, and no good could come of that. Either she would feel sorry for him and what he'd endured, or she'd grow more angry and bitter at the way he'd deceived her five years ago. The wisest thing would be to get him away from her, out of her backyard and out of her life.

Yet she couldn't seem to stop herself. "What am I, Michael? An idiot? You were in San Pablo with your thuggish *compadre* for one reason only—to find a criminal and haul him back to California so you could get paid a reward."

"Gallard was doing it for the money. The only reward I wanted was to see the man brought to justice."

"How noble." Lord, she hated the bitterness welling up inside her. She had never been a bitter person before, not even when she'd discovered herself pregnant and alone. Yet now…it was as if Michael's presence had lanced a boil inside her, and it was draining, spreading its toxic fluid throughout her. With every word he spoke, every new syllable of his outrageous story, the wound oozed more. She felt feverish, dizzy from the loss. "You lied to me, Michael. I fell in love with a liar. If you thought coming to see me all these years later would bring forgiveness, you were wrong. Instead of only knowing you were a liar, now I've got you standing in front of me, proclaiming yourself a liar—and trying to paint yourself as some kind of hero!"

"The man was responsible for my brother's death," Michael said. His voice had grown dangerously low, so low it was more emotion than sound. "Even knowing that, I regret that I killed him. I'm not a killer, Emmie." He lowered himself back onto the bench, as if having to rehash what had happened in San Pablo weakened him. "I didn't mean to kill him. But Gallard was bleeding, near death—and I guess I was in shock. I knew that if I didn't kill

Cortez he would kill Gallard and me both. I'm not pleased by what happened. And I sure as hell am not a hero.''

Emmie sighed. The monster tree had no answers in it for her. The night, the crickets, the first pinpricks of starlight perforating the sky—no answers anywhere.

"You should have told me," she said. The bitterness had left her voice, replaced by sorrow. It occurred to her that she, too, had been in shock, and now the shock was wearing off and the hurt was sinking in.

"I wanted to tell you why I'd come to San Pablo. But Gallard and I had agreed not to talk about it with anyone. We felt it would be safer that way."

"I wasn't just anyone," Emmie noted, moving back to her chair a safe distance from the bench. "I was in love with you."

"And I was going to tell you everything when it was all done. I was going to send Cortez and Gallard back to California and stay on, and tell you everything once it was over."

"So it took five years for this situation to be over?"

"I'm not sure it will ever be over." He tapped his fingers together, then gazed at them as if seeing them for the first time. Emmie was glad he wasn't looking at her. She didn't know what he saw when he stared at her, but she feared he saw more than she wanted him to know. "It took a long time for my shoulder to heal. The bullet had done more damage than I realized. But more than that, I was having nightmares. All the time. I thought—I was in so many pieces I didn't want to inflict myself on you.

I didn't want you to get stuck trying to put me back together.'' He pressed his fingertips together, shaping his hands into a rounded cage. ''By the time the nightmares stopped, I figured you were miles into a new life. You'd probably chalked me up as a selfish bastard and gotten on with your life.''

''You were right,'' she said.

To her surprise, he sent her a quick smile. ''But then some more time passed, and I realized that whether or not you'd gotten on with your life, I couldn't stand the possibility that you thought I was a bastard. So I tried to find you. I wrote to the Cesares in San Pablo, but they said you'd left years ago and hadn't kept in touch. I contacted the school down there, and they said the same thing. I tried to find you in Richmond, but there were lots of Kenyons and I didn't know where to start. So I hired a detective.''

''A detective?'' Had Michael paid someone to shadow her and snoop into her personal business? Just thinking about it gave her the creeps.

''There's a detective agency called Finders, Keepers. It specializes in reuniting separated lovers.''

She suppressed the impulse to retort that they weren't lovers. They had been lovers once, and they'd been separated, so maybe going to this detective agency hadn't been such a far-fetched notion.

''I thought, if only I could find you, I'd be able to explain what had happened, and why. And then, maybe…maybe *I* could get on with my life the way you'd gotten on with yours.''

''All right.'' She searched for residual stores of bitterness. She knew they were inside her, but she couldn't seem to tap into them right now. ''You've explained. Maybe I even forgive you. There's nothing more to say.''

''There is.'' His smile vanished. ''There's Jeffrey.''

Her heart seized for a moment, then recovered, pounding hard. Before coming outdoors and listening to Michael explain why she shouldn't consider him a bastard, she'd spent an hour with Jeffrey, watching him brush his teeth, helping him get into his pj's, reading a chapter of *Winnie-the-Pooh* and using funny voices for all the characters, feeling his solid weight against her bosom as he snuggled up to her, smelling his warm little-boy smell as she hugged him. Even knowing that Michael was waiting for her outside hadn't spoiled her time with Jeffrey. She hadn't let it.

She would never let anything spoil her time with him. Not housing woes, not parental disapproval, and not Michael Molina and his tale of guns and killing and lies.

''Jeffrey has nothing to do with you,'' she said with as much conviction as she could muster.

Michael opened his mouth and then shut it. What had he been going to say? she wondered. That he accepted her declaration? Or had he been going to call her a bigger liar than he was?

She would never know, because he was rising to his feet again. ''I've taken enough of your time,'' he admitted. ''I'm not sure I've said everything I need to say, but this is a start.''

No, she wanted to protest. *This is the end! Go away and don't come back!*

Yet when she saw the remorse in his eyes, the sadness and desolation as he gazed at her across the patio, she was forced to admit that perhaps he had experienced as much pain over the years as she had.

At least she'd surmounted her pain. She'd been blessed with a child she loved, and they'd made a good life together. What did Michael have?

Loneliness. Gruesome memories. Nightmares. The dreadful knowledge that he might never receive the forgiveness he so desperately wanted.

And he didn't have his son.

"I'll say good-night, then," he murmured, and for a strange, silent moment he looked as if he wanted to cross the patio to her, take her in his arms and cling to her. Or maybe it was her own yearning she saw, her own wish that she could give him as much forgiveness as he needed.

But before she could speak, he turned and stalked out of the circle of light, into the shadows, around her house and away.

He needed a kitchen.

Hell, he needed a lot more than that. But as he sat nursing his refill of coffee at the diner across the street from the Holiday Inn, he was forced to confront the undeniable fact that he didn't like diner breakfasts. He wanted a kitchen, where he could brew up a pot of strong coffee and refill his own cup instead of having to search a crowded dining room for an overworked waitress. He wanted a toaster, and fresh fruit from the supermarket, bought at a reasonable price. It galled him that for the price of a wedge of melon at the diner, he could buy an entire melon at the grocery store.

The issue wasn't money, though. It was that as long as he stayed in the hotel, he was a transient.

And as long as he was a transient, he had no chance of repairing things with Emmie, no chance of becoming a father to Jeffrey—assuming the boy proved to be his son.

It was only 6 a.m. in California, so he couldn't call Maggie Tyrell or her brother Jack at Tyrell Investigative Services for at least a couple of hours. He had no good reason not to linger at the diner while he waited for the West Coast to wake up.

On the table, the local newspaper lay open to the page with the listings of apartments for rent. He'd skimmed the ads once and would go over them more diligently with a pen after he'd decided that finding an apartment was the right thing to do.

Life had been easier when he'd been sure of right and wrong. Five years ago, he'd been sure that bringing Cortez back to face justice in California was right, and that whatever he and Gallard had to do to make that happen was right. He'd been convinced that hiding his mission from Emmie had been right, too. Yet last night, when she'd called him a liar…it didn't seem right in retrospect.

Could he have told her the truth back then? He'd promised Gallard he wouldn't discuss their plans with anyone except the local police department, but suppose he hadn't made that promise. Suppose he'd told Emmie what he'd come to San Pablo to do.

She would have rejected him, he was sure. She'd been a proper, well-bred Southern lady, not a woman who would want to pal around with a bounty hunter's assistant. She would never have agreed to have supper with him, never have danced in his arms on the plaza, never have taken him to church and her host family's *casa,* never have stood with him in his grandparents' dilapidated house. Never have made love with him.

It was worth being a liar to have had a chance with her. He wasn't even sure he'd lied, technically. But if he had, he didn't regret it. His lie had freed Emmie to love him.

And to hate him, if last night was any indication.

So much time had passed between her loving him and last night. He'd entered into his current mission—tracking her down—despite Maggie Tyrell's warnings about how he might not find what he was looking for when Finders, Keepers located Emmie. And he'd been okay with that prospect, fully prepared to accept that Emmie might not welcome him back into her life. He'd assured himself that all he wanted was to try to connect with her, not to force a reconciliation. He'd hoped she would be willing to hear him out so he could tell her what had happened, but he hadn't dared to wish for more.

That was before he'd seen the boy, though.

Now he had other ideas, other plans. Now he was scanning the listing of apartments for rent, thinking he ought to settle into Wilborough, Massachusetts, for a while.

He could work in Wilborough as easily as he'd been working in the Bay Area. He'd left academia to do consulting and discovered that private companies hoping for business in Latin America were eager to pay huge sums to people like him, who could interpret not just the language but the culture for them. Occasionally he oversaw research initiatives for the government, as well, helping to shape position papers and offering guidance to various departments—Agriculture and Commerce and sometimes one of the intelligence agencies. But the big money was in the private sector, and Michael earned a generous share of it.

He'd collected his voice mail before leaving his room for the diner. Nowadays all a person needed to do the kind of consulting he did was a computer with Internet access, a fax machine, a phone, occasional airplane tickets and an abundance of insider knowledge.

He had his laptop back at the hotel, with a built-in modem that enabled him to fax files and link up with the net. His room had a phone, and he was sure Wilborough had a travel agent or two. He carried his insider knowledge with him wherever he went.

But he sure would like a kitchen, so he could make his own breakfast.

He drained his cup of coffee and decided not to wait for another refill. After slapping some money down on the table, he folded the newspaper and headed back across the street to his room. The morning was damp with fog. Everything looked like a shadow of itself, as if he were observing his surroundings through smudged eyeglasses.

He'd never talked about fog with Emmie. Or rain. It rained so rarely in San Pablo in the spring he and she had never gotten caught in a downpour together. They'd never huddled beneath an umbrella, raindrops plastering their hair to their cheeks. Not once in their whirlwind romance had they ever discussed the weather.

How on earth could he have thought they'd be able to rebuild a relationship out of the splintered fragments he'd left behind when he fled from San Pablo? Just because she'd been so easy to talk to about the hard things, like Johnny's death and his father's pride, didn't mean she would be easy to talk to about the simple things, like whether it was going to rain that afternoon.

He reminded himself that he hadn't tracked Emmie down to Wilborough to rekindle their love. He'd come to ask her forgiveness—and so far, he hadn't even accomplished that. How could he even be considering finding a local apartment?

The boy.

He spread the newspaper out across his bed, next to it a map, and circled the rentals that sounded interesting in Wilborough and the adjacent towns. By the time he was done, it was nearly seven-thirty San Francisco time. Too early to call the Tyrells, but he was getting restless.

He dialed Maggie's number. After two rings, the phone was answered by her machine: "You have reached Finders, Keepers Detective Agency. Our office hours are 9 a.m. to 5 p.m. If you would like to leave a message, please wait for the tone."

Michael listened to a hiss, then a beep. "This is Michael Molina, calling from Massachusetts. Maggie, could you please tell your brother Jack that the boy's name is Jeffrey? Jeffrey Kenyon, I guess—but I'm not sure. Maybe Jeffrey Molina. Not likely, but maybe. Tell him to try Jeffrey Kenyon. Tell him if the boy is mine, he would have to be turning five years old some time in February. Tell Jack I'll call him later today, or he can call me here." He recited the Holiday Inn's phone number, then hung up and swore under his breath. The chance that the boy's name was Jeffrey Molina were zero to none.

The phone sat inert on the night table. He had to get out of the room.

After folding the paper open to the apartment listings, he pocketed the room key and left.

It was stupid to choose an apartment based on its proximity to Emmie's house, but hers was the only residential neighborhood he'd spent any time in, so he figured it was as good a place as any to begin his search. He drove through the dank morning, passing gas stations, fast-food joints and supermarket minimalls until he reached the intersection that would take him off the commercial strip into her community. He had memorized the route, and it took only a few minutes for him to reach Cullen Drive.

The fog snagged on tree branches like a gauzy cloth. The road shone beneath a layer of moisture. The houses looked brightly colored, their painted shingles and shutters vivid in contrast to the gray air around them. As he neared Emmie's block, he saw a blurred rectangle beside her driveway.

He slowed as he approached it, frowning as he tried to make out the object. A sign of some sort, he realized. Coasting closer, he began to decipher the words on the sign: a national realty chain, and in big block letters FOR SALE.

He slammed on the brake, but given how slowly he'd been driving, his car didn't screech to a halt. Tiny drops of water beaded on his windshield, and he flipped on the wipers, as if they could clear away the sight on the other side of the glass. But the sign remained at the foot of her driveway. FOR SALE.

Why hadn't she told him she was moving? Had she been so upset last night that she'd let this one trivial aspect of her life slip her mind? Or did she believe Michael had no right to know what was going on?

Had she planned to escape from town while he wasn't looking, and leave no forwarding address? Was it possible that she and the boy were already gone?

He turned off the engine and raced up the driveway, trying to ignore the unnatural thudding of his heart. He'd spent so much time searching for the courage to come after her—and more time searching for her. Could she have vanished during the flip of a calendar page?

If she had, would he have to start all over again in his search for her? Or would he do the smart thing and go home?

Shielding his eyes, he peered through one of the windows. Her living room was still furnished—not just furnished, but filled with signs of life—a news magazine on the coffee table, a couple of stuffed animals on the sofa, the coat closet open to display a rod full of coats and jackets in both adult and child sizes. Even if she'd left her furniture and magazines behind, she wouldn't have forgotten to take Jeffrey's and her own coats with her when she departed from Wilborough.

So she hadn't moved yet. But pivoting on the front porch, he saw the For Sale sign again, taunting him, reproaching him. *She's leaving,* it seemed to shout. *She's going away, and you aren't a part of her life. You have nothing to do with it.*

But he did. He was here. He'd found her, come clean with her, told her everything he could. Apol-

ogized. Agonized. Prayed that she would understand.

And he'd seen the boy, her son, who looked too
much like Michael.

He *was* a part of her life, damn it.

CHAPTER NINE

"WHAT'S THAT?" Jeffrey asked, aiming his finger at a sign posted near the driveway.

Emmie bit her lip. She could guess what it was, even from a block away. She'd been expecting it. But the reality of seeing it there, announcing to the world that the Kenyons were about to lose their home, made her stomach lurch and her throat go dry.

She swallowed and tried not to grimace at the taste of fear on her tongue. "It's just a sign," she said vaguely. Just a sign of how her carefully woven life was unraveling, strand by strand.

She could mope or she could get angry. She decided to get angry. Her landlord should have phoned and warned her that he'd listed the house with a real-estate agent. He could have discussed with her when the best time to start showing the house would be. Her lease didn't expire until the end of June. He hadn't had to put the house up for sale in mid-May, had he?

She liked her anger's heat, the way it scorched through her. But anger didn't come naturally to her, and she couldn't keep it burning. The gray dampness of the day doused it, leaving her weary and uneasy.

At least Michael's car wasn't parked in front of her house. Maybe he felt he'd accomplished his mission last night. He'd poured out his story, disturbing though it was, and taken his leave. If he'd expected absolution, too bad. Emmie wasn't sure she could forgive him for deceiving her—and she wasn't exactly enthralled by his experiences with guns and killing.

But if he'd killed that man in self-defense, if it was payback for the death of his own brother...

Damn. How could she think about the For Sale sign on her front lawn when she was so torn up about Michael?

Maybe she *did* forgive him, or at least understand why he'd done what he'd done. Maybe sometimes a man had to pull the trigger to protect his friend or avenge his brother. Maybe, when a man swore to keep a secret, he was bound to honor that vow.

And maybe last night, she'd refused him the forgiveness he was seeking not because she couldn't forgive him but because she honestly didn't know how to make room for him in a life she'd spent five long years constructing so there would never, ever be room for him in it.

"It's a sign, isn't it, Mommy? What kind of sign is it?" Jeffrey persisted as she drove slowly down the street to the driveway. He could recognize a few words, but not those that appeared on the sign, thank goodness.

"I'm not sure," Emmie said. "But once we get inside, I'm going to make a phone call and see if I can find out." The name of the real-estate company was printed on the sign. Perhaps Emmie could get information from the agent—although it still irked her that Mr. Arnett hadn't been courteous enough to notify her before advertising to the world that his house was for sale.

She got out of the car to open the garage, then got back in and drove inside. The engine echoed in the enclosed space, a pleasant rumbling sound. She suffered a pang of nostalgia thinking about how much she would miss everything she'd loved about this house—its echoing garage, the faint smells of motor oil and gardening supplies that hung in the air, the hairline cracks in the cement floor.

Jeffrey unfastened his seat belt as soon as she turned off the motor. He grabbed his Sesame Street lunch box from the floor of the car and swung open the door, blissfully unaware of his mother's angst. "What's for dinner?" he asked, waiting impatiently while she collected her tote bag and purse from the backseat and rummaged for her key.

"I don't know," she said with a bleak sigh. After a long, restless night remembering the days she'd spent with Michael in San Pablo, followed by a busy day teaching, an hour spent grading papers once the children were dismissed, a stop at Sunny Skies Pre-school to pick up Jeffrey and a drive home to discover the For Sale sign on her front lawn, she couldn't begin to think about food.

Jeffrey must have sensed her troubled mood, because once they were inside he carried his lunch box quietly to the kitchen and emptied it without being told, then rinsed the thermos in the sink and threw away the crumbs, crusts and crumpled cellophane left over from his lunch. He looked grave, intent on his chore, not his usual bubbling self.

Emmie felt guilty for bringing his spirits down to the level of hers. "How about if we have breakfast for dinner?" she suggested. Bowls of cereal, bagels and orange juice were one of Jeffrey's favorite din-

ners, not just because he loved breakfast food but
because eating morning fare in the evening struck
him as weird and therefore wonderful. Since Emmie
had little appetite anyway, she might as well let Jeffrey eat something that would make him happy.

"Breakfast! Yeah!" He perked up, clomping his
feet and smiling brightly.

"But first I have to make a phone call," Emmie
warned.

"Okay!" For the promise of cereal for dinner,
Jeffrey would gladly stay out of her way for a few
minutes.

He romped off, leaving silence in his wake. Emmie suppressed a shudder. It took so little to make
him happy; once they moved, she might be able to
buy his contentment with a bowl of Rice Krispies.
He might not mind living in an apartment or a
cramped condominium if he didn't have to eat meat
and vegetables at dinnertime.

Jeffrey's happiness came more easily than her
own, though. She was the one responsible for making a proper home—and nutritious meals—for him.
Once she was forced to evacuate this house, she
would feel like a failure.

Trying not to beat up on herself, she pulled the
telephone directory from a shelf, found the listing
for the realty office on the For Sale sign and dialed.

While the phone rang, she surveyed her kitchen.
One of Jeffrey's masterpieces, a crayon rendering of
what appeared to be lollipops but Emmie knew were
flowers, adorned the refrigerator door, held in place
by magnets. She wanted to believe that Jeffrey's artwork was what turned the house into their home,
and that if she hung his artwork on any other refrig-

erator, the decoration would magically turn that new residence into a home. It wasn't walls or floors or the arrangement of the windows—or even the garden, the monster in the crab-apple tree—that made this place a home. It was Jeffrey and her love for him.

A real-estate agent answered the phone and Emmie launched into a controlled tirade. She heard steel and the South in her voice as she began to recite her demands. Her drawl had eroded during her years in New England, but when she was riled it returned in certain words, certain inflections.

"Mommy?" Jeffrey hollered from another room.

Emmie tuned him out. She'd been trying to teach him all year not to interrupt her when she was on the phone, especially by bellowing from a distance. If he had a genuine emergency, he was either to find her or to shout "Emergency!" Otherwise he was to wait until she was off the phone.

Patience was not his long suit. Ignoring him only inspired him to shout louder. "Mommy! Someone's at the door!"

Emmie sighed, then turned toward the counter as if to shield the phone. "Mr. Arnett promised me he'd give us plenty of warning before he listed the house," she told the woman on the other end of the line. "I don't know why he jumped the gun—our lease doesn't expire until the end of June. He's always been very considerate."

"I assume you're speaking of Mr. Arnett Senior," the agent said. "It was his son who asked us to go ahead and list the house. I'm sorry there was a missed communication on your end, but Mr. Arnett's son is the one calling the shots."

"Mommy!" Jeffrey appeared before her, his eyes luminous with a combination of annoyance and excitement. "Didn't you hear me? There's a man at the door and he's got KFC!"

Emmie pursed her lips, contemplating her options. If Mr. Arnett's son was calling the shots, the damned For Sale sign would remain where it was. He was the one who wanted his father in Arizona and the house disposed of. As long as he was in charge, there was nothing she could do to slow the process.

And as if that wasn't enough, some man was standing on her front porch with food from Jeffrey's favorite purveyor of ready-to-eat chicken. "We'll discuss this further," she told the agent. "In the meantime, please make it clear that our house is not to be shown unless I'm present. As long as we're living here, I'm not going to have strangers traipsing through while I'm not home."

"I'll make a note of it," the agent promised.

"Thank you. Goodbye." She hung up the phone and felt her shoulders slump. Jeffrey might believe that no problem was so formidable that it couldn't be fixed with a serving of fried chicken, but Emmie knew better. Chicken or bagels and cereal, she still had no appetite.

However, she needed to see which kind neighbor of theirs had dropped by with food for her family. Probably it was Glenn Drinan from across the street. His wife might have sent him over with chicken and instructions to find out about the sudden appearance of the For Sale sign.

Jeffrey grabbed Emmie's hand and dragged her through the hall to the front door. She peered through the window in the door and saw a man on her front porch, armed with a shopping bag with the chicken vendor's logo printed on it. He wasn't Glenn Drinan, though. He wasn't any of her neighbors.

Michael Molina smiled crookedly and held the bag up to the window, as if to convey that he had indeed brought the chicken for her.

"KFC! KFC!" Jeffrey chanted.

Images flashed through Emmie's brain: Michael sitting on her patio last night, telling her how he'd lied to her in San Pablo, telling her how he'd allowed her to think he was a mild-mannered college professor rather than a bounty hunter. Michael in bed with her at that charming inn where they used to meet and make love. Michael shooting and killing a man. The For Sale sign, and breakfast for dinner because she lacked the strength to prepare a real meal.

She was overloaded. Overstressed. Too tired to fight both Michael and her exuberant son.

She opened the door a crack. "I thought this would be more practical than flowers," Michael said.

Damn him for looking so handsome. The past five years hadn't done any damage to his face or his physique. He was still tall and lean, dark and angular and irresistibly handsome. In a pair of jeans and a white oxford shirt with the sleeves rolled up, he looked neat and composed, the exact opposite of how she felt.

The hell with it. Let him and his chicken invade her house. She didn't feel like fighting with him or Jeffrey.

She swung the door wider. "This isn't a good day," she warned him, stepping back so he could enter.

He studied her in the afternoon light spilling through the doorway. "I have a feeling you haven't had a good day for a while," he murmured. And she cursed him again for being so perceptive. "How about you and Jeffrey joining me for supper?"

The entry filled with the aroma of fried chicken. Jeffrey did a victory dance around the living room, his boisterous activity registering at least five on the Richter scale. "KFC! KFC!" If she told Michael to leave and take his chicken with him, Jeffrey would probably accuse her of child abuse.

Besides, Jeffrey was likely to have some not very good days soon enough, when she broke the news that they were being forced to move. She might as well give him this much. "Jeffrey, stop shouting," she said, catching him on one of his circuits around the room and holding him in place. "This is an old...friend of Mommy's." She struggled over the word, but an old friend sounded safer than an old lover, or an old con artist. "His name is Mr. Molina."

"You can call me 'Michael,'" Michael interjected, shifting the KFC bag into his left hand so he could extend his right to Jeffrey.

Jeffrey gazed up at the tall man and earnestly shook with him. "I like KFC," he said.

"Then I guess it's a good thing I brought some for dinner." Michael smiled briefly at Jeffrey, then lifted his gaze back to Emmie. He appeared to be hoping for as much enthusiasm from her as he'd gotten from Jeffrey.

He would have a long wait, she thought coldly, turning from him and stalking down the hall to the kitchen, assuring herself that she was totally unmoved by his enigmatic smile, his soulful eyes, his beautifully male physique.

It occurred to her, as she entered the kitchen, that letting Michael into her house had been a major step. Just two days ago, she'd seen him and felt sick inside. Yesterday she'd granted him a hearing. She'd been distressed by what he'd said, but she'd listened.

She hadn't forgiven him. She was still determined to keep him from making any claims on Jeffrey. Yet…he was in her house. Bit by bit, he was making inroads.

She didn't like it. But she was too drained to fight right now.

"I can set the table," Jeffrey bragged, bouncing around the kitchen. He was obviously pleased with Emmie's guest. It was so rare that she had a man in the house—a man she would introduce as a friend. She didn't date; she didn't have the time, and she didn't really have the interest, either. On a few occasions she'd invited colleagues from the Oak Hill School over for wine and hors d'oeuvres, but the primary-school faculty included only two men, and they were both married and brought their wives. What little Jeffrey glimpsed of Emmie's parties before he was shooed off to bed would not have given him the impression that Peter and Hank were *friends,* and they certainly didn't pay Jeffrey any attention when they visited.

Michael was definitely paying Jeffrey attention. He kept his distance, but he was looking at the scampering boy intently. His observation of Jeffrey unsettled her even more. Did he know? Had he guessed?

As far as she was concerned, any suspicions Michael might harbor with respect to Jeffrey were irrelevant. He'd lost all claim to his son when he'd disappeared from San Pablo. She didn't care why he'd left. What mattered was that he *had* left, and he had no place in Jeffrey's life.

"If you're going to set the table," she reminded Jeffrey, "you'd better do it. This bucket of chicken is going to get cold."

"Stick it in the oven for a minute," Michael suggested, lifting the bucket out of the bag. "I bought some mashed potatoes and coleslaw, too. Oh, and sliced pickles." He pulled tubs and condiments from the bag and placed them on the table, doing a better job of setting the table than Jeffrey had accomplished with all his dashing around and boasting. Without awaiting instructions from Emmie, Michael put the tub in the oven and turned the dial to the warm setting.

He was taking over, and she didn't like it. "Here, Jeffrey," she said, handing him a stack of plates just so she could feel she was contributing to the dinner. "Put these around the table, please. Michael, what would you like to drink?"

"Have you got any beer?" he asked.

Cerveza, she thought, the Spanish word gliding naturally through her brain. She taught her class a bit of elementary Spanish each year, but *cerveza* wasn't a word they needed to learn at their age.

She had a few bottles chilled in her refrigerator. She poured a glass of Chablis for herself, deciding she needed to have the edges of her thoughts muted more than she needed to keep her guard up around Michael. He'd already insinuated his way into her home, and she'd been completely sober when she'd let him in. What difference would a glass of wine make?

Michael was still watching Jeffrey as he painstakingly folded three paper napkins from the yellow wooden dispenser on the table. Emmie watched Michael. She didn't sense any great rush of sentiment in him. The sight of this little boy who was his own flesh and blood didn't reduce him to a puddle of mush—if he'd figured out the connection between them.

How could he not? Every time she looked at Jeffrey she saw Michael. In his eyes, his coloring, the adorable quirk of his smile, she saw echoes of Michael.

She would probably need more than one glass of wine to get through this meal, she realized.

Michael donned the hot mitts that hung from a hook on the side of the oven and pulled out the bucket. They assembled around the table, Jeffrey with his milk in a Cookie Monster cup, Michael with a beer and a glass and Emmie with her delicate goblet of wine. She arranged the serving utensils in the containers of mashed potatoes and coleslaw, helped Jeffrey into his chair and pushed him close to the table. Then she sat, and Michael took his seat across from her. She reached for Jeffrey's left hand, and Jeffrey stretched his right hand to take Michael's.

"We like to say grace this way," Emmie explained in answer to Michael's questioning look.

He nodded and gathered her left hand in his right. If it was a rarity for her to have a handsome man in

her house, it was even more of a rarity for her to
have a handsome man holding her hand. She told
herself she was responding to the novelty of his
touch, not the familiarity of it. Surely, after so many
years, she had forgotten the strength of Michael's
hands, the shape of his fingers, their warmth and
power. She had forgotten what his hands had felt
like on her body, loving her. She had forgotten everything—and what she was feeling now had nothing to do with remembering.

"We are grateful for the food we eat," she murmured, lowering her eyes and giving Jeffrey's hand
a maternal squeeze. "Thank you, God, for the
bounty on our table tonight."

"Thank you, too, Michael," Jeffrey chimed in.

Emmie smiled faintly at Michael. "Yes, thank
you."

He glanced at her, then turned his gaze to Jeffrey,
studying the boy as he dug a heaping spoonful of
mashed potatoes from the bowl. "I love mash potatoes," Jeffrey announced. "They're like clay. You
can make stuff with them."

"Except, of course, that you know better than to
play with your food," Emmie chided gently.
"Would you like a drumstick, Jeffrey?"

"Yup! I love drumsticks," he told Michael.

Michael's attention shuttled back and forth between Jeffrey and Emmie. He probably didn't know
what to make of Jeffrey's passionate declarations.
Emmie could have explained to him that when a boy
was four and a half, he didn't shade his emotions
well. With equal fervor, he loved his mommy; his
stuffed bears, Teddy and Frumpy; his best friend,
Adam; and drumsticks.

But she didn't want to explain Jeffrey to Michael. She didn't want to give him that much access to her son.

"Mommy doesn't make mash potatoes too much," Jeffrey went on. "She says baked is healthier. She says there's vitamums in the skin and you gotta have vitamums so you can grow big. I bet you ate lots of vitamums when you were my age, huh?"

Michael smiled tightly. "I guess I did."

"And if I eat potato skins and all those other vitamums, I can grow up to be just as big as you. Right, Mommy?"

She didn't want to think of him growing up to resemble Michael in any way. But of course, she couldn't prevent it. He already resembled Michael too much.

"Are you moving?" Michael asked abruptly.

Panic gripped her. She'd been so worried about his making the connection between himself and Jeffrey she'd all but forgotten about the For Sale sign beside the driveway. She certainly didn't want to talk about it now, in front of Jeffrey.

Jeffrey's dark eyes grew round. "Are we moving, Mommy?"

She gritted her teeth and considered kicking Michael under the table. It was too late to signal him to shut up, but she wouldn't mind inflicting a little pain. "I'm not sure," she said, shooting Michael a lethal glare. "I haven't decided."

"If we moved to Florida, we could go to Disney World every day," Jeffrey said. "Can we do that, Mommy?"

"No, sweetie. Mommy works in Wilborough. We're going to stay here."

"Can we go to Disney World?" Jeffrey asked.

Thanks a heap, she wanted to snap at Michael. His tactless question had led to this. "I hope we can go someday," she said carefully, "but it's a big trip, and very expensive."

"Like, but if we moved to Florida it wouldn't be so 'spensive," Jeffrey reasoned. "It would just be a little trip, and then we could just pay a little money."

"I wish it were that simple," Emmie said with a sigh. She would be thrilled to take Jeffrey to Walt Disney World, but first she had to find affordable housing—which meant moving out of this unafford- able house. She glowered at Michael, who looked contrite but also confused, as if he understood that he'd done something wrong but couldn't fathom ex- actly what.

"Todd went to Disney World," Jeffrey prattled on, oblivious to the undercurrent of tension between the two adults at the table. "He goes to my school. Do you know him?" he asked Michael.

"Uh—no, I don't." Michael looked even more confused. Emmie smiled. Let him flounder. Let him realize how completely out of touch with Jeffrey he was.

"He said there's lots of scary rides, but he wasn't allowed to go on them, cuz they're so scary. They're not for little kids," Jeffrey reported solemnly. "Maybe next year I'll be big enough and then we can go."

"Maybe," Emmie said, relieved that Jeffrey seemed to have forgotten the subject of moving. If Michael had an ounce of sense in him, he wouldn't bring it up again in front of the child.

Apparently Michael had an ounce of sense. He ate in bemused silence, observing Jeffrey as he shoveled his food into his mouth and chattered about school: the collision he and Todd had created with their Matchbox cars, the yucky sandwich—some kind of pink meat with green olives stuck in it—that Adam had brought for lunch, the game of dodgeball Jeffrey had won in the yard outside the school. "I think we're making something for Mother's Day, but I'm not supposed to tell you," he reported.

Emmie smiled and ruffled his hair. "It'll be our secret," she swore.

"Some kids do Father's Day, too," Jeffrey said. "Not everybody, though. I don't," he told Michael without a moment's hesitation. He shrugged, used his fingers to pile the last small mound of mashed potatoes onto his fork, and devoured them. "Can I have cookies for dessert?" he asked. "Do we still have choco-chip cookies? Those are my favorite," he told Michael. "What's yours?"

"My favorite cookie?" Michael's voice sounded rusty. Emmie prayed with all her heart that he wasn't thinking about how Jeffrey didn't do anything for Father's Day.

"Yeah. I like choco-chip. You wanna hear something disgusting?" Jeffrey laughed gleefully. "Adam's favorite cookie is fig bars!"

"That's…really disgusting," Michael managed. "I prefer chocolate chip cookies."

"Me, too. Can I have some for dessert?" Jeffrey asked Emmie.

"We'll have dessert in a little while. Why don't you take your plate to the sink, and then you can be excused."

"Okay!" Jeffrey climbed down from his chair, carried his plate and cup to the counter by the sink and fled the room, happy not to have to sit at the table getting bored while the grown-ups lingered over their meal.

Emmie wasn't deliberately lingering. She simply didn't have much appetite. In fact, she hadn't had an appetite since Michael had arrived in Wilborough.

He scanned the room, as if to make sure Jeffrey wasn't lurking in the doorway, eavesdropping. Then he turned back to Emmie and leaned forward. "He doesn't know you're moving?"

"I haven't told him yet," Emmie admitted. She didn't owe Michael any explanations, but she saw no point in refusing to discuss her impending eviction with him. As long as it didn't have to do specifically with Jeffrey, she was probably safe talking about it with Michael.

"Why are you moving? Are you going back home?"

"Home?" A faint, sad laugh escaped her. "This is home."

"What about Richmond, Virginia?"

"There's nothing for me in Richmond," she said laconically. Maybe this wasn't a safe subject, either.

Michael wouldn't let it go. "Why not? Have your parents relocated?"

"My parents and I don't get along."

"Because of Jeffrey?" he guessed.

So much for avoiding the subject. "My relationship with my parents is none of your business," she said in as calm a voice as she could.

She didn't fool him. He must have known he'd

hit a bull's-eye. But fortunately, he also must have figured out that the subject was a painful one for her, because he reverted to the topic of her impending move. "So, you're selling this house and moving...where?"

"I'm not selling the house. It isn't mine to sell. I've been renting it, and now the landlord wants to sell it. Actually—" she recalled her conversation with the real-estate agent earlier that evening "—his son wants to sell it. I have no choice but to move."

"Why don't you buy it?" he asked.

"I can't afford it."

He sat back in his chair, regarding her. "It's not a mansion, Emmie. How much is the guy asking?"

She realized with a pang that she longed to unburden herself to another adult. Her life was full of work and Jeffrey, and although she had friends on the faculty at school, she couldn't confide in them about her precarious finances. "He's asking more than I can afford," she said, relieved to get it off her chest. "I could meet the monthly mortgage payments if I had enough of a down payment saved up. But I don't. So I'm going to have to find another place to live."

He tapped his fingers together the way he had last night. "Here's the irony of it, Emmie," he said. "I've been thinking I'd like to settle in the area, and now you're moving."

"Settle in the area?" Her voice sounded oddly breathless. "You mean, in Wilborough?"

"There isn't much available in Wilborough," he conceded. "A few apartments, but nothing exciting. Some of the neighboring towns have more units for rent. I hadn't really given much thought to buying, but I don't know…maybe I should.''

''Buying?'' She cleared her throat with a sip of wine. ''Why do you want to move to Wilborough?''

His gaze locked onto her, holding her captive. ''You know why, Emmie.''

''Michael.'' Still that strange breathlessness choked her voice. ''I don't want you living near me. You told me your horrible story last night, what happened to you, how awful it was. I appreciate all that, but it's history. *We're* history. I've moved forward with my life, and if you haven't you should.'' *I don't want you making claims on my son,* she thought desperately.

''I've moved forward with my life, too. I consult for companies doing business in Latin America and for the government. I get paid a lot for my knowledge. I can live wherever I want. Including Wilborough.'' His gaze circled the room. ''Including this house, even.''

An icy shudder tore down her back. ''Fine, then,'' she snapped. ''Buy the house. Our lease runs out at the end of June, and then you can have it. Talk about ironic,'' she added under her breath.

He sighed. He looked as solemn as Jeffrey had when he'd stated that scary rides were not for small children. ''I didn't mean I'd buy it right out from under you,'' he said, his voice low and earnest. ''All I'm saying is, we're connected, Emmie. I'm not convinced we're history. We made promises to each other five years ago—''

''And you broke your promises.''

''I told you why.''

''You said you wanted my forgiveness. All right.

Fair enough. If I forgive you, will you go away?''
*I don't want to share Jeffrey with you. Jeffrey is all
I've got, the one person in the world who brings me
joy and makes me feel whole. I don't want to turn
his life upside down—or mine.*

Michael shook his head. ''I changed my mind. I
want more than your forgiveness. We had something
five years ago. Something important.''

''Five years ago it was important. Now it's
dead.''

''I don't think so,'' he said. He reached across the
table and took her hand. Not to say grace this time,
but to force her to acknowledge him physically. If
he couldn't persuade her with his words, perhaps he
was hoping he could persuade her with his touch.

Her body responded to the light pressure of his
fingers around her hand, the warmth and strength of
his clasp. Her heart responded even more strongly,
more dangerously. This wasn't simply being
touched by a man. It was being touched by Michael
Molina, and unwelcome desire flared inside her.

She didn't want to be touched by him in any way.

''Emmie.'' He moved his thumb against hers,
gently, his eyes mesmerizing, so dark she could get
lost in them. ''What we had five years ago is very
much alive today. His name is Jeffrey, and he's my
son.''

CHAPTER TEN

IT HAD BEEN QUITE an interesting afternoon. He'd looked at a few apartments—nothing had bowled him over—and then gone back to the hotel to check his messages. One was from detective Jack Tyrell.

Michael had stared at the flashing light on his phone, pushing the pound button over and over to hear that one message: "Michael? This is Maggie's brother Jack from Finders, Keepers and Tyrell Investigative. Give me a call. I've got something for you."

Five times: *I've got something for you.*

Michael didn't want to know what Jack had. The problem was, more than he didn't want to know, he *did* want to know.

Eventually he'd pushed the star button to delete the message. He'd stepped outside his room into the cool, humid air and wished he were still a smoker. This was exactly the kind of situation where a man needed to scorch his lungs.

Instead he walked through the parking lot to the street and watched the traffic stream past the building. Across the way was the diner where he'd eaten breakfast that morning. He couldn't stand the thought of eating supper there tonight. He'd much rather go to a nice restaurant—although he wouldn't want to go alone.

He wanted to go with Emmie. So they could talk—or he could shake her by the shoulders and demand to know why she hadn't told him...

Assuming there was something to tell.

Of course there was something to tell. Jack Tyrell had said he had *something*.

Gathering his courage, Michael had marched back to his room and punched in the phone number for Finders, Keepers. Maggie Tyrell answered.

"This is Michael Molina. I got a message from your brother Jack. Is he in?"

"Oh—hi, Michael." He'd tried to assess her voice. Startled? Dismayed? Excited? "Sure, let me transfer you to Jack's office."

He'd heard a click, then a second click and Jack's voice. "Hey, Michael—how are you?"

"I don't know," Michael had answered truthfully. "You tell me."

"Your name is on the kid's birth certificate," Jack had said.

Michael had become acutely conscious of the weight and shape of the telephone in his hand. Smooth plastic, cool and hard. He'd noticed the way the late-afternoon sun wrestled through the dampness, spilling a milky light through the window. He'd heard the syncopation of his heartbeat, practically felt the blood moving from chamber to chamber and out into his body.

"You're listed as the child's father," Jack had reiterated, as if unsure whether Michael had heard him the first time.

Michael had heard him perfectly.

"The boy was born at Beth Israel Hospital in Boston on February 14. Valentine's Day."

Michael had felt oxygen passing through the membranes of his lungs and into his bloodstream. He'd felt the blood flow through the arteries to his brain, making his thoughts come in and out of focus with each pulse. He'd felt the blood in his extremities, keeping him alive—blood he shared with a little boy whose existence he hadn't even known about three days ago.

"Are you there?" Jack had asked.

"I'm here."

"Okay. This is a big one, I know. Kind of a shock. I should have had Maggie tell you. She's better at saying things the right way."

"There's no right or wrong way to say this," Michael had argued. "It just is."

"Well." A long silence, then Jack asked, "Is there anything I can do?"

"Not right now." Michael had tasted the saliva on his tongue. He'd felt the ends of his hair brush his nape. He'd been all physical sensation, as if his nerves were spiked, as if he were nothing but a bit of biological tissue, life itself, impulse and motion without reason or cause. "I'll be in touch," he'd muttered, then hung up.

Jeffrey Kenyon is my son. The idea had circulated through his body with the oxygen in his blood. It had mirrored his heartbeat, throbbing inside his skull, filling his mouth with the words that defined this simple, profound truth.

Just before he'd killed a man, he had created a new life. That morning in San Pablo, when he'd left Emmie's bed forever, she'd been carrying his son. And he'd gone out and shot a man to death.

There was a certain balance to it, he'd supposed. A certain gruesome symmetry.

It had taken him an hour to calm down, to feel like himself again. He couldn't face Emmie when he was so close to losing his mind. He had to be stable and focused for what was bound to be an even more difficult conversation than the one they'd had last night.

Food might help. He had no idea why he'd chosen the fried chicken over burgers or a pizza. In retrospect, he wondered if perhaps there was a genetic reason. Somehow, subconsciously, he must have known Jeffrey would love drumsticks and mashed potatoes. There could be a psychic connection between father and son.

Yet he had no idea how to relate to the boy. During dinner, as Jeffrey had prattled about all sorts of things Michael couldn't begin to fathom, he'd wondered whether he should even say anything. What did he and Jeffrey have in common, besides DNA and a taste for fried chicken? Michael had no experience in fatherhood, other than his observations of his own father. But that had been different. His father had known him from birth. He'd been a constant presence in Michael's life.

What had Michael been in Jeffrey's? Nothing.

But he was the boy's father. Emmie had listed him on the birth certificate. If she'd been willing to acknowledge his paternity, he would acknowledge it, too.

They sat in her cheery yellow kitchen, facing each other across the table, just the two of them. Her face was ghostly pale, her eyes wide. And then, with such suddenness it was as if someone had twisted a faucet, she began to weep. She cupped her hands over her cheeks and eyes, bowed her head and shuddered. Sobs filled the room.

He hadn't expected her to be overjoyed when he confronted her with what he'd learned. She'd been so annoyed by his reappearance in her life he'd just assumed that this added link would annoy her, too. Annoyance he could handle.

Not this heartbreaking grief, though.

"Emmie." He couldn't bear to watch the tremors racking her shoulders, to hear the hushed, plaintive moans that escaped her. He was seated only a few feet away from her, but he might as well be back in California for all the distance that loomed between them.

If it had taken enormous courage to return Jack Tyrell's call that afternoon, it took twice as much courage to rise from his chair and circle the table to her. Gently, not wanting to alarm her, he supported her elbows with his hands and eased her to her feet. Then he wrapped his arms around her and drew her against him.

She seemed to collapse into him, limp and bone-less, as if her body had dissolved into tears. She wept until his shirt was damp. She swayed and sighed and her breath was wet against his neck.

He wasn't sure what he'd been expecting. Hostility, perhaps. She'd been plenty hostile to him so far; he wouldn't have been surprised if she'd greeted his latest salvo with animosity or resistance. Or a stinging slap in the face. Or maybe denial. Since she'd gone out of her way to make sure he knew she wasn't welcoming him back, she might have lied and insisted he wasn't Jeffrey's father.

Or—less likely, but he'd hoped nevertheless—maybe she would smile and say, "Yes, he's your child. Let's figure out a way to make this work."

Or—least likely of all, but a man could dream—she would say, "I'm so glad you found us! Now we can be a real family!"

Assuming he wanted to be part of this family. Once again he realized he knew less than nothing about how to get along with children. Was he supposed to coach Jeffrey in soccer? Take him fishing? Talk to him? What did a person talk to a four-year-old kid about? He had no idea.

But if they were going to be a family, a four-year-old kid was the reason. If not for Jeffrey, this would just be about Emmie and Michael, two people who'd once meant something to each other a long time ago.

They'd been good together in San Pablo, perfectly attuned to each other. He still remembered the first time they'd made love—with only their hands—and how astonishingly fulfilling it had been. And every other time after that. They'd been better than good.

He hadn't searched for her with sex in mind. But now that he had her body pressed to his, her head nestled beneath his, her lovely curves fitting against him, he wanted sex, too. He wanted to carry her to her bed and strip her naked and slide deep into her, feeling her hot and tight around him, feeling her come.

Thinking about it made him hard. He shifted slightly so she wouldn't notice his arousal, but she clung to him even more, shaking with sobs. She was probably too hysterical to realize what her nearness was doing to him, what effect her soft, womanly fragrance had on him, and the swells of her breasts pressing against his chest.

He had loved her in San Pablo. It had been a crazy love, instantaneous, magical, totally illogical—but he'd believed that it could evolve into something real and lasting, something that would grow stronger each day until, at some undefined point, he and Emmie would no longer remember what life had been like without each other. With time, he'd been sure, that was the kind of love they could have had.

But they'd been apart for so long. Like two strands that had once been coiled into an unbreakable cord, they'd since become uncoiled, separated back into single threads, and rebraiding the cord might be impossible. He hadn't needed Maggie Tyrell's admonishment to know that finding Emmie would offer no guarantees.

Could he share Jeffrey with a woman who had made it quite clear that she loathed him? Could they be parents to that little boy together? He couldn't ask her. She was crying too hard.

"Emmie," he whispered. Her hair was silk against his lips. He longed to kiss her so badly he could taste it.

"I don't want this," she mumbled. He could barely make out the words. "I don't. I don't want you here, Michael." Yet she held on to him, her hands clutching his sides, her face buried in the hollow of his neck.

"I know." He didn't, really, but he thought the words might comfort her. If she stopped crying, they could talk about their situation. He needed to understand precisely what about this whole mess had her so upset—that he'd found out about Jeffrey, or that *he* was Jeffrey's father, or that he'd killed Edouardo Cortez, or that he'd misrepresented himself to her in San Pablo...or that he was in her kitchen, embracing her and wanting her the way a starving man wanted bread. Or all of the above.

He had to cool off. His nerves were bristling, his muscles tensing. He stroked his hands up and down her back in a consoling rhythm. He could feel the ridge of her spine through her blouse, and it made him want to slip the blouse off her shoulders, to lower his head to her breasts and kiss them. He had to will his hands not to cup her bottom and move her against him.

She made a small, whimpering noise, deep in her throat, then shifted her head, slid her hands to his chest and nudged him back. When she leaned away, her cheeks were mottled, her eyelashes spiky from her tears. A true gentleman would have offered her his linen handkerchief, but Michael didn't happen to have one. He reached around her for a paper napkin and handed it to her.

She dabbed at her eyelids and cheeks. Her eyes continued to well up; every time she wiped a streak of moisture from her face, a tear fell and left a new one.

"Mommy?" Jeffrey shouted from the doorway behind Michael. "Can I have cookies now?"

Instinctively Michael shielded Emmie from her son. He didn't think Jeffrey should see his mother falling apart like this.

"Not yet," she said in a weak, wavering voice.

"What'sa matter? Mommy, are you okay?"

Michael heard Jeffrey step into the room. Again acting on instinct, he gathered Emmie back into his

arms and pulled her against him, hiding her face
with his shoulder. "Your mom will tell you when
it's time for cookies," he said brusquely.

"How come she's crying?" Jeffrey asked.

"She had something in her eye," Michael replied,
assuring himself that it wasn't a lie. She *did* have
something in her eye: oceans of tears. "It hurt," he
added, knowing that that wasn't a lie, either. Whatever had set Emmie off, she was hurting badly.

"Is she gonna be all right? Mommy, are you
gonna be all right?"

Emmie leaned back and forced a smile before she
peered past Michael's shoulder to let his son see her.
"I'll be fine, Jeffrey," she said hoarsely. "If you'd
like, you can take three cookies and eat them while
you watch TV."

"Really?" Jeffrey sounded ecstatic. Evidently the
privilege of eating cookies in front of the television
set was so thrilling that he forgot all about his
mother's emotional outburst.

Michael released Emmie, giving her the chance
to stand on her own. She watched as Jeffrey pulled
three cookies out of a ceramic cookie jar shaped like
a clown's head. He put them on a plate and tore out
of the room.

Alone with her once more, Michael eyed her war-
ily. She seemed more in control, her lower lip no
longer trembling, her eyes still moist but not over-
flowing. She crossed to the sink and turned on the
tap.

He watched her splash water on her face, then dry
herself with a paper towel. When she turned, she
looked relatively composed. "I haven't cried in five
years," she said.

"Why not?"

A lopsided smile tugged at her mouth. "Who had time? I was too busy earning a living and raising my son."

My son, he heard. Not *our* son. "Even with all that, you could have found time to cry if you needed to."

"Maybe I didn't need to," she said, though the sarcasm edging her tone indicated that she'd needed to plenty of times.

"But you needed to now."

"Yes, I did. I don't suppose it has anything to do with your being here, does it?" she asked, her smile turning ironic.

He accepted the insult without letting it wound him. "I know you're not happy with me," he said, then smiled, too, realizing what an understatement that was. "But I *am* here, and we've got to work things out."

"There's nothing to work out," she retorted. "I'm Jeffrey's mother. I've raised him. I've loved and guided and taught him, and we've gotten along fine in spite of everything. All you did was donate the sperm. That doesn't make you a father, Michael."

He nodded, even though her honest words stung in a way her insults never could. "I haven't been a father because I didn't know I was a father," he explained. "Didn't it ever occur to you to inform me?"

"You walked out on me," she reminded him. "Obviously you weren't interested in staying in touch. What should I have done? Hired a detective to find you?"

"Didn't you even want child support?"

"I didn't want anything from you," she said with surprising vehemence.

"And it doesn't matter that I might have wanted to support my son?"

"No," she said bluntly. "It doesn't." She sighed, her smile gone, and crossed back to the table. Her wineglass was nearly empty, and she carried it to the refrigerator for a refill. "Do you want another beer?" she asked.

Beer might make this conversation less painful. But he'd rather suffer the pain than drift through it feeling nothing.

He shook his head and resumed his seat, waiting for her to return to the table with her refilled glass. She sipped, once again composed, her cheeks dry, her gaze reserved. He saw no sign of the emotions she'd vented just minutes ago, no sign of the vulnerable woman he'd been holding.

"You need my help now," he observed.

"No, I don't."

"You're about to be forced out of this house because you can't afford it."

A flicker of anger lit her eyes, and he counted it as a triumph. He'd rather have her furious than impassive and chilly. "We'll figure something out," she said tensely.

"We—meaning you and Jeffrey? You aren't going to raid his piggy bank, are you?"

Another flicker, hotter than the first. He tried not to smile. "I'd be perfectly able to afford this house if I'd gone to my parents and begged for some money. Or if I'd started working sooner, or took a second job, or...I don't know." Her fire seemed to burn itself out, doused by remorse. "I couldn't take a second job. I needed to spend whatever time I could with Jeffrey. A boy needs his mother. And a mother needs her son, too. I love him so much, I—" Her voice broke, and Michael braced himself for more tears. She didn't cry, though. She took a deep breath, sipped some wine and managed another smile, so poignant it made him want to take her in his arms again and assure her that she didn't have to act brave and tough to impress him. He was plenty impressed by what she'd accomplished on her own.

"What would it take for you to be able to stay in this house?" he asked.

"A down payment." She relaxed in her chair, so slightly he wouldn't have noticed if he hadn't been watching her. Her shoulders seemed marginally less stiff, her jaw marginally less clenched with tension. "Before Jeffrey was born, I was able to find substitute teaching jobs, but they didn't come with any health insurance. So his birth wiped out my savings. I did part-time subbing for another year and a half, until he was old enough to go to a preschool and I was able to land a job here in the Wilborough School District. I've managed to save a little money, but not much. Not enough to buy this house. My landlord wanted to sell it to me, and I can afford the monthly mortgage, but I don't have enough for a down payment."

"I could supply the down payment," he said.

The combative fire returned to her eyes. "No."

"Why not?"

"Do you think you're going to buy your way into our lives, Michael? Or is it guilt money?"

"Call it child support," he suggested, deciding then and there that he would insist on helping her out with the house. If she let him do nothing else, she would have to allow him that. Had he known of Jeffrey's existence, he would have been sending money all along. He wasn't a deadbeat. He would have paid enough so that Emmie could have stayed home with Jeffrey until he was older, if that was what she'd wanted. He would have paid the hospital bills. He would have done what a father was supposed to do.

She opened her mouth and then closed it. After lifting her glass, she studied him above the rim, then sipped. Evidently she thought his offer was worthy of serious consideration.

"It's a big chunk of money," she said.

"Not a problem."

"If I agreed to let you do this," she asked, leveling her gaze at him, "what would you expect in return?"

He cursed. He'd been keeping himself reined in, letting her pour out her emotions. But for God's sake, he had emotions, too. Just that afternoon he'd learned that he was a father, that a woman he'd once loved had given birth on Valentine's Day four years and some months ago and he'd never known about it. His son had been on this earth, living and growing, and Michael had been left completely in the dark. He deserved to throw a fit as much as she did.

"I'm his father," he growled, rage surging inside him. "If I want to support him I'll damned well support him."

"You don't even know him," she pointed out.

That silenced him. She was right, of course. He

drummed his fingers on the table and sorted his thoughts. "Okay, tell me this. What would be the ideal situation for you? To own this house and have me out of your life?"

"That sounds nice." She tempered her words with a grin.

"Why do you want me out of your life? Do you hate me that much, after so many years?"

She shook her head and traced the edge of her glass with her fingertip. "I've built something here, Michael," she said hesitantly, as if speaking the words the instant they took shape in her mind. "I did it all by myself. I had no help from my family or from you. And I've done a pretty good job of it, all things considered. But it's…delicate. I've worked awfully hard to get everything balanced just so. You destroy the balance."

He reminded himself that she had once been an upper-class girl from a cozy, conservative home. She liked stability. Traveling to San Pablo had been the most daring thing she'd ever done—and she'd done it under the auspices of a church. Then she'd gone and done something even more daring: she'd fallen in love with Michael.

And that had turned out badly.

So she didn't want to take chances. She didn't want to risk anything on him. She wanted to protect what she had.

He was the opposite, maybe because he'd never had much to begin with. He'd never been afraid of taking chances and forging into new territory. If he had, he'd be working in a warehouse side by side with his father in Bakersfield, instead of consulting with the leaders of industry and the government.

"I'm not going to promise you that your life and Jeffrey's will be the same if I'm here. But I'm his father. You can't just shut me out like that."

"Do you have any idea what it means to be a father?" she asked.

"I'll learn."

"Do you know how to kiss a boo-boo and make it all better? Do you know how to bring down a child's fever? Do you know how to take the itch out of chicken pox? How to make sure sneakers fit properly? How to make Eeyore's voice when you read *Winnie-the-Pooh* out loud? Do you know what to feed an imaginary monster that lives in a tree?"

Michael slumped in his chair, trying not to succumb to defeat. No, he didn't know how to make Eeyore's voice and what an imaginary monster might eat. But he knew a few things. "I know my son likes KFC chicken and mashed potatoes. I'll learn the rest."

She eyed him speculatively. "It's not easy."

"Easy doesn't interest me."

Another long stare, and then she blinked. Her eyes glistened with new tears, but they didn't fall. "I don't love you, Michael," she said, her voice as clear and pale as the wine in her glass. "I did once, but I don't anymore. That's not going to change."

"Another thing I know," he continued, refusing to flinch at the bald challenge in her words, "is that predicting what's going to happen is a waste of time." He refused to shift his gaze from her. "I didn't come here to make you fall in love with me, Emmie. I came here…" He'd come because Maggie Tyrell's advertisement had promised that lost lovers could be found. He'd come because there had been

loose ends hanging between Emmie and him—more
loose ends than he'd even known about—and because he didn't want to live the rest of his life wondering about what had become of her, whether she
ever thought about him, whether San Pablo was as
special as he'd believed at the time.

He'd come because sex with her had been incredible and he wanted that again. Because talking with
her had been just as incredible. Because every time
he bit into a peach he thought of her. Because every
time he saw a pink rose, every time he dug into one
of his grandmother's native-cuisine feasts, every
time he thought about his brother Johnny, he remembered the intense, soul-shaking days he'd spent
with Mary-Elizabeth Kenyon five years ago.

Maybe he'd come not to make her fall in love
with him but to see if he could fall in love with her
again.

LONG AFTER MICHAEL had gone and Jeffrey was in
bed, she sat out on the patio, a final glass of chilled
wine in her hand. The moon was waxing, a bright
silver crescent cut into the sky like a cosmic smile.
The crickets chirped, the cicadas buzzed and a few
fireflies flickered near the hedges.

The monster in the tree ate shredded carrot peels.
She supposed Michael could learn that much.

She wasn't going to have to move. Jeffrey wasn't
going to lose his monster. She had given Michael
permission to help her buy the house.

She couldn't make herself feel bad about her decision. Michael was right: he was Jeffrey's father,
and if he hadn't provided for the boy before, now
was as good a time as any for him to start.

If accepting money from Michael meant accepting Michael himself, well, maybe she could do that, too—for Jeffrey's sake. Jeffrey had asked her about his father a few times over the years, and she'd never answered him with lies. She'd told Jeffrey that she'd loved a man very much but that man wasn't ready to settle down and return her love so he'd gone away. But Emmie was grateful to him because he'd given her Jeffrey.

She *was* grateful to Michael. If she was still a bit unsettled about what he'd done in San Pablo, she knew her greatest anger was over his having deceived her, presenting himself as a sweet, gentle professor instead of someone bent on revenge. But maybe his revenge was justified, and if the man he'd killed had been about to kill him and his friend, the killing had been justified, too.

She'd hated Michael because he'd left her. She'd hated him because she'd trusted him and loved him and he'd betrayed her. But she'd spoken the truth when she'd told him she didn't hate him anymore.

Somehow she was going to have to make room for him in her life and Jeffrey's. She wasn't going to trust him—it was always possible that he would leave again, the way he had before. And she wasn't going to tell Jeffrey who Michael was, at least not right away. She couldn't bear to let Jeffrey grow attached to the man who was his father when she had so little faith that that man would stick around. One betrayed Kenyon in the family was quite enough.

Yet she would accept Michael's help. She'd accept his money so she could keep her home.

And she would try with all her might not to let him upset her delicately balanced world.

CHAPTER ELEVEN

WHAT A PARADOX: Michael was going to spend the morning looking at apartments for himself and the afternoon helping Emmie to buy her house. He hadn't seen much of her house beyond the entry, the living room and the kitchen—he'd glimpsed the dining room and a hallway leading off to what he assumed were the bedrooms—but he could gauge the size of the house from the exterior, and by his estimation it had three bedrooms.

More than enough room for him, even if Emmie didn't want him in her bed.

He didn't dare to suggest moving in with her, though. It was nothing short of a miracle that he'd gotten her to agree to accept some money from him. But she trusted him about as much as a field mouse might trust a snake.

He was supposed to meet her at her school at three o'clock that afternoon. From there they would drive to a local bank, where she had already processed a mortgage application, and she would reapply for the mortgage with Michael by her side, explaining to the mortgage guy that Michael would contribute the down-payment money. Michael should have been swallowing hard at the understanding that if the application went through, he would be writing a sizable check and handing it over to the bank on Emmie's behalf. But when he thought of her struggling to keep Jeffrey clothed and fed and supplied with books and toys, not only didn't he mind the idea of writing that check, but he actually was looking forward to it.

He wasn't buying Emmie, he told himself. Nor was he buying access to his son. What he was buying was his own peace of mind, a sense that although he'd been less than honest with Emmie five years ago, he was at bottom an honorable man.

The apartments he looked at were uniformly depressing. The first one was large but dark; trees and surrounding buildings seemed to swallow the sunlight before it could reach the windows. The second apartment was so small he reflexively hunched his shoulders as he wandered through the cramped, stagnant rooms, feeling the walls closing in on him. The third apartment overlooked what had to be the busiest street in the eastern half of the state. In less than a minute he counted eleven eighteen-wheelers wheezing and grinding gears through the intersection outside the living-room window.

He wanted to live in Emmie's house.

With Emmie.

And with Jeffrey, too—although the idea of spending every day with a little boy he didn't know, but who was his own son, scared the hell out of him.

He returned to his hotel room, edgy but vaguely excited. He'd grown up in an environment bathed in uncertainty—his parents' rocky marriage, their shaky finances, the friction between their Anglo and Latino cultures, his brother's bad choices, his own frightening foray into higher education, a world no one in his family knew anything about. A little more uncertainty now shouldn't bother him. But it did.

He did his best to tune it out and focus on a report he'd been hired to prepare for a client hoping to market snack crackers in Central America. He worked for a couple of hours, then grew restless. Trying not to think about Emmie and Jeffrey was tiring; he could lock them out of his thoughts for only so long before they broke down the door.

Two-thirty. Too early to go to Emmie's school, but he wasn't going to sit squinting at the screen of his laptop in his dreary hotel room anymore. He scooped up his keys and headed outside.

Downtown Wilborough contained its share of national chain outlets, but Main Street also boasted a fair number of mom-and-pop shops. He parked by a meter, inserted a coin and strolled up and down the street, wondering what it would be like to live in a pretty New England town. Springtime was balmier here than in Southern California, and infinitely more green. Trees exploded with leaves. Flowers cascaded from planters and window boxes. The previous day's humidity had left everything fresh and dewy.

A sporting-goods store caught his eye. He wandered in and grinned at the display of hockey sticks and pads beneath a sign that read Hockey Gear For Summer Leagues On Sale. Summer hockey? In California, hockey seemed out of season even in the winter.

He worked his way through the store until he came upon a section filled with baseball equipment. He'd never taken much interest in hockey, but baseball was something he could understand. He and

Johnny had played sandlot ball through the summer months of their childhood.

He wondered if Jeffrey owned a glove or a bat. Emmie might read *Winnie-the-Pooh* in Eeyore's voice to the boy, but had she ever bought him baseball gear?

It was something every American boy ought to have—American girls, too, Michael allowed, but at the moment he was thinking about just one particular American boy. He was thinking about that boy's father, too, about how baseball was something a father taught his son.

Maybe Michael could do that.

He searched the store for a clerk, spotted one in the soccer department and waved him over. "What size bat should I get for a four-and-a-half-year-old boy?" he asked.

The clerk eyed the wood and aluminum bats and shook his head. "Hollow plastic, I'd guess. A whiffle-ball bat, maybe—but we don't sell those. Most kids that young, you don't want to encourage them to swing a clublike object around."

"I see your point." But Michael still wanted to buy something for Jeffrey. "How about a glove?"

"We've got some small gloves, sure," the clerk said, leading Michael to a wall full of pegs with gloves hanging from them. "Is he a rightie or a leftie?"

Michael didn't know. But he himself was right-handed, and he was pretty sure Emmie was, too. "Rightie," he guessed.

"Good thing. I don't have too much to choose from for lefties." The man pulled a few small leather baseball gloves from the wall and handed them to Michael.

He examined them. They were too tiny for him to try on, and they seemed stiff and rigid. He would have to teach Jeffrey how to break a glove in. Maybe he ought to buy some glove oil, too.

By the time he'd left the store, he had purchased a glove, a bottle of oil and a can of tennis balls. Jeffrey wasn't ready for hardballs yet. He wasn't even ready for softballs. Michael wasn't sure what he was ready for, but he felt more like a father now than he had a few minutes ago.

He got back into his car and drove to the Oak Hill School. It was a pretty suburban primary school, a one-story redbrick building with broad windows and a flat roof. The circular front driveway was jammed with bright-yellow buses, and children streamed from the building in a formation just this side of chaos.

He drove to the parking lot, parked and got out. Approaching the front door, he saw only an endless torrent of children—children who might stand as tall as his shoulders and children who would have to rise on tiptoe to come up even with his hip. They chattered, shouted, shoved one another and used language he would have gotten slapped for using at their age. Suddenly the new child-size glove sitting in the trunk of his car didn't make him feel like a father anymore.

Again it hit him that he knew nothing about children. Nothing about their gaudy clothes, their shrill voices, their oversize backpacks, their untied sneakers. Why had he forced the parenthood issue with Emmie last night? Why hadn't he left things alone?

He wanted to believe it was because he was at heart a moral, responsible man. But maybe it was also because he desired Emmie. The only way he could possibly win her respect at this point was to prove how moral and responsible he was.

He would prove it. He would figure out kids. He'd gotten the fried-chicken part right last night. He'd introduce his son to baseball today. In time, with practice, he'd figure out the rest.

Like swimming against the current, he worked his way through the stream of exiting children to the front door of the school and inside. A secretary was posted behind a broad desk in a glass-enclosed office overlooking the lobby, but she was on the phone and didn't notice him, so he decided not to check in with her. Instead he turned down one of the corridors, searching for Emmie.

The walls were decorated with juvenile artwork and neatly typed poems and essays. The water fountains were navel-high and the floors durable linoleum. Most of the classroom doors were open. He peeked into each one as he passed. Chairs were perched atop desks; bulletin boards were cluttered with more primitive art and school papers; chalkboards were sponged down. This school wasn't so different from the school he'd attended as a child, but he felt as if he'd entered an alien universe.

Around a bend in the corridor, he peered into yet another open classroom and spotted Emmie. Dressed in a flowing skirt with a cheerful floral print and a crisp white blouse, she was seated on the edge of her desk, talking to a boy who stood before her.

Not wanting to intrude, Michael remained half-hidden outside the doorway. He heard Emmie's voice, low and soothing, and the boy's voice, also muted. He couldn't make out the words, but he sensed from the way they faced each other, the way Emmie patted the boy's shoulder, the way she tilted her head and smiled, that the conversation was serious but not deadly. Eventually the boy hoisted a bulging backpack off the floor, slung it over his shoulder and jogged out of the room, his huge sneakers clomping against the floor.

Following the boy with her gaze, Emmie noticed Michael. Her eyes widened slightly, and she pushed away from her desk.

Yes, he thought, taking in the sway of her hair, the ethereal beauty of her eyes, the gentleness with which she'd talked to the boy. What he wanted had to do with Jeffrey, but it also had to do with Emmie. It had to do with the fact that Michael felt exactly the same way he'd felt five years ago, when he'd glimpsed her shopping for peaches in the town market in San Pablo. She'd worn a loose, feminine skirt then, too, one that only hinted at the proportions of her hips and legs. Her skin had been a bit darker from exposure to the tropical sun, and her eyes had contained more laughter, but she was just as enchanting today as she'd been five years ago. He had known on that fateful Saturday morning in San Pablo that he wanted the lovely blond woman with the elegant hands and the slender build. He wanted her now, just as much, and it seemed just as fateful.

"I thought you were going to wait for me at the front desk," she said, crossing the classroom to him.

"The secretary was busy, so..." He shrugged. He didn't trust his voice not to blurt out how much he longed for Emmie. He didn't trust his arms not to reach out to her, to haul her to himself and devour her with a kiss. "Is that kid okay?" he asked, motioning toward the hall, where the boy had vanished. If he talked about Emmie's student, he might be able to control the troublesome yearning that kept threatening to overtake him.

"He's lazy," she said, returning to her desk and packing a folder of papers into her tote. "He's fallen behind in his work. He's a bright boy, but he needs self-discipline."

"The way you were talking to him—it didn't look as if you were chewing him out for being lazy."

"Well, I don't want to scare him off or make him angry. I just want him to do the work he needs to do." She pulled a key ring from the top drawer of her desk, locked the desk and joined Michael at the door. "Let's go see my buddy at the bank," she said, preceding him out of the room.

He thought about what she'd said. She made taking responsibility sound so easy: just do what you need to do. If Michael did what he needed to do, if he taught Jeffrey how to throw a ball and how to catch it in the pocket of his glove, if he made taking ownership of their Wilborough home economically feasible, would that be enough? Would Emmie stop trying to scare him off, stop resorting to anger and see him for the man he was?

He could think of one way to find out: do the work he needed to do.

HER MEETING WITH Ronald Petit at County Savings and Trust went better today. She had been to the realty office during her lunch hour and had the sales contract for the house written up. Mr. Arnett Senior

was thrilled she would be able to buy his house—
she had no idea what his son thought about it, and
she didn't care. The real-estate agent was delighted,
too. She would be getting her commission without
having done more than hammer a For Sale sign into
Emmie's front lawn.

Armed with the sales contract and backed by Michael and his money, Emmie glided through the
mortgage application process with minimal effort.
Obviously it was a lot easier to get money out of a
bank if you began the process with an adequate supply of funds in hand. The irony didn't escape her,
but Ronald Petit was so happy she could now qualify for the mortgage that she kept her observations
to herself.

By four o'clock, she and Michael were outside,
strolling across the parking lot to their cars. The
bright sunlight contrasted with the deep black of his
hair, and his expression was inscrutable as he
strolled beside her.

As she had when he'd shown up at her house the
other night, she acknowledged how handsome he
was. She had forced herself to forget a long time
ago, because remembering anything good about him
had hurt too much. But more than just his generosity
that afternoon in the bank softened her opinion of
him. She was aware of the easy grace of his gait,
the swing of his arms, the breadth of his shoulders,
the sheer physical beauty of him.

In truth, she had never really forgotten how attractive he was, even when she'd tried. The difference was that now she was letting his striking appearance stir something inside her, something deep,

something she had buried the day he'd abandoned her.

Their cars were parked in adjacent parking spots. They halted in the narrow space between the two vehicles. She wasn't sure what was supposed to happen next: he'd just promised her a huge chunk of money, so anything she suggested—that he join her and Jeffrey for dinner or that he leave them alone—would be tainted by that. Not having enough money was a disaster, but having a lot of money complicated matters, too.

"Thank you," she finally said.

A playful breeze deposited a strand of her hair onto her face. Michael lifted it away, his thumb brushing her cheek. He focused his gaze on her, his eyes so dark they seemed bottomless. "Does that mean I'm being dismissed?" he asked.

She wasn't sure what it meant, other than thank you. And she wasn't sure she was dismissing him, either. She ought to, in view of how her cheek burned in the wake of his light touch.

But he'd given her money. To acknowledge that she welcomed his touch would imply that he'd somehow purchased the right to touch her. And she didn't really feel affectionate, she assured herself. She felt grateful and friendlier than before, and...warm. Inexplicably warm.

"I have to go pick up Jeffrey at his preschool," she said, wondering if Michael could hear the odd thickness in her voice.

"I'd like to see where he goes to preschool, if that's all right with you."

She shook off the wistful mood that threatened to overtake her. Michael's wanting to see Jeffrey's school so soon after he'd helped her buy her house carried a threat. He *had* bought access, after all. He'd bought a home not for her but for his son, and now he wanted to forge deeper into Jeffrey's life.

She had known this might happen, yet she'd accepted his money anyway. Now she was going to have to accept the rest of it—and maybe convince herself that bringing Michael and Jeffrey together wasn't the worst thing in the world. But still... "Jeffrey doesn't know," she warned.

"About me being his father?"

She nodded. "I'm not ready to tell him."

He digested this. Even though there was hardly any room to move between the two cars, he put a bit of distance between them. "When will you be ready?"

His impatience rankled. "This isn't something I'm going to rush into," she retorted. "As far as I know, you might disappear on me again. You might hand me a check and then go back to California. And then what would I tell him? 'Oh, by the way, Jeffrey, that guy who blew through our lives last spring was your father.'"

He didn't smile. "I'm not going to blow through your lives. He's my son."

"I tried to tell you last night—you have no idea what that means."

"I want to learn."

She sighed. It would be good for him to learn, and good for Jeffrey. But the more Michael became a father, the less Jeffrey would belong to her.

He was still a child, though, who needed both parents. If Michael was seriously willing to accept

his son, she owed it to Jeffrey not to deprive him of
his father.

"All right," she muttered, swallowing the dread
that formed a knot in her throat. "If you want to see
his preschool, follow me."

During the drive, she labored to keep her eyes on
the road ahead of her instead of on her rearview
mirror, which was filled with the reflection of Michael's rental car as it tailed her through town. She
repeated to herself, over and over, that Jeffrey deserved to have a father, and if that father turned out
to be his actual genetic father, it wasn't the end of
the world. She told herself that what had happened
five years ago was history, that Michael had had a
good reason for what he'd done, that as violent and
frightening as it was, she could accept his need to
kill that man—at least, she could intellectually.
Emotionally, it was still hard, but she was trying to
be fair.

And even if he hadn't shown up in Wilborough a
few days ago, she knew Jeffrey wasn't really hers.
Children were merely on loan to their parents. They
grew up and grew away. Sooner or later Jeffrey
would bond with other adults, find other role models, idolize both men and women. Whether or not
Emmie let Michael back into her life, Jeffrey would
grow up.

Michael stuck close to her when they emerged
from their cars outside the preschool. He looked ap-
prehensive but determined as she led the way into
the building. He flinched at the swell of noise from
the big playroom, where Jeffrey was sure to be.
Young children didn't have volume controls on their

voice boxes; whether they were excited, happy, miserable, full of energy or tired, they tended to shriek.

She was used to the din. Michael clearly wasn't. Well, he'd better get used to it if he wanted to be Jeffrey's dad, she thought with a superior smile.

After he recovered from the shock of the noise, he followed her into the big playroom. What might appear like bedlam to the uninitiated was actually a fairly organized playtime, but Michael's lips thinned and his brow furrowed as he sidestepped a few tots, halted to avoid colliding with a three-year-old darting across the room wielding a toy rocket ship and winced at an off-key chorus of the alphabet song being performed by a small circle of girls in one corner. Tuning out the commotion, Emmie scanned the room, then zeroed in on Jeffrey crashing toy cars with Adam and Todd, as usual. At her wave, he smiled and carried his car to the shelf where it was stored. Then he scampered over to her.

"Hi, Mom," he said, beaming up at Michael. "That's your friend."

"Yes. He's still here," Emmie said, wondering if she sounded irritated or relieved. She felt a little of both, actually.

It took Jeffrey a few minutes to gather his lunch box and an art project that involved a paper plate, feathers, construction paper and scraps of cloth. Emmie sought his teacher for a quick conference on how his day had gone, and then she and Jeffrey left, Michael at their heels as if he couldn't wait to clear out.

"Can I play pirate?" Jeffrey asked, modulating his voice. He knew shrieking wasn't effective with his mother.

"I don't know," Emmie hedged, then made up her mind. "Okay." She didn't want to invite Michael back to her house, but she wasn't ready to send him on his way, either. "He plays a pirate game at a town park," she explained as the three of them crossed the parking lot. "If you want to follow us there…"

"Sure." He seemed a bit more certain now that they were outdoors. "I'd like that." He glanced at Jeffrey, who charged ahead to Emmie's car, too excited about a trip to the community center to wait for the adults. What was Michael looking for when he stared at Jeffrey? Emmie wondered. Recognition? Love?

Whatever it was, he'd better not pressure Jeffrey into giving something he wasn't prepared to give. She might be reluctantly willing to let Michael get to know Jeffrey, but she was a mother, protective and prepared to fend off anything and anyone who posed a danger to her child.

They drove the short distance to the park, Michael's car once again filling her rearview mirror. She'd barely applied the parking brake when Jeffrey tugged at the belt on his booster seat, eager to race to the jungle gym and become a marauding pirate. He was already charging across the grass when she locked her car and turned to search for Michael.

He had parked a few spaces away, and he, too, was locking his car. He held a bag that appeared to contain a lumpy object. "What's that?" she asked, joining him at his car.

Michael smiled hesitantly. "It's something for Jeffrey."

"What?" she demanded, once again the protective mother. Did he think he could bribe her son? Bad enough he'd secured her tolerance with the down-payment money; he'd better not be planning to buy Jeffrey's affection.

"A baseball glove." He pulled it out to show her. "A child's size. I hope it's small enough."

"A baseball glove?" She experienced a surge of conflicting emotions—and anger and resentment weren't among them. The gift was so kind, so generous. So appropriate. Yet it reminded her of her limitations. She should have gotten her son a baseball glove. All little boys had them, didn't they? It had just never occurred to her—because she was a mother. Baseball gloves were the sort of thing fathers took care of.

She wanted to cry again—for Michael's thoughtfulness and her shortcomings—but she'd done enough crying last night. With a few discreet blinks, she cleared the tears from her eyes and turned to the playground. Jeffrey had scaled the jungle gym to a high platform, where he waved his hand and shouted, "Ahoy! Prepare to board!" He didn't exactly know what that meant, but he'd seen a cartoon about pirates once, and the characters in the show had spoken those lines.

She turned back to discover that Michael had left her side and was jogging across the grass to the jungle gym. He might have needed her support at the preschool, but apparently he didn't need it now.

She crossed the grass but kept her distance, once again buffeted by contradictory emotions. She wanted Jeffrey to be happy with the glove, but she didn't want fatherhood to come too quickly to Michael. She knew from personal experience how easy it was to fall in love with Michael, but it wouldn't be fair if Jeffrey fell in love with him after just one game of catch.

Yet if Jeffrey rejected Michael's gift, Michael would feel terrible, and she didn't want that, either. She didn't want him hurt.

That realization took her aback. He'd hurt her, hadn't he? He'd abandoned her and her son, and she'd spent five years healing. And now she was feeling as protective of him as she was of her son. She didn't want Michael hurt.

It was absurd. She loved Jeffrey—of course she wanted to protect him. But Michael?

She'd loved him once. And he was trying, putting his ego on the line, making himself vulnerable, taking a chance with Jeffrey. If it worked out, if they hit it off…Jeffrey wouldn't love or need her less. He'd still be her beloved son. But he would have something he deserved: his father. And Michael would have something he would have had long ago if his life had taken a different turn: his son.

He stood at the bottom of the jungle gym and called up to Jeffrey, his words lost in the distance between the playground and the spot where Emmie stood. Jeffrey looked down. Michael extended the glove up to Jeffrey. Jeffrey reached for it, and Michael shook his head. They talked a bit more, and Jeffrey climbed down. Only when he was on the ground did Michael hand him the glove.

Michael knelt down next to Jeffrey. She watched as he eased the glove onto Jeffrey's left hand. She wanted to move closer so she could hear what they were saying to each other, but she didn't dare. This was Michael's first real foray into the world of fatherhood; if she got too close, she might distract Jeffrey or wind up as an intermediary between them. If they were going to do this, they'd have to do it without her.

Michael stepped back from Jeffrey, who gazed at the huge leather mitt on his hand. She could tell by the way he angled his head that he was giggling— she could conjure the sound in her mind, even if she couldn't hear it. She guessed he was also perplexed, unsure of what to do with the glove now that he was wearing it. He swung his arm back and forth, held up his hand in front of his face and giggled some more.

Michael dug into his bag and pulled out a can of tennis balls. He snapped the can open, took out a ball and tossed it to Jeffrey. It bounced off the glove's fingertips and dropped to the grass.

Michael picked up the ball and threw it again. This time it glanced off the thumb part of the glove and fell.

She moved to a bench and sat, her attention never straying from Michael and Jeffrey. She watched as Michael rotated Jeffrey's left hand so it was palm up and dropped the ball into the pocket of the glove. He squeezed the glove around the ball, then took the ball and stood behind Jeffrey, reaching around him so he could cup his left hand under Jeffrey's. He dropped the ball into the glove again, squeezing Jeffrey's hand around it.

Jeffrey gazed up over his shoulder at Michael. He looked puzzled but intrigued—and utterly fearless. This man he had only met a day ago was practically hugging him, and Jeffrey trusted him enough not to recoil.

"Go ahead," Emmie whispered, knowing Michael wouldn't hear her. "You can put your arms around him. You're his dad."

Last night, she wouldn't have said that. Last night, she'd been terrified by Michael's invasion into the snug little world she'd created for Jeffrey and her. But watching him today, observing how patient he was as he tossed the ball to Jeffrey and Jeffrey dropped it and Michael tossed it again, she admitted that maybe he *did* have what it took to be a father: the willingness to keep trying, to keep teaching, to build a connection, one toss of the ball at a time.

This was good. She wouldn't fight it. She would let Michael be Jeffrey's father.

CHAPTER TWELVE

SHE MADE A GRILLED CHICKEN for dinner, with saffron rice and a fresh salad. A real meal, not fast food, nothing that came in soggy cardboard or paper wrappers with a cheap toy prize tossed in.

Jeffrey didn't complain. He was too busy chatting man-to-man with Michael about baseball. "Who do you think is the greatest player that ever lived?" he asked Michael between mouthfuls of drumstick. "My friend Adam says it's Mo Vaughn, cuz he's nice to kids. He does all kinds of neat stuff with them, like take them places and stuff."

"That would put him pretty high on the list," Michael conceded, then took a sip of wine.

Emmie wished she had a better vintage to reflect the celebratory aspect of the evening. Maybe the night called for champagne—if only she had a bottle of bubbly lying around. Jeffrey certainly seemed to consider this dinner a festive occasion. He was essentially unaware of the housing crisis that had just been averted. To him, what made the day miraculous was that he now owned a baseball glove.

"I think maybe Babe Ruth," Jeffrey continued. "'Cept Babe is a silly name for a guy."

"I agree."

"Did you ever go to a real game? I mean at Fenway Park,'' he clarified, naming the ball field where the Boston Red Sox played.

''I've never been to Fenway Park,'' Michael told him, ''but I've seen some Dodgers games in Los Angeles.''

''I don't know about the Dodgers,'' Jeffrey said. ''I know about the Red Sox.''

Emmie listened, astonished by her son's enthusiasm. He'd never said a word to her about baseball. If he had, she would have acted on his interest—taken him to a game at Fenway, maybe, or if that had been too expensive to some of the Little League games right in town. Several of her students played in the younger levels of Little League. She'd bet Jeffrey would love to watch a game in which the teams were composed of children only a few years older than him.

Why hadn't she known he was a baseball nut? Had he kept this from her because she was his mother and he didn't want to discuss baseball with a woman? Or because she'd never picked up on any subtle signals from him?

She would have felt miserable about having failed her son in some way, except that she was too fascinated by the interplay between him and Michael. Michael didn't exactly look relaxed. He answered Jeffrey's questions but didn't appear to know how to pose questions in return. If it weren't for Jeffrey's natural ebullience, the conversation would have petered out.

''Who do you like better?'' Jeffrey was asking. ''Sammy Sosa or Mark McGwire?''

''They're both good guys,'' Michael said.

"They hit homers. I wanna hit homers, too. Will you teach me how to hit homers?"

"When you're older," Michael promised, then shot a glance in Emmie's direction. His eyes seemed to ask, *Can I teach him how to hit homers when he's older? Will I still be in his life? Will you allow it?*

Instinctively she nodded. She might fear having her world overturned by Michael's presence, but her first concern was Jeffrey. Jeffrey, she acknowledged, needed a man in his life, someone who would teach him how to make a pocket with his glove and who would analyze with him the relative merits of assorted home-run sluggers.

She ate her meal, watching Michael dutifully answer Jeffrey's endless questions, and she wondered whether perhaps she needed a man in her life, too.

She had loved him once—and she'd loved no one since. She'd made a good life for herself and her son, gotten a rewarding job, proved she could do everything on her own. No, she didn't need a man. But it was nice having Michael at her table. The room felt more complete with him in it.

She cautioned herself not to think along those lines. She'd barely decided to let him get to know Jeffrey. She couldn't complicate matters even more by letting herself get to know Michael all over again.

"I have fruit and cookies for dessert," she announced, realizing that Michael and Jeffrey had polished off just about all the food she'd served. "I'm afraid it isn't fancy, but—"

"I can't believe you threw this meal together after a whole day at work," Michael said, pushing back his chair. "When I've had a long day at work, I always wind up eating takeout or microwaving something.''

"We do that more often than I'd like to admit," she said with a grin, recalling that just last night she'd been prepared to serve Jeffrey cereal and bagels for dinner.

"Well, I'll skip dessert. I'm full," Michael told her, rising and gathering some of the dishes to carry to the sink.

"Not me," Jeffrey piped up. "I gotta keep eating so I can grow as big as Mo Vaughn. Besides, dessert is *cookies*," he emphasized, as if he couldn't believe that Michael would turn down such a treat.

"And fruit," Emmie reminded him. "If you want to grow up to be as big and strong as Mo Vaughn, you've got to eat a healthy, well-balanced diet."

Jeffrey rolled his eyes and glanced at Michael for support. Michael appeared to be struggling against a smile. "You'd better have some fruit," he said.

All three of them cleared the table together. Almost like a family, Emmie thought, then shoved the notion away. It was too tempting—and too soon—to think of them that way. Just because she wanted to trust Michael didn't mean she could.

He refilled his wineglass and hers as she filled the sink with soapy water and left the dishes to soak. While Jeffrey gobbled up cookies and lingered over a banana, the adults sipped their wine and listened to him babble. "I wanna be a pitcher when I grow up. Is Mo Vaughn a pitcher? I don't think so. I wanna pitch like Babe Ruth, only I don't know if he was a pitcher, either. Will you teach me how to throw like Babe Ruth, Michael?''

"I'll teach you how to throw like Jeffrey Kenyon," Michael said.

Not Jeffrey Molina, Emmie noted. Michael was being careful, respecting her wishes and not declaring his paternity. She sent him a private smile to let him know she appreciated it.

He smiled back.

It occurred to her that perhaps this didn't have to be hard. If they clicked as a family, if Michael was willing to fit himself into the Kenyon world, why not? Why not trust her instincts the way she'd trusted them five years ago?

She knew the answer to that question. She mustn't confuse what she wanted with what was. Take it slow, she warned herself, even if her gaze kept drifting to his fingers cupped around the bowl of his goblet, to his long, athletic legs, to the broad, sturdy shoulders that had supported her yesterday when she'd wept.

"Can we go outside and play some catch?" Jeffrey asked, his banana finally consumed. "It's not dark out yet, Mommy—"

"It's getting dark, and it's getting late," she said. "You've still got to take a bath, and then we're going to read a little."

"And I gotta brush my teeth, too," Jeffrey said with a long-suffering sigh. He rolled his eyes at Michael, who suppressed another smile. "I bet your mommy doesn't make you brush your teeth," he muttered.

"When I was your age, she did," Michael told him.

"I'm going to do the dishes," Emmie announced, pushing to her feet, "and then it's bath time. If you two want to play catch for a few minutes, I guess it would be all right.''

''No,'' Michael said abruptly. ''I'm going to help you with the dishes.''

She chewed that one over for a minute. She thought he was trying to build a relationship with Jeffrey—and what man would rather wash dishes than play catch?

A man who wanted to build a relationship with Jeffrey's mother. ''All right,'' she said. ''You can help with the dishes.''

''I wanna play catch!'' Jeffrey whined.

''Your mom needs some help right now,'' Michael insisted.

Jeffrey gave him a querulous stare, as if appalled that his former ally had turned on him. Michael remained unmoved. Sulking, Jeffrey trudged out of the kitchen.

''You could have played with him,'' Emmie said in a soft voice.

''I didn't want to. I'm not...'' He paused, searching for the right words. ''I'm not used to dealing with children. I'm sort of maxed out on him at the moment.''

Well, that was honest. ''All right,'' she said. ''I'll wash. You dry.''

They carried their half-empty wineglasses to the sink to sip while they worked. Emmie handed Michael a towel, then plunged her hands into the hot suds.

''Have you ever thought about buying a dishwasher?'' he asked.

She made a face. ''Why would I buy a dishwasher for a house I never dreamed of owning?'' She scrubbed one of the plates. "Even if I owned the house—"

"You will," Michael reminded her. "You practically do already."

"Dishwashers are expensive. I live on a tight budget. And no—" she cut him off before he could speak "—I won't have you buying me a dishwasher."

"Why not?"

"I'm already in too much debt to you."

He took the rinsed plate from her and wiped it dry. "I'm in too much debt to you," he argued. At her quizzical look, he explained, "You raised my son. I owe you so much for that."

His heartfelt words seeped into her, as warm as the water in the sink, as glistening as the rainbow-flecked bubbles. She groped for a knife at the bottom of the pile and rubbed it with the dishcloth, all the while trying to locate the source of her resistance to him. She knew it was in her somewhere, but she couldn't seem to find it.

"I'm sorry," she said, scrubbing the knife until it shone like a mirror. "I'm sorry things happened the way they did five years ago. I'm sorry everything got botched so badly."

"I'm sorrier than you."

She handed him the knife to dry. "I'm not sorry we met, though," she admitted. "I'm not sorry we made Jeffrey."

"He's a good kid," said Michael.

"He's a demanding chatterbox and sometimes a brat." She set to work on another plate and grinned. "He's also the best kid in the world."

"Emmie..." He took the plate she handed to him,

but instead of drying it, he put it on the counter and turned to face her. "I want this to work." He sounded earnest, the words rising from him as if they'd been born deep in his soul.

Two days ago, even a day ago, she hadn't been sure she wanted it to work. But today she did. Not because of the baseball glove, but because Michael was trying so hard, and because when she looked at him, she felt a warm, rippling sensation in her gut, a rainbow-glistening, sweetly scented, cleansing heat.

"It's going to take time," she said, her voice muted to contain the emotions churning inside her. "I don't want to rush into anything." That was a lie. She *did* want to rush into something with Michael, just as she had in San Pablo. But she was older now, and she hoped wiser. She had responsibilities. She couldn't take chances with her heart the way she could back then, when she was young and on her own and the world lay open and inviting before her.

"Then we won't rush," Michael promised. "I just want you to know where I'm going with this. I hired that detective at Finders, Keepers for a reason, Emmie. I wanted to make things right with you. I was thinking only of the past. It never occurred to me that I might belong in your life today. But I do. There's a very specific place for me here. So don't count on me leaving you."

She turned away, feeling tears burn in her eyes. She didn't want to dissolve into sobs again. One big cry every five years was enough.

In any case, these tears weren't like the ones she'd shed last night. Those had been tears of distress and fear. These were tears of hope—hope that Michael could live up to his promises, hope that after so many years her life could be made whole again. Hope that Michael could be the one to make it whole.

HE KEPT HIMSELF OCCUPIED while she gave Jeffrey his bath. She didn't know where he was—in the living room, thumbing through a magazine, or snooping in her bureau drawers, or perhaps outdoors on the patio, savoring a final glass of wine. If she didn't trust him, she'd be distracted, worrying about where he might be and what he might be up to. But she wasn't distracted or worried.

She supposed that meant she trusted him.

Jeffrey wouldn't stop talking about baseball. Seated in the center of the tub, the outlines of his legs wavering beneath the water as he created eddies and small tides with his plastic tugboat, he babbled on about his new obsession. "Adam says the Red Sox are the best team in the world, and they're cursed, too."

"Cursed?"

"It's the curse of the banana or something."

"The curse of the Bambino." She had heard her colleagues joke about that in the faculty lounge at school. "People say the Red Sox will never win the World Series because they traded Babe Ruth to the New York Yankees. Ever since then, the team has played under a curse. At least, that's what people say."

"What does bananas have to do with it?"

"Bambino. That was Babe Ruth's nickname—the Bambino."

"His name was Babe and they called him 'Bambino'?" Jeffrey found this hilarious. He laughed uproariously, capsized his tugboat and scooped a double-handful of water out of the tub, letting it spill onto his head. Once the water had run off, leaving his hair plastered to his scalp, he gazed up at Emmie in wonder. "How do you know that?"

"I know a few things," she said.

"About baseball?"

"Yes." She knew *very* few things about baseball, but apparently what little she knew was enough to impress her son. His eyes were bright with awe. Taking advantage of his reverent regard, she grabbed the washcloth and swiped under his chin, scrubbing away the rings of dirt that settled into the creases of his neck.

He squealed. "Don't do that! It tickles!"

"Well, you're clean. And if you stay in there much longer, you just might turn into a pickle." Usually she liked him to soak in the tub for as long as possible, but not tonight. Not when she knew Michael was somewhere in her house, waiting for her.

She wrapped Jeffrey in a fleecy towel as soon as he climbed out of the tub, turning the act of drying him off into an excuse to hug him. "So, you had fun playing ball today, didn't you?" she said, kneeling in front of him and pulling her arms around him to dry his back.

"Yup! I'm gonna be a baseball player when I grow up, Mommy. I want to be in Fenway Park, and nobody better call me 'Babe.'"

"Sounds like a plan." She handed him his pajamas, then released the stopper in the tub and sponged down the sides.

Emerging from the steamy bathroom, she spotted Michael down the hall in the living room, staring out the window at the front yard. He seemed lost in his thoughts, so she didn't interrupt him. She longed to know what he was thinking, what he was feeling. Was he sure he wanted to stick around and make this thing work, or was he wondering if he'd gotten in over his head and promised more than he could deliver? Was he thinking that contributing the down payment to the purchase of her house had been enough and he should cut out before he got sucked in?

Or was he deciding that he was truly over his past, that the nightmare he'd lived five years ago no longer cast a shadow into his future? That he was healed and ready to move forward—and that moving forward would bring him back to Emmie?

Jeffrey broke into Emmie's musings. "Will you make Eeyore's voice?"

"Of course. I always make Eeyore's voice." She followed him into his bedroom, leaving Michael to gaze out the window into the dim dusk light.

She read to Jeffrey, monitored him while he brushed his teeth, then tucked him into bed. It occurred to her, as she nuzzled her son's clean, soft cheek with a kiss, that Michael could never take Jeffrey away from her. He could only enhance her closeness with him and make it even more precious.

She turned off the lamp, switched on the night-light and left Jeffrey's room. Michael was where she'd last seen him, in the living room, assessing the view from the window. "I'm sorry that took so long," she apologized, realizing her evening rituals with Jeffrey had consumed nearly an hour.

Michael turned and smiled. His eyes were somber, reflecting the depth of his thoughts. "No apology necessary."

"There's a lot of work involved in raising a young boy," she said, almost as a warning. She couldn't have faith in Michael's commitment unless she was positive he knew what he was committing himself to.

He seemed to understand what she was saying. "I'm flexible. And I'm a good learner." He crossed the room to her, his enigmatic smile still in place. "This is a good house. I'm glad you'll get to stay here."

"I'm glad, too. Thank you for making it possible."

He laughed. "What's going on, Emmie? First you're apologizing, then you're saying thank you. Is this the etiquette hour?"

She would have laughed, also, except that her emotions were too tangled for laughter. "I'm trying to learn how to be with you again," she said. "My mother always told me courtesy was the best way to deal with a situation."

"You're still a daughter of the South," he joked, but there was a serious undertone to his voice. He closed the space between them and planted his hands on her shoulders. "We don't have a situation, Emmie."

"We don't?" He was so close to her, not the way he'd been close to her yesterday when she'd bawled like a baby in his arms, but close as a man to a woman, close in a way that felt like a very dangerous, intriguing situation indeed. "What do we have?" she asked, peering up at him.

"Each other," he answered, then lowered his mouth to hers.

She tried to remember the first time he'd kissed her in San Pablo, in that alcove near the plaza at the center of town. She tried to remember if his kiss had inundated her with sensation the way this one did, if the persuasion and possession of it had sent currents of heat and need spinning through her entire body, making her ache, making her feel weak and powerful all at once.

It didn't matter what that first kiss had been like. They'd been different people five years ago, younger, wilder, freer to take chances and seize opportunities. Yet she felt just as free now, just as willing to take a chance.

She parted her lips to welcome him. He accepted her invitation, thrusting his tongue into her mouth, conquering it with deep, greedy strokes. He moved his hands around her shoulders to her back and pulled her tightly to himself. She felt his palms flat against her shoulder blades, then sliding down to her waist, to her hips and up again, roaming all over her back, exploring, claiming.

She hadn't been touched like this in such a long time. She'd met a few men, dated a few, but none had made her feel this way, delicate and strong and womanly all at once. None of those men had been Michael.

His hands continued their journey, rounding her bottom and pressing her to him, then gliding to the outer surfaces of her thighs, up past her hips to her waist, higher under her arms so his thumbs could brush the swells of her breasts. She wanted to pull away so he could caress more of her, but she wanted

the closeness of him, too, the sleek warmth of his
chest against hers, the solidity of his shoulders, the
hardness of his arousal evident through his jeans and
her skirt as he pressed into her.

She wanted him. She wanted his body, his love.
She wanted his promises. She wanted to feel whole.
Jeffrey wasn't enough to make her life complete, she
acknowledged with a wistful resignation. She hadn't
felt complete in five years. But now she had Michael.

I don't want to rush into anything. Her words echoed in her mind, haunting, nagging. She wanted so
much—but she didn't want to be a fool. She didn't
want to get hurt. She didn't want to jeopardize what
she had, even if it wasn't complete.

She wanted to trust Michael, but he hadn't earned
her trust yet.

"Michael?" Her voice sounded strange to her,
her lips tingling, her tongue thick and sluggish, as
if reluctant to waste energy talking when it could
instead be gliding over Michael's, venturing into his
mouth and feeling him groan.

He sighed, a hint of surrender in the sound. He
let his hands drift back to the safer territory of her
shoulders and rested his cheek against her brow.
"You want me to leave," he guessed. She felt the
rough texture of his jaw, a day's growth of beard
scratching her forehead as he spoke.

"I don't want you to leave," she murmured. "But
I think you should."

"Okay." He held her for a minute longer, then
relented, letting his arms drop to his sides and taking
a step back. She risked a glance at his face and was
shaken by the raw hunger she saw there, the mes-

merizing darkness of his eyes, the sharp line of his
nose, the dazzling curve of his lips, not a smile so
much as a question.

She knew what he was asking. She knew he already knew the answer. Yes, she wanted him, as
much as he wanted her. But she wasn't sure of him,
not yet. She wasn't going to make the same mistake
she'd made with him last time.

He nodded, as though to acknowledge her tacit
answer, then took another step back and turned to
face the door. His steps seemed labored, as if he
were fighting against the impulse to return to her
side, but he honored her request and kept going until
he had his hand on the latch. "Say good-night to
Jeffrey for me," he said, then swung open the door
and strode out, apparently counting on momentum
to get him away from her.

She released a broken breath, which was followed
by a small, dazed laugh. It didn't matter that Jeffrey
would be fast asleep by now; that Michael had remembered him was a minor miracle. And she didn't
really mind that Michael hadn't also wished her a
good-night. He probably knew that as long as they
weren't going to spend it together, their night
wouldn't be good.

She chastised herself for that absurd thought. She
hadn't pined for Michael five years ago, and she
wasn't going to pine for him now. She was going
to sweep the kitchen, review her lesson plan for tomorrow, take a shower and get some sleep.

She swept. She went over her notes. She tiptoed
into Jeffrey's room and pressed a kiss to the crown
of his head as he clung to Teddy and Frumpy and
snored contentedly. Then she retired to her own bed-

room, where she stripped off her clothes and stepped into a hot shower. Maybe she ought to have taken a cold one, but she needed the heat more than she needed to douse the embers that continued to smolder inside her, still glowing from Michael's kiss. She hoped the steaming water would relax her, massage her flesh, tranquilize her twitching nerves, soothe her yearning heart. She washed her hair and remembered the sensation of his breath ruffling the strands. She felt the shampoo suds slide down her back and remembered his hands following the same route along her spine, down to the hollow of her waist.

She mustn't be reckless. Not this time. She was a mature woman. She desired Michael because she hadn't been with a man in far too long, and she knew he was a wonderful lover, both fierce and sensitive, daring and tender—the most magnificent man she'd ever been with, even if he'd broken her heart.

She was too smart to let her heart get broken again.

She rinsed her hair, then shut off the shower and scrubbed herself dry with a towel. She moved briskly, calmly, doing her impersonation of a smart, mature woman. She brushed out her hair, blow-dried it, pulled her nightgown from the hook behind the door and put it on. She cleaned her teeth and rubbed a moisturizing lotion onto her hands. Then she reentered her bedroom.

Her bedside clock read ten-thirty. She was tired. She climbed into bed, set the alarm for tomorrow morning and shut off the lamp.

The room was eerily dark and still. Through the open window she heard a faint breeze ruffling the new spring leaves. Maybe it wasn't leaves, she thought whimsically—maybe it was the monster in the tree, stirring to life.

She closed her eyes and waited for sleep to come. Her nightgown bunched around her legs. When she tried to adjust it, it pinched at her neck. She lifted her hips, smoothed out the gauzy white cotton and settled back into the mattress.

The pillow felt as if it was stuffed with pebbles. She sensed every lump, every strange bulge. She sat up, punched the pillow into shape, lay back down and then had to lift her hips and smooth out her nightgown again.

Her toes were cold.

She groaned. There was nothing wrong with her toes, nothing wrong with the pillow or her night-gown or anything else but herself. She wasn't going to get any sleep tonight, not when her body wanted Michael. Not when her heart wanted him even more.

Yet if she was foolish enough to try to get him to come back, she wouldn't be able to. She didn't know where he was staying in town. Some hotel…hadn't the baby-sitter mentioned where he was staying? The day he'd shown up in town, Claire had been here with Jeffrey and Adam, and she'd spirited the boys inside to keep them away from Michael. But she'd jotted down where Michael was staying on the message pad next to the phone in the kitchen. Emmie had thrown out the note.

Unable to stop herself, she tossed back the blanket and stalked down the hall in her bare feet. When she snapped on the kitchen light her eyes burned from the glare, but a few blinks soothed them. She grabbed the notepad. Claire's message was gone, but its imprint remained on the new top sheet.

Emmie tilted it against the light. "Holiday Inn," she read.

This was insane. She should just go back to bed. If she couldn't sleep, she could at least try to get some rest. She mustn't be reckless. If she and Michael were destined to build a new relationship from the remnants of their old one, it would take time. She could be patient.

As she recited that sensible lecture in her mind, her hands hauled down the telephone directory from the shelf. She riffled through the pages until she found the listing for Wilborough's Holiday Inn. *Be smart,* she told herself. *You don't want to rush into anything. You know you don't.*

She dialed the number.

Hang up, Emmie. Take your time. Get to know him better. Make sure you're sure.

A clerk answered the phone. "Please connect me with Michael Molina's room," Emmie requested.

He's going to turn your life upside down. He did it before and he'll do it again, even worse this time. This time you've got Jeffrey to think of. You have to be strong for Jeffrey. You have to play it safe.

"Hello?"

Michael's voice silenced the nattering voice inside her skull. Her mind went blank, then filled again with an image of him, the sheer male presence of him, the implacable demands of her soul for him.

"Come," she said.

CHAPTER THIRTEEN

SHE'D SAID SHE DIDN'T want to rush into anything. But his mind and body were begging him to rush. He felt like a kid facing his very first time, anxious and excited but afraid to linger, because if the lady in question had a minute to think it over she might change her mind.

"Come," Emmie had said. Just that one word.

She wasn't going to change her mind, not about this.

It took all his willpower not to break every speed limit between his hotel room and her house. He needed not to rush—not only when he arrived at her house but now, closing the distance between them. This wasn't about sex, he knew. It was about Emmie's decision to trust him, and about his resolution to live up to her trust.

This was it. He could never betray her again. No matter what happened to him, what he stumbled into, what disasters befell him, he could never, ever leave her after this, because if he left her he would destroy himself even more than her.

A single light glowed above her door, a beacon guiding him where he needed to be. He pulled into the driveway, parked and walked one painstakingly controlled step at a time when all he wanted was to sprint across her lawn. As he reached the front step, the door swung open.

She stood framed in the doorway, clad only in a white nightgown of some diaphanous material. He saw the shadow of her body through the cloth, her long legs and narrow waist, her breasts taut against the fabric, already aroused. Her eyes were round with what he interpreted as panic, but she pushed open the storm door and let him inside.

They stood in the entry, illuminated only by the glow of the light above the front door. He heard her deep breaths and his own. He heard his heart pounding, and he believed that if he listened carefully he'd be able to hear hers, too.

"Are you sure?" he finally asked.

She nodded. That would have to be enough.

He took her in his arms and lowered his mouth to hers. He felt certainty in her kiss, in the possessive strength of her arms around him, in the wild yearning of her lips, her tongue. He felt it in the heat of her body pressing into his. He was hotter than she was. He was burning up, right there in her doorway.

He kicked the door shut, then scooped her into his arms. She looped her arms around his neck and continued to kiss him, her hair spilling over his arm and her bare feet bumping against his hip. Her house was dark except for the night-light spilling a velvet-soft amber glow through Jeffrey's open door.

Michael wondered whether they should close it. He didn't know. He had never made love to a mother before.

Emmie would have shut the door if she'd felt it

necessary. He continued down the hall to the room at the end—her bedroom.

Like the rest of the house it was dark, except for the angular red digits of her alarm clock and the moonlight tracing shimmering silver outlines along her furniture. His eyes were accustomed to the dark, and he could see that her modest double bed had been slept in—or, more likely, tossed and turned in. The sheets were rumpled, the blanket thrown back, the pillows lopsided. Just like his bed back at the hotel.

He lowered her onto the mattress, then stretched out beside her. Her fingers scrambled over the buttons of his shirt, yanking them free. Every time she skimmed his chest with her hand he felt his temperature soar higher. He wanted to tear the damned shirt off and let her touch him, really touch him, not accidentally glance off his skin.

I don't want to rush, she'd said just a few hours ago in her kitchen. God, but he wanted to rush. He wanted her to want to rush. He wanted her naked, but to remove her nightgown would require him to lift himself off her, and that would mean she would stop touching him.

Rush, he thought, gathering handfuls of her nightgown and tugging it up over her hips. *I've waited years for this. I want to rush.*

At last his shirt was completely undone. He released her long enough to slide it off and toss it onto the floor. Then he went back to her nightgown, eased it up over her breasts, over her head, and hurled it in the vicinity of his shirt.

She was so beautiful. The moonlight now outlined her—her slender throat, her smooth shoulders, her creamy skin. Her breasts were fuller than he'd re-membered, the nipples darker. Because of Jeffrey, he guessed. That little boy had changed everything.

Would her body feel the same? he wondered. Would it respond as it had before? It wasn't the same body he'd loved five years ago. She had car-ried a life inside it, nurtured and protected his son in her womb. He skimmed his hand down to her belly, wishing he could feel the difference through her flesh, a mystical warmth where his child had lived for nine months.

All he felt was Emmie, soft and smooth. He slid his hands back up to her breasts, stroking them, then kissing them. He took one swollen nipple into his mouth and wondered if she had nourished his son this way. Did she understand that right now she was nourishing Michael?

She shifted restlessly beneath him, her hands ranging across his back, down to the waistband of his jeans, up again and down, her fingers pinching the denim in apparent frustration. He knew she wanted him to take the jeans off—hell, he wanted them off, too—but he couldn't stop kissing her breast, rubbing that soft, sweet nub with his tongue, sucking on it and hearing her gasp.

"Michael," she whispered. The first word she'd uttered since he'd entered her house: his name. For that alone he would stop kissing her long enough to finish undressing.

He had brought protection with him. That morn-ing, in a moment of defiant optimism, he'd stopped into a drugstore and bought a package between the second and third apartments he'd looked at. After tossing the box onto her night table, he stripped off his jeans and shorts and sent them onto the floor with the rest of his clothing. Then he rejoined her in the bed.

It was heaven, touching her. Heaven, feeling her hands on him, her lips, the strength of her legs weaving through his. He no longer felt like rushing, now that they were in her bed and he could actually believe she was his.

He caressed her shoulders, her sides, her abdomen. He strummed his fingers down her legs and up again, rolled her onto her stomach and grazed a path along her spine. He had never lost his astonishment at how soft a woman's body could be, how delicate her bones could feel beneath her skin. Even a slim woman like Emmie had heft in places—the roundness of her bottom, the gentle curves of her thighs. He had always adored the female body—but Emmie's body more than any other. And Emmie tonight more than he'd ever adored her before.

She turned back to face him, her gaze imploring. As he propped himself above her, she ran her hands down his chest to his groin, molded her fingers around him. He closed his eyes to savor the friction of her strokes, then opened them again. He wanted to see her, wanted to read in her face how much she wanted him, how ready she was for him.

He moved between her legs, caressing her, feeling her dampness. She arched against him and moaned impatiently, but still he watched her face, wanting to see it in her mouth and her eyes, wanting to hear it in the rhythm of her breath.

"Michael," she whispered again, "Michael..." And his heart broke a little because she was so open to him, because her trust moved him more than he could have imagined.

He reached for the packet, grabbed a sheath and readied himself. Then he pressed into her, trying not to rush—but oh, she felt so good. So hot and tight, so right. His heart broke a little more, just from the pleasure of it.

She relaxed, seemingly satisfied finally to have him inside her. He rocked her slowly, surprisingly relaxed himself. Minutes ago, driving over to her house, he'd felt his urges storming inside him, threatening to tear him apart, but now that he was here, now that their bodies were locked intimately together and he saw a dazed, blissful smile shaping her lips, he stopped feeling so frenzied. This was theirs for as long as they could make it last. If he rushed it would end sooner, so he wasn't going to rush.

Loving her was like a dance—one where he was graceful and able, where he knew all the steps. He and Emmie moved like silk and sinew, like fire and love, burning higher with each surge, giving more to each other, taking more. Beyond them only the night existed, dark and silent.

She drew her legs around his waist, gripped his shoulders with her hands, and the smile faded from her lips. He kissed her and she groaned, clinging to him. Realizing how close she was made him want to let go, but he waited, bringing her along, holding back until she was there.

Heaven, he thought as he thrust one final time, sinking onto her and letting the sensation sweep through him.

For a long time they lay quietly, their limbs entwined, their hearts pounding and their breath coming in ragged bursts. He felt Emmie's hands floating vaguely over his back and combing into his hair. He was too tired to move. Too happy.

Then she spoke again. "Michael."

"Yes." It occurred to him that he might be crushing her, and he raised himself on his hands. "Are you okay?"

Her eyes glistened. "I want this to work," she said, her voice hushed and throaty.

"It will," he promised.

"I'm scared."

"Don't be." How could he be so positive? They'd never really had a regular courtship. They'd never built a relationship the normal way, taking their time, getting to know each other. All they had between them was a brief, almost unreal stretch of time in San Pablo and five years of sorrow, disappointment and loneliness. And now this: a night in a charming ranch house on a half-acre plot in the suburbs, with a child fast asleep just down the hall. Their child.

Why was he making such crazy promises?

Because the alternative—losing Emmie—was unbearable.

"We'll make it work," he vowed. He settled on the bed beside her, pulling her against him and wrapping his arms around her. Her hair smelled of lavender. Her skin smelled only of her, a salty, musky scent that turned him on all over again.

They had all night. He wasn't going to rush, not anymore. If he was going to make this work, he was going to have to do it right—slowly, gradually, becoming a father as he became Emmie's lover and partner.

Her respiration grew deeper, more regular, and her hand moved in a gentle pattern against his side. Yes, he would make this work. But he had to admit that he was as scared as she was.

TWO DAYS LATER, he moved into their house.

He'd been looking at apartments for rent, but Emmie just didn't see the point in that. He wanted to be a part of their family, and she wanted him to. And it wasn't a huge move. He wasn't bringing furniture with him—in fact, all he had was a single suitcase, his laptop and a few folders of notes. The day after he moved in, he purchased a printer-fax machine—a remarkable extravagance, she thought, but one he said he would need if he was going to keep up with his work.

It amazed her that he needed so little: just a few changes of clothing, a computer and a printer-fax. But when she thought about it, she realized that what he really needed was nothing he could pack in a bag or a box and move into the spare bedroom. What he needed was already in her house: her and Jeffrey.

"I still feel awkward with him," he complained one evening after she'd put Jeffrey to bed and then joined Michael out on the back patio for an icy lemonade.

"It takes more than a few days to build a relationship," she reminded him. The night was balmy, heavy with a premonition of summer. The grass smelled like summer, too, green and tangy. The foliage on the trees was thickening. In just a few

weeks the school term would be over—and this
year, maybe she wouldn't have to do any private
tutoring. One summer-school class would tide her
over, now that Michael was available to help out
with her finances.

She was growing dependent on him, and it
alarmed her. She depended on him to keep her
budget from collapsing into debt, and to share adult
conversations with, and to hold her at night. Before
he'd come back into her life, finances had been her
biggest worry—and yet of all the needs he met, the
financial support struck her as the least important.
Even the sex, while splendid, wasn't the best thing
about having him around.

It was the conversations. She loved talking to him.
She hadn't realized how much she'd been craving
adult company. Jeffrey was still the center of her
universe, but it was so gratifying, after listening to
one of his long-winded descriptions of a Matchbox
car crash at school or Adam's disgusting lunches or,
more often now, the significance of the Red Sox in
the grand scheme of things, to be able to unwind
with Michael over a glass of wine or a soft drink
and talk about the day's newspaper stories or her
concerns about a student, or the latest policy pro-
posal the Oak Hill School principal had cooked up.
Or Michael's work. He didn't talk about it much,
but what little he shared fascinated her. He was currently working out a strategy for a California firm
that wanted to market its snack-food product in
Latin America. Michael was writing a report on how
to approach the import officers in each of three
countries, how to get the U.S. ambassadors involved, which markets showed the most promise

and which were better avoided. "Lots of money exchanges hands in these deals," he told Emmie. "One of my jobs is to make sure the executives I'm working for are getting the money into the right hands."

She felt as if a room had been opened in her brain, one locked for five years. It was musty and dusty, but Michael had shoved open the window and let in the sun-brightened air. Emmie could talk about grown-up things with a grown-up, and it was invigorating.

So she was delighting in adult conversation. But the novelty in Michael's life—juvenile conversations with Jeffrey—was apparently not so invigorating. "All he wants to talk about is baseball," Michael complained. "I feel like I've unleashed a monster."

Emmie chuckled and propped her bare feet up on the picnic-table bench. "The only monster he knows about is the Green Monster," she said, using the nickname of the green outfield wall in Fenway Park. "He used to be friends with an invisible monster in that tree over there—" she gestured toward the crab-apple tree "—but now all he thinks about is baseball."

"Is it me, then? Do you think if I left he would find something else to talk about?"

She shot him a quick look. Did he want to leave? Did he think Jeffrey's obsession with baseball was bad? "Kids sometimes get fixated on things. It will pass."

Michael used his finger to trace a line in the condensation misting the surface of his glass. "I want to talk to him about other things. I want to get to know him, but I just don't feel it's happening. Maybe…'' He measured her with his gaze. ''Maybe if I told him I was his father—''

''No,'' she said quickly.

Michael frowned. ''I don't see why you're so dead set against it. He sees me here all the time now. I'm at the table for breakfast. I'm there for dinner. I've got my work set up in the spare bedroom. He's probably figured out where I'm sleeping.''

''He doesn't know what our sleeping arrangements mean,'' she argued, then took a deep breath. She knew it was too soon to tell Jeffrey that Michael was his father. What she didn't know was *why* it was too soon. She just knew it was.

If she told Michael it was because she still didn't trust him, he would be hurt. And she wasn't sure that was the real reason anyway. She did trust him. She wouldn't have let him move into her house if she didn't.

She trusted him because she wanted to, because trusting him brought so much joy into her life— because it brought *him* into her life and kept him there. She had decided she was prepared to risk her heart on him. But Jeffrey… She wasn't going to take risks with her son's heart.

''You're too impatient, Michael,'' she finally said, then sipped some lemonade to cool her throat. ''Everything will come in its time.''

''You're afraid for him to know, aren't you?'' he said.

She took another long sip, trying not to react visibly to the accuracy of his guess. ''I'm afraid for us all,'' she admitted. ''Something terrible happened to you five years ago.'' Closing her eyes, she pictured the scar on his shoulder. The first time they'd made love, she'd felt it with her fingertips. The following morning, she'd seen it with her eyes. It wasn't big or ugly, but it was there, a permanent reminder that violence had torn Michael from her, and torn him apart inside.

"Do you think something terrible will happen to me again?" he asked. "Do I have a target on my back?"

"You made choices," she reminded him. "You weren't just an innocent target. You made choices, and what happened to you was a result of that."

"I'm making different choices now."

She sighed. "If it works out, we'll tell Jeffrey. Please give me enough time to be sure."

"All right," Michael said, relenting. She knew he wasn't pleased, but he was backing off to show his respect for her—or else because he didn't feel like arguing. He rose from his chair, moved behind her and placed his hands on her shoulders, his thumbs digging into her nape. "Just tell me how to talk to him," he asked as he massaged the taut muscles at the base of her skull. "Tell me what to say so I don't feel so out of my depth with him."

"As long as you talk about baseball, he'll be happy."

Michael snorted. "What else does he talk about? With you, I mean."

She sighed again, this time from pleasure, and bowed her head so he could dig deeper with his fingertips. "Things he'd never talk to you about," she said, trying to keep her mind focused on the conversation while her body melted into a deeply relaxed state.

"Like what?"

"Like things that frighten him. Or classmates who bother him."

"Why can't he talk to me about those things?"

"He hardly knows you, Michael. And anyway, you're a man. He idolizes you. He's not going to tell you he's afraid of lightning."

"Is he?"

"Yes. But don't tell him I told you."

Michael pressed his fingers into her shoulders, working out the knots. "When I was a kid, I was afraid of lightning, too."

"Really?"

"I told my father."

"And what did he do?"

Michael's hands went still, and his voice sounded colder when he said, "He told me I was a big boy and I ought to act like one. He told me only babies were afraid of lightning." He resumed rubbing her shoulders, more gently this time, apparently distracted by his memory. "I wouldn't do that to Jeffrey."

"He doesn't know that. He doesn't know you well enough to trust you with his fears."

"That's my point. How can I get him to know me well enough?"

"Be patient, Michael," she repeated, pushing herself to her feet and facing him. "You want too much."

"Yes," he agreed, then hugged her close and kissed her lips. "I want too much," he whispered.

THE WEATHER TURNED HOT and thick, a premature taste of summer. All weekend, the air was muggy and stagnant and dense clouds slid across the sky. Michael spent both days with Jeffrey and Emmie, observing their interplay, envying the ease with which they talked and joked with each other. Emmie was right, of course—Michael couldn't expect to build a rapport with the boy instantly, especially since he knew so little about kids to begin with.

But he wanted it.

Saturday morning, they went to the supermarket together. Emmie had warned Michael that the outing wouldn't be fun, but he'd insisted on accompanying them, determined to learn everything he could about Jeffrey. What he learned in the Super Stop-&-Shop was that Jeffrey took delight in darting up and down the crowded aisles, scooping junk food and cookies from the shelves and tossing them into Emmie's cart, whereupon she would pluck Jeffrey's contributions out of the pile and replace them on the shelves. "Why don't you strap him into the seat?" Michael suggested, noticing that other people had their children secured in the wagon seats.

"He hates it," Emmie said. "He's gotten too big to fit in comfortably."

"Well, he shouldn't be running around like that. He'll get hurt, or hurt someone else."

Emmie shot him a look of annoyance. "Thanks for the input. Maybe you'd like to chase after him and hold his hand while I finish shopping."

Michael caught up with Jeffrey in the deli aisle. At the end of the aisle stood a murky tank of water with live lobsters lolling inside. "Look," Michael said, figuring the ugly blue creatures would interest Jeffrey. "See the lobsters?"

Jeffrey was underwhelmed. "I wanna go see the Red Sox."

"We're in the supermarket now," Michael said unnecessarily.

"I wanna go to Fenway Park," Jeffrey said, just as unnecessarily.

The shopping took an hour. "Saturday's always the worst day to shop," Emmie muttered as they waited in an interminable line to pay for their groceries. "Everyone who works during the week comes here on Saturday."

Michael nodded. Not just everyone who worked during the week was there, but most of them seemed to have brought an obstreperous child or two with them. He recalled his shock the afternoon he'd entered Jeffrey's preschool. Why were kids so noisy? Why did they shriek when talking in a normal voice would be much more effective? Children never shrieked in his neighborhood when he was growing up. All the kids used to hang out outdoors, playing games like baseball or pickup basketball that didn't require shrieking. When they got older, they kept their voices down, maintaining a low profile so their elders wouldn't catch them sneaking smokes in the far corner of the playground. By the time they were teenagers, their cars were much louder than they were.

He wanted to connect with Jeffrey. He also wanted to teach the boy how to turn down the volume, or else to teach himself how to tolerate the kid's high-decibel energy. As Emmie deftly negotiated the crowded parking lot with her shopping cart and her rambunctious son, he acknowledged how very much he had to learn about being a parent.

Maybe she was right not to want Jeffrey to know he
was Jeffrey's father yet—not because he had any
intention of abandoning them, but because it might
be easier for Jeffrey to accept him as a dad if he
was a bit more at home in the role.

In the afternoon, they attended a free movie at the
town library, and in the evening dinner at a restaurant that featured pizza and an indoor play area for
children. The pizza was mediocre and the noise level
in the room was nerve shattering. Michael began to
wonder if Emmie had plotted this day for the specific purpose of making him go deaf.

He did his best to smile. He gamely ate his pizza
and watched as Jeffrey scampered through the maze
of tubes and slides and ladders in the play area. He
visualized the bottle of aspirin in his toiletries bag
back at Emmie's house and imagined swallowing
two pills, or maybe four, or a dozen—whatever it
took to make the throbbing between his temples
fade.

"Is this a test?" he asked Emmie at one point,
having to shout above the din.

"A test?" She pulled a string of mozzarella from
her plate and popped it into her mouth. "What do
you mean?"

"Baptism by fire. You dragged me through the
supermarket and made me sit through *Mary Pop-
pins,* and now this. Is it a test, to see if I can stand
living with Jeffrey?"

She smiled uncertainly. "This is what living with
Jeffrey is like," she said. She didn't seem to be
shouting at all, yet he had no trouble hearing her.
"Do you think you can't stand it?"

"It's…too loud," he said.

Her smile relaxed slightly. "Children are loud." She reached across the table and patted his hand. "Don't expect everything to happen at once, Michael. You'll get used to it if you want to. If you don't…" She let her hand come to rest on the table barely an inch from his, but that inch felt like a mile. "If you don't want to get used to it, you won't."

"I want to," he assured her, trying to persuade himself, as well. He had to want this. Jeffrey was his son. "Maybe if I could just have a little time with him on my own—away from circuses like this," he added, gesturing toward the maniacal children squawking and giggling and dangling by their knees from the bars of the climbing apparatus in the center of the restaurant. "The only thing he wants to talk about with me is baseball. Maybe I could take him to a ball game."

Emmie looked intrigued but mildly doubtful. "Just by yourself?"

"Him and me. No screaming kids."

"Just screaming adults," she joked, although she still appeared dubious. Then she shrugged. "If you want to give it a try…"

He bought Red Sox tickets for Wednesday night. Just two, for him and Jeffrey. He asked if Emmie would go with them, but she declined.

"It's hot and sticky out," she said. The heat wave had continued, giving the region an August feel although June was still days away. "And I'm really not that big a baseball fan. Besides, this is your chance to go one-on-one with him."

He wasn't ready to go one-on-one with Jeffrey. What, other than baseball, would they talk about? Would he have to listen to one of Jeffrey's inter-

minable monologues about toy-car collisions at
school? What if he started to whine? What if he
cried for his mother?

Obviously Emmie trusted Michael enough to let
him solo with Jeffrey. Or else maybe she trusted
Jeffrey not to fall apart with Michael. In either case,
she was revealing a degree of trust he took pride in,
even though he spent most of Wednesday worrying
about how the evening would go.

Emmie seemed utterly calm as she waved them
off at around five that evening. She'd armed Michael
with a map and handwritten directions to Fenway
Park, told them to have fun and walked blithely into
the house as Michael backed down the driveway to
the street. She was probably thrilled to be done with
them for a while, Michael thought churlishly. She
would have a tranquil dinner, then relax with a book
or a good TV show and not give a thought to Michael for the evening.

It was his own impatience that had led to this, he
conceded, glancing over his shoulder at Jeffrey, who
sat strapped in his booster in the center of the backseat, wearing his Red Sox cap and clutching his
baseball glove. "Is Mo Vaughn gonna be there?"
he asked.

"Maybe." Who the hell knew if Mo Vaughn
would be there? Who knew how Jeffrey might react
if he wasn't? Michael struggled to think of something else to discuss, something that wasn't baseball.
"Do you like hotdogs?"

"Nope."

Great. What was he going to buy Jeffrey to eat?

"Are you too hot?" Emmie had insisted that Jeffrey wear long pants, despite the muggy afternoon.

She'd predicted that once the sun set the temperature would drop.

"Nope."

"We're going to be out past your bedtime," Michael continued valiantly. "Does that bother you?"

"Nope."

He gave up. "So, I bet you're looking forward to seeing Mo Vaughn."

And Jeffrey was off, chattering nonstop about Mo Vaughn and the Red Sox and the curse of the banana, whatever that was.

The stadium was pretty full for a weeknight, but not packed. Michael was glad. He didn't want Jeffrey to be surrounded by rowdy yahoos drinking beer and making fools of themselves. A vendor approached, and Michael bought a bag of popcorn and a bottle of water for Jeffrey, who sat forward in his seat, his eyes as round as soup bowls as he surveyed the illuminated field. "Which one's Mo Vaughn?" he asked. "You think someone's gonna hit a ball over here? I could catch it if they did. I brought my glove."

Michael settled in for a long night. While Jeffrey ran at the mouth, Michael occasionally answered his questions about what was going on down on the field, but mostly he meditated on the demands of paternity. He'd never thought it would be easy, but he'd always assumed, on the basis of absolutely no experience, that when you became a father, parenting skills blossomed naturally inside you. He had never thought he'd have to work at them and exert himself to be a dad. Then again, he hadn't given much thought to being a dad at all. It had been a remote idea, strictly hypothetical.

There was nothing hypothetical about Jeffrey. He was warm and squirming next to Michael, smelling of popcorn and butter, sticky from the ice-cream pop Michael later bought him, sweaty from the heat and wired from the excitement. He was a real boy, and when Michael wasn't suffering from abject dread about his ability to fulfill his role as a father, he was proud to think he'd had something, however trivial, to do with the creation of such a lively, cheerful, relentlessly noisy boy.

"Who's that guy? Who's that one?" Jeffrey asked, pointing all around the field. "Which one's the pitcher? I wanna be a pitcher when I grow up."

The game ended with a Red Sox win. Jeffrey left the stadium toting a pennant, the half box of popcorn he'd been unable to eat, the bottle from his water, a souvenir program and his glove. Although it was after ten, he was revved up, not the least bit sleepy. The air carried the scent of auto fumes and city grime mixed with the sour aroma of impending rain.

"That was fun!" Jeffrey exclaimed, skipping because he apparently had too much energy to walk. "It was cool. When that guy slid into second, that was so cool. I wanna slide. Will you teach me how to slide, Michael?"

"When you're a little older," Michael promised. Unlike Jeffrey, he was tired. He wished he didn't have a half-hour drive ahead of him. He wasn't in any danger of falling asleep at the wheel, but he knew Jeffrey would babble the whole way home, and the prospect didn't thrill him. A man could be proud of his paternity and fatigued by it at the same time.

He had just unlocked the car doors when a clap of thunder shook the air. Jeffrey had been in the middle of an oration on the excitement of sliding, but the rumble rattling the sky caused him to freeze and gasp.

"Get in the car," Michael urged him, swinging the door open as the first fat drops of rain splattered onto the ground. He helped Jeffrey into his seat, strapped the seat belt on and then slipped in behind the wheel less than a second before the skies opened up. "Wow," he said as the windshield turned into a sheet of water. "That was good timing."

Jeffrey said nothing.

Michael ignited the engine and flipped on the headlights. Their white beams cut through the downpour, illuminating the rain so it looked like dense silver threads. As he navigated through the crowded lot to the street, a flash of lightning lit the sky, followed by another rumble of thunder.

"Lucky this didn't start during the game," Michael observed, switching the windshield wipers onto their highest speed. "They would have had a rain delay. Do you know what that means?"

Not a word from the backseat.

Stopped at a red light, he peered over his shoulder. Jeffrey's eyes were as round as they'd been at the stadium, but this time they glowed with unadulterated terror. He was afraid of lightning, Emmie had told Michael.

"Lightning used to scare me when I was your age," Michael said.

Jeffrey didn't speak.

"I used to run into the bedroom I shared with my brother and hide under the covers."

The wipers clacked rapidly back and forth.

"I didn't want to come out until the lightning stopped. It really scared me."

Finally, in a tiny voice, Jeffrey asked, "Was your brother scared, too?"

Michael felt something pierce his heart, as sharp and hot as a needle, locating the most tender spot and stabbing it clear through. "My brother wasn't scared of anything," he admitted. "And that wasn't good. Sometimes being scared is the right thing to be."

"It's good to be scared of lightning, isn't it?" Jeffrey asked, barely audible beneath the drumming of the raindrops on the roof of the car.

"It's better to be scared of lightning than not to be scared of anything," Michael assured him.

"Yeah," Jeffrey agreed. He said it in less than a whisper, but Michael heard. The next time he had to stop for traffic, he glanced back again. Jeffrey no longer appeared aghast. A few minutes later, another glance informed Michael that Jeffrey had fallen asleep.

Hours of baseball hadn't accomplished as much as a single bolt of lightning, Michael realized. But that bolt of lightning had accomplished everything he'd hoped for and more.

Teaching your son that it was all right to be afraid sometimes—*that* was what fatherhood was all about.

CHAPTER FOURTEEN

"MAX GALLARD IS IN TOWN."

Michael tossed this news out so casually Emmie wasn't sure she'd heard him correctly. He and Jeffrey were seated at the dining-room table, hard at work solving a seventy-five-piece jigsaw puzzle. Actually, Jeffrey was hard at work. Michael seemed to have limited his contribution to handing Jeffrey piece after piece.

When completed, the puzzle would depict a scene of two dinosaurs drinking from a pond edged in palm trees and ferns. Right now, the puzzle was a jumble of color—a bit of leg here, an arching neck there, a bright-green frond in the corner—interrupted by amoeba-shaped gaps where the polished maple surface of the table showed through.

Emmie stood in the kitchen doorway, having just finished grading a stack of math tests. She was grateful to Michael for occupying Jeffrey after dinner so she could get her work done. Without him, she would have played with Jeffrey until his bedtime, and only then—too late for her own well-being— would she have gotten to the folder of test papers.

But now she was done and ready to rescue Michael from his child-care responsibilities. Except that he'd just dropped this bombshell. "Max Gallard?" she repeated.

"He's in Boston."

She took a deep breath. Why on earth had the bounty hunter who'd brought such grief to her and Michael come to Boston? And if he had, why did Michael know about it? Why did he even care?

Her memories of Max Gallard were surprisingly vivid. After all this time, she would probably recognize him if she passed him on a busy street. She remembered keenly the Sunday afternoon she'd met him in San Pablo. He'd been drinking a *cerveza* at the tavern overlooking the plaza, and he'd looked tough and brawny and dangerous. She hadn't realized how dangerous he was at the time, but his appearance had provoked her.

His being in Boston, and Michael's knowledge of it, provoked her again. She pressed her hand against the doorjamb to keep from storming into the dining area and demanding an explanation from Michael. Her emotions churned, but she held them inside, hoping he'd mentioned the man only in passing, one of those "small world" coincidences.

"He'd like to see you," Michael said, shattering any hopes she'd had that Max's presence in the area didn't mean anything.

She and Michael had been doing so well, she thought disconsolately. Three weeks had passed since he'd moved in, and she could scarcely remember what life had been like without him. He fit into her life so perfectly. He made everything sweeter, richer, more intense. He gave her support when she needed it, privacy when she wanted it, and love, so much love she actually believed in it. Her doubts had thawed like ice beneath a hot sun. She'd finally come to terms with the fact that, just as he'd promised, this was going to work.

He'd made progress with Jeffrey, too. He'd learned how to relax around the boy, how to accept the relationship on Jeffrey's terms. Only about half their conversations dealt with baseball now. Emmie had even begun to contemplate a time in the not-too-distant future when she and Michael might get married and Jeffrey might learn that Michael was his father.

The future looked auspicious—but suddenly Max Gallard was in Boston, a nasty bit of the past chasing after them, twisting in on them like a snake, its fangs bared.

"I need a head," Jeffrey announced, nudging Michael's hand away from the puzzle pieces spread across the table. "Where's the head, Michael? It's a growly head, with big teeth."

"A growly head," Michael said thoughtfully, scanning the pieces.

Emmie used the distraction to retreat into the kitchen. Maybe if she pretended Michael had never brought up Max Gallard's name, he would let the matter rest.

She crossed to the kitchen table, gathered up the math tests and stashed them in her tote bag. In just two weeks the school year would be over. Perhaps she and Michael could take Jeffrey on a real vacation trip, something more exciting than a day at the beach in Rockport. They could drive up to Maine and explore the islands, or they could head west into the Berkshires and go to a concert at Tanglewood. Or take a four-day weekend on Cape Cod. They could bond as a family, all three of them, without the distractions of work and preschool.

If only Max Gallard would go away...

She glanced at the wall clock and turned back toward the dining room. "Jeffrey, it's bath time," she called from the safety of the kitchen. If she went into the dining room, Michael might mention that man's name again.

"I'm not finished yet," Jeffrey complained. "We gotta finish this puzzle. I need the growly head."

She planted her hands on her hips, as if that would lend her voice more authority. "You can finish it tomorrow. Right now, it's time to get you into the bath."

"You mean, I don't gotta clean up the table?"

"Don't *have* to. You can leave the puzzle out overnight."

"Okay," he said, so delighted to be spared the chore of cleaning up that he skipped through the kitchen, whirling past Emmie on his way to his room to get undressed.

The nightly rituals of bath time and story time consumed the next hour. Michael had indicated no interest in participating in either activity, and Emmie was glad. No matter that he had become a deeply ingrained part of their lives—bathing her son and reading to him were special activities for her and Jeffrey, and she didn't want to share them with anyone, not even Jeffrey's father.

But eventually the bath was over and Jeffrey was dried off and in his pajamas, his teeth brushed and his bladder empty. Eventually Emmie finished a chapter in *The House on Pooh Corner,* tucked him in, kissed him on the cheek and whispered that she loved him. Eventually she ran out of ways to avoid Michael.

After clicking on the night-light, she left Jeffrey's room. She found Michael in the living room, reading the sports section of the newspaper, several stuffed animals keeping him company on the sofa. He glanced up at her entrance, then stood and smiled. "Hey, there," he said in a low, sexy voice. His smile carried a hint of astonishment, as if he couldn't believe his good luck in having worked his way back into her life.

Sometimes she couldn't believe her good luck, either. But at the moment she wasn't feeling terribly lucky.

He tossed down the newspaper, stood and came to her, his arms outstretched. She moved into his embrace, wishing she could find comfort in it. They'd started the day so gloriously, she reminded herself. She'd awakened before him, eased out of his arms and propped herself up so she could study his face. In his sleep he'd been smiling, the same astonished smile he'd given her just now. She'd wondered if he'd been dreaming about their love-making. Recalling it made her smile, too—and left her astonished. Her memories of him hadn't been exaggerated. They were as good together now as she'd remembered them being then. Even better than she'd remembered.

They'd had cereal and fruit for breakfast, and then she'd left the house with Jeffrey to drop him off at Sunny Skies before she drove to the Oak Hill School. Her students had been well behaved today. Even Josh, Will and Tommy had been relatively calm, a minor miracle considering how summery the day had been. At four o'clock, she'd picked up Jeffrey, and they'd stopped at the bakery on the way home, just because it had been such a perfect day and she wanted to celebrate. She'd intended to buy a cake, but Jeffrey had insisted on cupcakes, three of them. "For me, you and Michael," he'd said simply, as if there was no question in his mind that Michael was a part of their family.

Dinner had been leisurely. Michael had had a productive day, he'd told her. Jeffrey had described the thing he'd made at preschool: "It's clay and it's suppose'ta be a baseball bat, only it looks kinda like a hotdog. I don't like hotdogs, so I'll prob'ly give it to Adam."

Why couldn't the day continue being perfect? Was that really so much to ask for?

"Can we talk about it?" Michael asked, his lips half-buried in her hair.

"Talk about what?" *Anything but Max Gallard,* she pleaded silently.

"Max Gallard." Michael loosened his embrace so he could lean back and peer into her face. "He wants to see you, Emmie."

"I don't want to see him," she said bluntly.

Michael nodded, then led her to the sofa and nudged her to sit. He pushed away Mr. Rabbit and Elmo, then lowered himself onto the cushion next to her and arched an arm around her. "I know you don't," he said. "I could read your expression, loud and clear. But think about it, Emmie, okay? He flew all the way to Boston to see you."

That startled her. She had assumed he was in town for some other reason and simply thought he'd drop by. "To see me? How did he even know I was here?"

"I've kept in touch with him over the years."

"You have? Why?"

Her question surprised him. "Why shouldn't I have kept in touch with him? We went through something significant together, Emmie. Something traumatic. He thinks I saved his life—"

"I think you did, too. I'm not sure what he did to yours, though."

"He gave me the chance to settle accounts for my brother," Michael said. His voice was even, but she had learned that when he appeared at his calmest on the surface was when his emotions were churning most violently inside, out of sight.

He twirled his fingers through her hair, collecting his thoughts before he spoke. "I told him when I began my search for you. He knew about my attempt to find you on my own, and about my hiring Maggie Tyrell at Finders, Keepers when I couldn't get anywhere with the search myself. I e-mailed him once I realized things were going to work out between us, because I knew he would want to know. And he decided to come."

What Michael had said made sense, up until the last sentence. "Why would he decide to come here?"

Michael shrugged. "I think he wants to apologize. He felt it was his fault we got separated in San Pablo—"

"It was," she interjected.

"And he wants to tell you he's sorry things went wrong then. He wants you to know how glad he is that we've gotten past it." His fingers continued to wander in her hair, twining through the strands. "We have gotten past it, haven't we?"

She was ready to say yes. Yet if she'd gotten past it, why would she be so resistant to a visit from Max Gallard?

Michael seemed to understand her hesitation. "Emmie?" he murmured.

"Yes," she forced herself to say. She loved him. She'd come to depend on him, to need him and want him and enjoy him. She thought of him as her family, and she wanted nothing to threaten the peace she'd found with him in the past few weeks.

If she honestly feared that letting Max see her could threaten that peace, how strong could her faith possibly be?

"All right," she said, then sighed and closed her eyes, resolving not to let the idea of a visit from Max bother her. "He can come and say he's sorry."

Michael pulled her snugly against him. "I love you, Emmie," he whispered.

He loved her. That alone gave her the confidence to face anything: her past, her loss, her rediscovery of Michael, of love, of the ability to trust. She supposed she could even face Max Gallard if she had to.

TWO DAYS LATER, Michael picked Max up at the commuter rail station a town away from Wilborough. Michael had seen Max a few times back in California, although Max had remained in Los Angeles, while Michael had moved north to the Bay Area. Max was no longer the husky, well-muscled iron man he'd been when Michael had known him five years ago. His wound had taken a toll on him.

He was thinner, a bit more haggard, but also calmer and more reflective. His hair was longer and generously streaked with gray, and he'd grown a stylish goatee, also well seasoned with gray.

They shook hands on the station platform, and then Max pulled Michael into an awkward hug. "You look better than I've ever seen you before," he said. "This thing is going well, huh?"

"It's going well," Michael confirmed. He could have said it was going splendidly, magnificently—he could have shouted to the skies that he and Emmie belonged together and destiny had been kind to bring them to this point after so many years. But talking about his feelings would trivialize them, so he kept it simple. "It's going real well."

"How about the kid?" Max asked as they descended the stairs to the parking lot. "What does he think of having you as his father?"

"He doesn't know yet," Michael told him. He'd mentioned Jeffrey to Max in his e-mails. Max had been sympathetic when Michael had admitted that fatherhood didn't exactly come naturally to him. "We're getting along better. It's a slow process, but it's coming. I really want to tell him the truth." Michael unlocked the car and sighed. "I want him to know, but Emmie isn't ready yet."

"Why not?"

Michael sighed again. "We screwed up bad, Max. She's skittish." He got in behind the wheel and contemplated the idea that had been lurking in his mind: that if tonight went well, if a reunion between Emmie and Max put the past to rest once and for all, she would be willing to let Michael tell Jeffrey he was his father. But if tonight didn't go well, if she took one look at Max and remembered all the bad things, all the grief and resentment of Michael's deception, she might not let him get close to her son.

Their son, he reminded himself. This was about his son as much as hers.

During the drive to Wilborough, Max talked about the private security work he was doing, and his flight to Boston, and his utter lack of jet lag. "There's a technique to avoid jet lag," he insisted. "You can train yourself out of it." Even thirty pounds thinner and significantly more weathered, Max still enjoyed pretending he was impervious to the kinds of physical challenges that felled mere mortals.

"This is a nice town," Max observed as Michael steered into Emmie's neighborhood. "Nothing like what we're used to, huh? Look at all the greenery."

Michael smiled. California's climate was semi-desert dry. The sprawling emerald lawns and foliage-dense trees of New England were rarities back home.

But this was his home now, not California. This was where he'd thrown his lot; this was where the woman he loved had set down roots, and this was where he was going to stay.

He wondered if he should warn Max that Emmie wasn't looking forward to his visit. Max wouldn't be scared off, but he might become defensive, prickly, as likely to pick a fight as to make amends.

He kept his mouth shut except to say, "Remember not to let anything slip out with Jeffrey."

"Don't worry."

Michael turned onto Cullen Drive and steered up Emmie's driveway. The evening would go well, he assured himself. He and Emmie had come so far; a few hours with Max wasn't going to undo what they'd accomplished.

She was waiting for them, watching through the screen door as they strolled up the walk to the front porch. She had on the simple cotton jumper and white T-shirt she'd been wearing that morning when she'd left for school. Michael was always amazed by how fresh she managed to look after hours cooped up in a classroom with her pupils. He usually wound up rumpled and weary after a few minutes in the company of just one small boy. Obviously she was a professional when it came to dealing with kids.

She scrutinized Max cautiously as Michael ushered him into the house. Max immediately seized her hand and pumped it. "She's still beautiful," he said to Michael. "I could see why she turned your head five years ago—and I can see why she turned it again now." He turned back to her and released her hand. "Emmie, I don't know if you remember me, but—"

"I remember you," she said, her voice soft and reserved, laced with a vestige of her Virginia drawl. "You're looking well, too, Max."

"I look like sh—" He cut himself off, smiling sheepishly. "I look lousy, but you're polite enough not to say so. Emmie, I really appreciate your letting me come by."

"It's all right." She seemed mildly uneasy. Michael knew how much letting Max come by had taken out of her. If Max didn't know, he could guess. "I'm just going to throw some burgers on the grill outside," she said, pivoting and heading toward the kitchen. "Michael, why don't you get Max something to drink?"

"Where's Jeffrey?" Michael asked, gesturing for Max to join him as he followed Emmie down the hall to the kitchen.

"He's down the street at Adam's house. I told him to be home for dinner by six."

Relief swept through Michael, unexpected but real. Not that he didn't want to see Jeffrey, but given Emmie's tension and Max's determination to see this reunion through, Michael didn't have much energy to concentrate on Jeffrey.

Emmie pulled the fixings for a salad from the refrigerator. Michael wanted to kiss her, or at least just touch her shoulder and thank her for letting Max come, but he felt odd with Max watching them. Instead he asked, "Would you like a hand with anything?"

"No, thanks." She exuded a brisk, businesslike attitude, cool and off-putting.

"Then I guess we'll stay out of your way." Michael's offer won him a fleeting smile from her. "How does a beer sound, Max?"

"I'd love one."

Michael grabbed two bottles from the fridge and led Max out through the kitchen door onto the patio. There, in the balmy late afternoon, they sat and drank, surrounded by more New England greenery. Max commented on the simple charm of small-town life—maybe it took a hardened urban cynic to appreciate the peace of suburbia, he said—and Michael focused on the woman inside the house, tearing greens and slicing tomatoes for her salad, her blond hair held back from her face with a tortoiseshell barrette. He thought about her reticence and her trust, and how much he loved her, how sweet the world seemed when she was nearby.

Max broke into his thoughts. "She's not happy I'm here."

Michael sipped some beer. "You remind her of a bad time in her life," he pointed out.

"I remind *me* of a bad time in *my* life, too." The sun was fading from yellow-white to rose, heightening the ruddy undertone of Max's complexion. "I remember when you first met her. I was so ticked off. I thought she was going to ruin our plans."

"As it turned out, we ruined them without any help from her." Michael heard a trace of bitterness in his tone.

"But now you've got the chance of a lifetime, Molina. The chance to undo the past, to overcome everything that got ruined. A woman, a home, a family—I envy you that. You don't know how lucky you are."

"I do know."

A familiar shriek roiled the air, high and filled with laughter. Jeffrey appeared around the side of the house, galloping at full speed, his Red Sox hat askew and his denim overalls bearing grass stains on the knees. "Michael!" he whooped, barely acknowledging the stranger seated on the patio. "Mommy says we're eating outside!" He held out his hand, and Michael slapped him five. Jeffrey loved eating outside. It was almost like camping out, he thought, and it didn't matter so much if crumbs dropped off his plate onto the ground.

Jeffrey slapped Michael's palm back, then paused to acknowledge Max. Before Michael could introduce them, Emmie swung open the back door, poked her head out and said, "Jeffrey, I need you to wash your hands and then you can bring out some plates and napkins."

Michael exchanged a look with Max, who didn't seem too ruffled. If he could face down a murderous thug like Cortez, Michael supposed he could cope with a protective woman exuding enough arctic vibes to give him the chills on a late-spring evening.

Insisting she didn't want any help from the men, she organized Jeffrey to assist her in bringing food outside to the picnic table. Michael fired up the gas grill without being asked, but once it was hot she took over, broiling the burgers. He would have asked her to sit and relax, maybe have a beer while he cooked the meat, but then she would lose her excuse to avoid Max. He wouldn't deny her that.

But in a few minutes the burgers were done, sandwiched in their toasted rolls and carried to the table, which Jeffrey had set with a colorful plastic tablecloth, napkins and plates. A garden salad glistening with Italian dressing was heaped in a wooden serving bowl, and bottles of ketchup, mustard and relish pinned the tablecloth down so the breeze couldn't steal it.

Max fixed Emmie with a determined smile. "Michael tells me you're a schoolteacher, Emmie."

"That's right."

"Just like you were in San Pablo."

"What's *sampablo?*" Jeffrey asked.

"It's a place down in Central America where your mom, Michael and I all knew one another before you were born," Max explained. Michael glanced at Emmie. She sat poised, as though prepared to grab Jeffrey and flee if necessary.

"Before I was born?" Jeffrey had a lot of trouble

conceiving that the world existed before he was in
it.

"That's right." Max returned his gaze to Emmie,
even as he addressed Jeffrey. "I ran into some trouble down there, and it caused your mom a lot of
sorrow. And I came here to apologize to her."

Michael continued to watch Emmie, angling his
gaze so he wouldn't seem to be staring. She appeared to relent slightly, her posture just a little less
rigid, her muscles a little less primed to pounce.

"My mistakes caused a lot of pain for Michael,
too," Max continued to explain, even though Jeffrey
looked bewildered and not too interested. "They
would have been friends all along, except that Michael was busy saving my life. And because he was
such a hero to me, he and your mom kind of lost
each other. I've always felt bad about that."

Jeffrey appeared marginally intrigued. "He saved
your life? How?"

"The details don't matter," Michael said quickly.
"We were friends, and then I met your mom, and
she became a very special friend to me, too. But I
lost her."

"Because of me," Max interjected. "So I was
about the happiest person when Michael told me he
found your mom again."

Jeffrey bit a mouthful of burger and chewed on
it, his round, dark eyes searching his mother's face.
"You knew Michael before?"

"Yes, I did." She picked at a lettuce leaf on her
plate, then smiled at Max. "You didn't have to
travel all this way to tell me you were sorry."

"Oh, yes, I did. For my sake, if not for yours.
I've had to stand by and watch Michael miss you

and try to find you for so long. I always felt it was my fault.''

"Well." Her smile was genuine. "Consider yourself forgiven.''

Michael let out a long breath. That was it, then. The past had finally been sorted out and locked into storage where it couldn't cause them any more problems. He and Emmie had each other, Max had the absolution he'd wanted and Emmie was smiling. He dug into his food, his soul glowing as warmly as the twilight sun.

As if he sensed the grown-ups were done talking, Jeffrey took over the conversation. He described a game he and Adam had invented at Adam's house that day, a convoluted make-believe adventure involving invisible cops and a pirate named Mo Vaughn, with gold hoop earrings in both ears. He offered a comprehensive analysis of a toy-car crash he and Adam and Todd choreographed at school, and a critique of several of his classmates' lunches. As he talked he ate, slurped his milk and separated the shredded carrots out of his salad. "Can I feed these to the monster?" he asked Emmie.

"I'd rather you eat them," she suggested.

"I wanna feed them to the monster. I haven't fed him in days. I bet he's hungry.''

"What monster is this?" Max asked with an amiable grin.

"It's a big monster with poker-dot hair and he lives in that tree." Jeffrey used his fork to point out the crab-apple tree at the rear of the yard. "And if I don't feed him, he might starve to death.''

"You'd better feed him, then," Max said. "As a matter of fact, I'll help you feed him." He picked a few bits of carrot out of his salad and added them to the pile on Jeffrey's plate.

Emmie grinned, apparently touched by Max's kindness toward Jeffrey. Michael's soul grew even warmer. He understood why Max had needed to come here. It was one of the reasons he, too, had needed to find Emmie. When he'd hired Finders, Keepers to locate her, he hadn't expected that they would reconnect as lovers. But he'd needed to see her, to apologize, to put the past away. Max needed the same thing.

He watched as Jeffrey solemnly led Max across the grass to the tree and left the carrot scraps on a branch. He could hear Jeffrey's high-pitched voice, an incomprehensible babble. His gaze met Emmie's across the table, and he reached for her hand and gave it a squeeze. "How are you doing?" he asked.

"Fine."

"I love you," he murmured.

"I love you, too."

"So you know monsters?" Jeffrey was chattering as he skipped and Max walked back to the patio.

"Well, the kind of monsters I've known don't live in trees, and they don't have polka-dot hair," Max told him.

"What kind of monsters do you know?"

"The kind of monsters who do terrible things to people," Max answered.

Michael shot Max a quick look, but Max didn't notice. His attention was on the bubbly boy at his side. Emmie slid her hand out from under Michael's. Her smile chilled a few degrees. "Max," she said, "I don't think—"

"What kind of terrible things?" Jeffrey persisted.

"Well, do you know what criminals are?" Max asked.

"Bad people on TV."

"In real life, also," Max emphasized.

"Don't scare him," Michael said when Max failed to acknowledge his quelling look.

"I'm not scaring him," Max said genially, sitting on the bench and patting it for Jeffrey to sit next to him. "He's asking me questions, and I'm telling him the truth. There are bad people in this world, and some of them are monsters. And I've dealt with them. So have you."

Michael gave his head a subtle shake, but Jeffrey hoisted himself to his knees so he could get a better view of Michael above the salad bowl. "You know monsters, Michael?"

He didn't want to lie to Jeffrey, but sometimes a lie was better than the truth. "No, I don't."

"He did once," Max said, almost bragging. "He saved my life by killing a monster."

"You killed a monster?" Jeffrey seemed about to burst with excitement. "You killed a monster, Michael? How? With your bare hands or with a big sword like a pirate?"

"Jeffrey," Emmie warned.

"I don't want to talk about it," Michael said.

But Jeffrey wouldn't be silenced. "How'd you kill him? Did you blow him up with a big bomb?"

"He used a gun," Max said calmly. He was accustomed to guns; they'd been a part of his life and his work for years. "He shot the bastard—excuse me, he shot the monster. He was a very bad man, and Michael shot him."

"Was there blood?" Jeffrey asked, his eyes so wide they seemed too big for his face. "Lots of blood? Did the man scream? Was it exciting? I bet it was exciting!'' He aimed his fingers like guns and made exploding noises with his mouth. ''*Blam! Blam!* Like that! And blood everywhere, and screaming, and—''

''That's enough.'' Michael shoved back from the table, suddenly nauseated. Yes, there had been explosion noises and blood everywhere, and probably screaming, as well. Screaming inside Michael's head, if nowhere else. Screaming in his black, black dreams for months afterward. Screaming and blood and death, so grotesque that Michael had never believed he would ever feel clean enough to deserve Emmie's love.

Jeffrey didn't appear to hear him. ''I wanna be a hero, too!'' he shouted, leaping off the bench and scampering around the patio. ''I wanna kill monsters and save lives just like Michael! I wanna shoot a gun like Michael did!''

''No,'' Michael said. He felt as if he were yelling, but the word came out choked, blocked by the tension in his throat. ''No, you don't want to be like me. You never want to do what I did.'' He felt he had to say something to Emmie, also, and Max, but he couldn't even look at them. The nightmares were rushing at him, sweeping down on him like icy shadows, reclaiming him. He did not want his son to be like him.

Unable to speak, he stalked into the house. He could escape from Jeffrey, from Emmie and Max. But he couldn't escape from what he'd done five years ago. He could never escape from that, and he knew it.

And, God help him, he knew Emmie knew it, too.

CHAPTER FIFTEEN

"WE'RE GOING IN THE WATER!" Jeffrey bellowed.

Emmie glanced past him to peer out the jet's rounded window. As it approached the runway at the San Francisco airport, it did seem to be flying awfully close to the water. She patted Jeffrey's hand and said, "We're not going in the water. We're going to the airport, just like I told you."

It was his first flight, and she couldn't blame him for being excited. During the entire five and a half hours, he'd marched up and down the aisles, inspected the plane's tiny lavatories, made buddies with the flight attendants and stolen an hour's nap. All the while, Emmie had tried to keep her mind on him. But it traveled on its own secret route, backward and forward, following an itinerary she couldn't control.

She hadn't tried very hard to convince Michael to stay. She hadn't been sure she'd wanted him to, not after that night. No matter what had happened in the years since they'd first met, no matter how much he'd healed, no matter that the love they'd kindled once had instantly reignited when Michael had found her, the ugliness of his experience in San Pablo could not be erased.

She'd been sure she could accept it. She'd been sure Michael had made peace with it, too. But that night, when she'd seen her son—*Michael*'s son—so enraptured with the brutality of it, charging around like a homicidal maniac and swearing that he wanted to be just like Michael, that he wanted to shoot a gun and kill people, too...

When Michael said he had to leave, she'd let him go.

She'd been regretting it ever since.

School ended for her the second week in June. The third week in June, she'd purchased two tickets on a flight bound for San Francisco. Thank goodness for credit cards and children's discount fares.

The plane touched down with a light bump. Michael squealed with delight. "That's cool. I wanna fly in a plane again."

"You will." In a matter of days, no doubt. She'd bought round-trip tickets with the intention of returning to Massachusetts once she and Michael had seen each other—assuming she was able to find him. She had no idea whether she would, let alone whether she could convince him that she loved him.

Despite what had happened. Despite what he'd done. Maybe because of it. She loved Michael Molina.

Max Gallard had been beside himself. When he'd gotten back to Los Angeles, he'd telephoned her, distraught. "I'm going to spend the rest of my life apologizing to you—" he'd said.

She'd cut him off. "No. That won't be necessary."

"I came between you and Michael once, and now I've come between you two again. I'm like the kiss of death to you."

"Maybe our relationship just wasn't meant to

be,'' she'd argued, swallowing her tears. How could she love Michael? How could she possibly include him in the safe, secure world she'd created for Jeffrey?

"I told Jeffrey about Michael because he saved my life. Both our lives. He *is* a hero."

She'd wanted to press her hands to her ears to shut out Max's voice. "I'm sure you're glad for what he did, but—"

"What he did was brave and honorable. What he did was right! How could you let him leave you?"

"He wanted to go. It was his decision."

"You let him go."

Because I realized I couldn't deal with his past, she'd wanted to say. *Because I couldn't let my son idolize a man who had done what Michael had done.*

"Cortez was responsible for Michael's brother's death," Max had reminded her. "It could just be that I'm not the only life Michael saved. There could be lots of other people, street kids who are alive today because Cortez didn't flood Los Angeles with more illegal guns. People's baby brothers could be alive today because of Michael."

I know this, she'd sobbed inwardly. *But I can't stand it.*

"He risked everything, Emmie. He risked his own life to put an end to that man. Even worse, he risked your love. How could you let him leave you?"

"It was his choice," she'd said weakly.

Long after she'd hung up the phone, her words had echoed hollowly inside her. What choice had he had but to leave? He'd found her because he wanted her forgiveness, and that horrible night in the backyard, he learned that even if he had her love, he didn't have her forgiveness. No wonder he'd left.

But she *did* love him. He *had* done something noble and courageous. And now she might have lost him forever because she hadn't been able to give him what he'd needed that night, what he would always need.

He'd come to Wilborough from somewhere in the Bay Area, but she had no idea where he lived or how to reach him. She didn't even have Max's number to call him back and ask. She'd learned something vital from Michael, though: how to find a lost lover.

"It's still early in the day here," she pointed out to Jeffrey, not bothering to explain the time-zone differences. "So when we get off the plane, we're going to visit an office."

"What office?"

"It's a detective agency called Finders, Keepers."

THEY TOOK A CAB NORTH from the airport into the city. Jeffrey was beside himself. Before today, he'd done so little traveling—but in the past six hours he'd been on a jet plane, flying three thousand miles from home, and now he was riding in a car through a city so exotic even Emmie gaped at her surroundings. "Oh, boy! Another hill!" Jeffrey would cheer each time the cab vaulted over another of San Francisco's roller-coaster roads. They caught glimpses of the Bay, the water so turquoise it looked unreal to Emmie, who was used to the North Atlantic's green and gray hues. They ogled tidy stucco buildings, multihued Victorians, town houses stacked along the slanting sidewalks like dominoes. Emmie wondered if the slight nudge of a building at the top of the hill would push it into the next building, and into the next, until they all tumbled down to the water's edge.

Van Ness was a reasonably level street, and the building that bore the address of Finders, Keepers, which she'd found in a phone book at the airport, looked interchangeable with any number of office buildings in Boston. Emmie and Jeffrey rode up the elevator and stepped out to find themselves face-to-face with the front door of Tyrell Investigative Services, which was evidently the parent company of Finders, Keepers.

She approached a secretary inside and asked for Finders, Keepers. With an appealing casualness, the young woman didn't inquire if they had an appointment or tell them to wait while she contacted some inner office by phone but simply said, "Follow me." She was a sturdy, energetic woman with lush brown curls of hair tumbling around her face. Emmie felt skinny and pallid next to her, and dowdy in her wrinkled cotton dress. The woman's slacks were crisp and fresh looking—but then, she hadn't just disembarked from a transcontinental flight.

"Where are we going?" Jeffrey asked in a stage whisper that could probably have been heard across the bay in Oakland.

"To talk to a special detective," Emmie whispered back, holding his hand so he wouldn't wander off. They passed two offices with their doors open and were led into a third one. The walls were clean and white, a side counter held a computer with its screen saver swirling, the window overlooked the traffic on Van Ness and the broad desk at one end faced a framed poster of two ballet dancers performing a pas de deux.

"Have a seat," the young woman said, gesturing toward two upholstered chairs near the desk. As Emmie sat, the woman circled the desk and sat facing them. "I'm Maggie Tyrell," she said, "the president of Finders, Keepers. You caught me at a quiet moment. What can I do for you?"

Emmie blinked and sat up straighter. This effervescent young woman was going to save her life?

Well, she'd found Emmie for Michael, hadn't she? If she could do that, surely she could find Michael. "I understand you find missing lovers?"

"That's correct."

"Well, I—I'm missing someone."

"You miss Michael?" Jeffrey piped up, squirming in the oversize chair. "I miss him. He taught me all about baseball. Ask me a question about baseball," he boasted to Maggie Tyrell. "I know everything about baseball."

She grinned. "Do you think the Giants have a shot at the pennant this year?" she asked.

"I don't know. I only know about the Red Sox."

Maggie chuckled. "I guess you're from Boston, huh?" She turned back to Emmie, her smile expectant.

Emmie nodded. "And I guess we both miss Michael," she said. "He was a client of yours. He hired you to find me, and you did...and now he's gone and I need to find him. Michael Molina is his name."

Maggie's expression changed. She gazed curiously at Jeffrey and then back at Emmie. "You're Mary-Elizabeth Kenyon, the teacher," she said. Emmie was surprised that the detective remembered, and even more surprised when she added, "And this must be Jeffrey."

"Yes, this is my son Jeffrey." Emmie ruffled his hair.

Maggie leaned back in her chair and shook her head in bewilderment. "I suppose it's none of my business why he left you. He went to an awful lot of trouble to find you, and the last I heard it was going well. I believe in true love, Ms. Kenyon—but though it breaks my heart to admit it, sometimes it just isn't meant to be."

"This is meant to be," Emmie insisted. She'd never been surer of anything in her life. "I love him, and we thought—we both thought there was something insurmountable standing in our way. But it's not insurmountable. I need to find him, to tell him that."

"Well." Maggie studied her for a minute, then shrugged. "This is so simple I'm not even going to charge you. Let me just give him a call—"

"No." Emmie leaned across the desk, prepared to block Maggie's hand before it reached the phone. "He might say he doesn't want to see me. Please— if you could just tell me where I could find him— he lives somewhere around here, doesn't he?"

"Across the Bay, in Berkeley." She regarded Emmie for another minute. "I feel a little funny about this. If he really left you, maybe he doesn't want to see you again."

"Maybe I didn't want to see him when he showed up at my house six weeks ago," Emmie shot back.

Maggie conceded with a nod. "All right." She swiveled to her computer, called up a file and located his address. She copied it onto a sheet of paper and handed it to Emmie. "It's about a twenty-minute drive from here. Do you have a car?"

"No. We can take a cab." Emmie didn't want to think about how much money she was spending. She would gladly live in debt for the rest of her life if it gave her a chance to make things right with Michael.

"Okay. Do me one favor, though."

"Anything."

"Let me know how it goes, all right?"

"All right." Emmie stood and shook Maggie's hand. Then she turned to Jeffrey, whose energy had flagged. He sat lethargically in the chair, apparently suffering the aftereffects of a long, long day that was not yet close to being over. "Come on, Jeffrey. Let's go find Michael."

"Okay," he said, dragging himself out of the chair.

"He's adorable," said Maggie as Emmie took his hand. "I can see why Michael…well, just go and find him. Good luck."

Jeffrey fell asleep during the drive across the Bay to Berkeley. Emmie gently shook him awake as the cab stopped in front of a courtyard of pretty garden apartments. The buildings were Spanish-style, white stucco with red-tile roofs, arched doors and windows and attractive grillwork with flowering vines twining through the wrought iron. The architecture reminded Emmie of San Pablo.

San Pablo, when everything had been possible. When the future had spread before her, golden and beckoning. When she had trusted her heart.

Just like today.

She led Jeffrey up the walk to the door with Michael's number on it and rang the bell. He might not be home—or, worse, he might be home and not alone. But she'd come this far, and she wasn't going to retreat. Even if he had a woman with him—if he could be brave enough to fly across the country to find her, not knowing what he might find, she could be brave enough to ring his bell.

After a minute, the heavy oak door swung open, and there he stood. Alone, dressed in blue jeans and a wrinkled white shirt with the sleeves rolled up, his hair disheveled and his eyes as dark as onyx. He was clearly startled. But before he could speak Emmie said, "We have something to tell Jeffrey."

"We do?" He peered down at the sleepy boy clinging to his mother's leg. Then he knelt in front of Jeffrey and said, "Hey. How are you doing?"

"I'm tired," Jeffrey said. "We miss you."

Michael stared at Jeffrey for a moment, then stared at the floor, at the wall, at the terra-cotta courtyard beyond his front door. Everywhere but at Emmie.

"We miss you," she echoed. "Maggie Tyrell at Finders, Keepers gave us your address. Can we come in?"

Michael straightened up. She saw his neck move as he swallowed. "Sure," he said, stepping aside and gesturing for them to enter.

His town house disconcerted her. Everything was so neat and clean—not that she'd ever seen any evidence that he wasn't a neat, clean person, but the furniture was sparse and tasteful, the tile floors shiny and the rugs devoid of mud or brown grass clippings, the sofa cushions in place and the tables all matching. It occurred to her that he was quite well-off—and that he didn't have a child living with him. "This is your home?" she asked, amazed, then embarrassed by her amazement.

"I guess so," he said enigmatically.

She turned to him. "What do you mean, you guess so?"

He watched as Jeffrey let go of Emmie's hand and crossed to a deep-slung leather easy chair. He climbed into it and curled up, his eyes open but bleary with sleepiness. Once Jeffrey was settled, Michael steered his gaze back to Emmie. "Do you really want to tell him?"

She nodded, aware that revealing the truth to Jeffrey would be one of the riskiest, most difficult things she'd ever done. "I was going to tell him myself, but I thought we should do it together. Besides..." She averted her eyes and admitted, "I didn't have the guts to do it myself."

He touched her cheek, cupping his hand around her face and tilting it until her eyes met his. "Are you sure you want him to know?" he asked in a hushed voice. "He knows so much else about me—"

"We'll deal with that," she said. "He took the wrong things from your story. I can try to teach him the right things—but I need you with me, Michael. You can teach him better than I can."

He scrutinized her face for a long minute. "I don't want him to turn out like me," he whispered.

"I do."

His hand trembled against her face, and he let it drop. Then he turned to the drowsy boy, crossed the room and hunkered down in front of the chair. Emmie joined them, dropping to her knees next to Michael. "Are you still awake, Jeffrey?" Michael asked.

Jeffrey nodded. "Whatcha whispering about? Is it a secret?"

"It was," Michael told him. "But not anymore." He glanced at Emmie—seeking support, she thought, gathering his hand in one of hers and Jeffrey's hand in the other. "I'm your father, Jeffrey."

Jeffrey's eyes widened. He said nothing.

Emmie nodded. "It's true, Jeffrey. When we knew each other, so long ago—remember when that man Max told you about San Pablo? We knew each other then."

"I loved your mom," Michael said, his voice wavering slightly as if straining beneath the weight of his emotions. "But I had to leave her. And I didn't even know it when you were born. I didn't know where you and your mom were. It took me years to find you."

Jeffrey gazed at Emmie, questioning. "I have a daddy?"

"You always had a daddy," she reminded him gently. "You asked me, and I said your daddy was a man I loved, but he went away. But he left me with you, which I always considered the greatest gift I'd ever received."

Jeffrey thought this over. He shifted to stare at Michael, then twisted back to Emmie. "He killed a man."

"It was a terrible thing," said Michael, drawing Jeffrey's attention back to him. "And I'm sorry it happened. But at the time it was the only thing I could do, and so I did it.''

''He was a bad man.''

''Yes.''

''And you're a hero.''

''I'm just a man, too, Jeffrey. I'm not a hero.''

''You're my daddy,'' Jeffrey declared, his tone leaving no doubt that he considered that synonymous with being a hero. He smiled, then closed his eyes and drifted off to sleep.

Michael and Emmie remained on the floor near Jeffrey's chair for a long while, until he started to snore. Then Michael stood and, offering his hand, helped her to her feet. The light had faded, throwing long shadows across the elegant living room. Emmie was tired, too—but more than tired, she was edgy, her nerves jumping, her heart drumming. She'd just gotten through one of the riskiest, most difficult conversations she'd ever had—but she was facing another just as risky, just as difficult.

She started with the most important part. ''I love you, Michael.''

He smiled sadly. ''Love was never the problem between us.''

''You wanted my forgiveness.'' She took his hands in hers, ran her thumbs over his warm, smooth palms, sought strength in his grip. ''What happened in San Pablo happened. The only thing I had to forgive was your leaving me the way you did—and I forgave that long ago. You couldn't help it. You had to go.''

''But—''

''The rest, Michael…it's not for me to forgive. Your friend Max convinced me that what you did *was* heroic—but I didn't need much convincing. He only told me what I knew in my heart.'' She felt tears welling up, crowding her eyes, but kept going. ''It's you who have to forgive yourself. I didn't stop you from leaving Wilborough, and I should have. But you were the one who left—because you couldn't forgive yourself.''

He inhaled, gazed down at her, sighed. ''Emmie. It used to haunt me. I couldn't get it out of my head. I thought I was over it, but…I'm not. It still haunts me.''

''I know. You're still haunted by your brother's death, aren't you?''

''Yes, but—''

''Some things you aren't meant to get over. Your brother, San Pablo…you learn to live with them. You learn to forgive yourself and go on.''

He sighed again. ''Emmie.'' He touched his lips to her brow. ''I missed you, too. God, I missed you.''

''Why did you say you *guessed* this was your home?'' she asked.

He glimpsed Jeffrey, deeply asleep on the chair, and then smiled crookedly. ''I had a wild dream that Wilborough could be my home someday. I wanted to believe that could happen.''

''Believe it,'' she murmured to him. ''We want you home.''

''If you want me home…'' He closed his arms around her and held her tight, making her feel safe and secure, letting her know she was in the arms of a hero. ''I'll come home.''

They held each other in the fading light, just steps

from their sleeping son. So close to each other, Emmie knew that they had both come home. And this was also something they would never get over. It wasn't a wild dream. It was simply love.

HARLEQUIN®
SUPERROMANCE®

From July to September 1999—three special
Superromance® novels about people whose
New Millennium resolution is

By the Year 2000: CELEBRATE!

JULY 1999—*A Cop's Good Name* by Linda Markowiak
Joe Latham's only hope of saving his badge and his reputation is
to persuade lawyer Maggie Hannan to take his case. Only Maggie—
his ex-wife—knows him well enough to believe him.

AUGUST 1999—*Mr. Miracle* by Carolyn McSparren
Scotsman Jamey McLachlan's come to Tennessee to keep the
promise he made to his stepfather. But Victoria Jamerson stands
between him and his goal, and hurting Vic is the last thing he wants
to do.

SEPTEMBER 1999—*Talk to Me* by Jan Freed
To save her grandmother's business, Kara Taylor has to co-host a
TV show with her ex about the differing points of view between men
and women. A topic Kara and Travis know plenty about.

By the end of the year,
everyone will have something to celebrate!

HARLEQUIN®
Makes any time special ™

"Fascinating—you'll want to take this home!"
—**Marie Ferrarella**

"Each page is filled with a brand-new surprise."
—**Suzanne Brockmann**

"Makes reading a new and joyous experience all over again."
—**Tara Taylor Quinn**

See what all your favorite authors are talking about.

Coming October 1999 to a retail store near you.

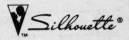

HARLEQUIN®
Makes any time special ™

WIN A DREAM

In celebration of Harlequin®'s golden anniversary

Enter to win a *dream!* You could win:

- A luxurious trip for two to **The Renaissance Cottonwoods Resort** in Scottsdale, Arizona, or

- A bouquet of flowers once a week for a year from **FTD**, or

- A $500 shopping spree, or

- A fabulous bath & body gift basket, including **K-tel**'s *Candlelight and Romance* 5-CD set.

Look for **WIN A DREAM** flash on specially marked Harlequin® titles by Penny Jordan, Dallas Schulze, Anne Stuart and Kristine Rolofson in October 1999*.

FTD

RENAISSANCE.
COTTONWOODS RESORT
SCOTTSDALE, ARIZONA

K·TEL

COMING NEXT MONTH

#858 TALK TO ME • Jan Freed
By the Year 2000: Celebrate!

When Kara Taylor left her husband on their disastrous first anniversary, she figured she'd just call her marriage a bad experience and move on. Sure, Travis was handsome and charming and wonderful, but they were mismatched from the start. He was a true outdoorsman, and she was the ultimate city girl. Success mattered more to her than it did to him, so who would've thought that nine years later he'd be the only person who could save her business?

#859 FAMILY FORTUNE • Roz Denny Fox
The Lyon Legacy

Crystal Jardin is connected to the prestigious Lyon family by blood—and by affection. And she's especially close to Margaret Lyon, the family matriarch. Margaret, who's disappeared. Whose money is disappearing, too. At such a critical time, the last thing Crystal needs is to fall for a difficult man like Caleb Tanner—or a vulnerable young boy.

Follow the Lyon family fortunes. New secrets are revealed, new betrayals are thwarted—but the bonds of family remain stronger than ever!

#860 THE BABY AND THE BADGE • Janice Kay Johnson
Patton's Daughters

Meg Patton, single mother and brand-new sheriff's deputy, has finally come home to Elk Springs. It's time to reconcile with her sisters—and past time to introduce them to her son. And now her first case has her searching for the parents of an abandoned infant. But Meg can't afford to fall for this baby—or for the man who found her. No matter how much she wants to do both....

#861 FALLING FOR THE ENEMY • Dawn Stewardson

When crime lord Billy Fitzgerald, locked away in solitary confinement, arranges to have prison psychologist Hayley Morgan's son abducted as a bargaining tool, Hayley's life falls apart. To ensure her son's safety, Hayley has to rely on Billy's lawyer, Sloan Reeves, to act as a go-between. Trouble is, he's the enemy and Hayley is smitten.

#862 BORN IN TEXAS • Ginger Chambers
The West Texans

Tate Connelly is recuperating from near-fatal gunshot wounds. Jodie Connelly would do anything to help her husband get well—except the one thing he's asking: divorce him. Maybe the Parker clan—and Jodie's pregnancy—can shake Tate up and get him thinking straight again.

#863 DADDY'S HOME • Pamela Bauer
Family Man

A plane crash. An injured woman. A courageous rescue. All Tyler Brant wants is to put the whole thing behind him. But the media's calling him a hero. And so are the women in his life: his mother, his six-year-old daughter and Kristin Kellar—the woman he saved. If only they knew the truth....

HARLEQUIN ● CELEBRATES

FIVE DECADES OF ROMANCE

Starting in September 1999, Harlequin Temptation® will also be celebrating an anniversary—15 years of bringing you the best in passion.

Look for these Harlequin Temptation® titles at your favorite retail stores in September:

CLASS ACT
by Pamela Burford

BABY.COM
by Molly Liholm

NIGHT WHISPERS
by Leslie Kelly

THE SEDUCTION OF SYDNEY
by Jamie Denton